Avis Blackthorn: Is Not an Evil Wizard!

(Book 1)

Jack Simmonds

Jack Simmonds'

Avis Blackthorn: Is Not an Evil Wizard!

Copyright © 2015 by Jack Simmonds

Cover copyright © 2015 by Jack Simmonds

Third edition.

ISBN: 1502345498

ISBN-13: 978-1502345493

Thank you for supporting my work.

CONTENTS

CHAPTER ONE

The Blackthorn Family

From the outside you would think my family exceptionally strange. They pride themselves on being the most evil family in all of the Seven Magical Kingdoms, a title which no one is due to question. We, the Blackthorns, are pretty notorious.

My name is Avis Blackthorn and I am twelve years old. I am currently at the end of my summer holidays and due, in six and a half days, to start at Hailing Hall School for Wizards. It's a school for other young Wizards like myself from all over the Magical and Non-Magical lands.

As most of you reading this will probably be from the Non-Magical lands, or *The Outside*, as we call it, I suppose I had better explain: we, Wizards, live in a similar dimension to you, but separate and kind of invisible. Happendance is the Kingdom I live in and it's probably the second worst, after Farkingham — which is just a black dustbowl. Happendance is all forest and filled with stupid annoying fairytale creatures.

I can't wait to start school and get out of this draughty castle and away from my stupid family. Can you believe it, Hailing Hall is a boarding school, so I get to actually stay there, like actually live there! My last school was just a magical theory school for youngsters just down the road, so I had to come back every night.

The castle that my parents insist on calling *Darkampton Manor* is cold, damp and in major need of repair. My parents never seem to have the time to do much about it (I think they like the cold). Anyway, they are too busy working for their beloved, evil high master - Malakai. He is the most evil high master Sorcerer these Seven Kingdoms have ever

1

seen. He's killed more people than a Wolfraptor (a huge, flying, killer wolf). In fact, if a Wolfraptor came face to face with Malakai, it would probably scream like a girl and fly away (no offence to any girls). My parents are totally and utterly in love with him and think he does tiny golden nugget poo's. They are always talking about him.

I've only ever seen him once and had nightmares ever since. He wears this dark black hood like Death and has these horns on his head and his hands... his hands are like black charred skeletons hands, all bony and disfigured. He even spoke to me once. He asked me, in his deep rasping voice like splintering wood if I, like the rest of family, would be coming to work for him when I left school. I didn't say anything. My Mum had tried to hide me upstairs, not because she thought I would be scared, she couldn't care less about that, but because she is ashamed of me.

They all are. Ashamed of me because I am not inherently *evil* like they are. My Mum is a hard woman, not one to cross. She's a terribly fierce witch who works constantly. I have three older sisters, almost identical to her in looks and personality. Then there's my three older brothers, all terribly handsome, fiercely competitive and unashamedly evil.

I am not good looking, Mum says I have a sloped, unsymmetrical face. I am not competitive or good at anything at all, apart from reading, but you can't be competitive at reading can you? Unless there's a *'how many books can you read in a week'* competition. I'd probably win that. And to cap it all, I am in no way evil. I don't even have the heart to kill a fly. They all joke that they think I am either adopted or was accidentally swapped at birth. I'm not sure.

My parents do all sorts for Malakai. They run meetings with other Malakai supporters and organise evil things.

Toppling the government seems a priority currently.

Right now I am in one of the topmost towers, one of the least draughty ones, seeing how long it is before they come and drag me downstairs. The youngest sister is getting married to some poor deluded Prince who doesn't have a clue what's happening. He's under some kind of Spell, I just know it. They are having some pre-engagement party and I have to go and 'mingle'. They should be up here soon, I felt a *Searching Spell* shoot around my feet about twenty minutes ago.

The older sisters: Marianne, Gertrude and Wendice arrived in separate carriages last night, along with the poor Prince. My brother's not far behind. Rory and Gary arrived with their friends Danny, Larry and Stan. My other brother Ross still lives at home with me and is the bane of my life. They all made such an entrance and palaver when returning home last night, that Wendice (the one who's getting married) pretended to feint until everyone's attention was directed back on her. This is normal.

This all proceeded with around three hundred guests pilling in from all over the Seven Magical Kingdoms. Our poor Irish butler Kilkenny had been making beds for the last three months.

BANG! My door flies open. I've been rumbled. It's Gertrude, the fattest of my sisters.

"What are you doing up here when it's Wendice's big day?!" she calls, loud enough for the entire castle to hear.

"I am not… just about to…" I stutter.

Her face wobbles as it talks, which is pretty funny. "Well get your bony backside downstairs and mingle… there's people down there who want to take the mick out of you. There's people expecting *entertainment*!" She cackles.

I am treated like a kind of performing monkey. They ask me to perform Magic sometimes because apparently it's *so hilarious watching someone so rubbish.* Mum stops it if she sees, because she doesn't want me upstaging the family. I don't know why they don't just give me up for adoption, it would be the best thing for everyone.

I follow fat Gertrude, her wobbly bottom barely fitting inside a huge blue dress. I thought about telling her that she needn't worry if she falls down the long stone spiral staircase, because she'll have an equivalent of about fifty cushions to soften the fall. I don't, just in case she sits on me and squashes me to death.

The party was just as I expected, lots of horrible people I know I hate who all look at me and smile gleefully as Gertrude announces my arrival, while stuffing three eclairs in her big wobbly gob.

I hid as best I could, keeping my head low to avoid all dark gazes, I even hid under a table as Nasty Luke came my way. Mind you, most people get out of the way when Nasty Luke's about, he stinks.

Music started soon, with some classic Happendance folk. My brothers were all in a corner doing mini-duels until Dad came over, his presence enough to make them scatter. Dad is a cool guy, and an impressive figure. Standing over six feet tall, with a stare that could topple a giant troll. He always dresses smartly, and has recently grown a beard, which suits him. I like my Dad - I just wish he liked me. People in the party treat him with reverence, while others are jealous of the trust that Malakai has in him, I just know it.

I grabbed a plate and helped myself to some food, narrowly avoiding Mum's homemade trout and tomato rolls (don't ask). I sat in a corner eating my second helping of trifle, my favourite, and just about the only normal food around here. I noticed that there was no one my age here. Oh well, in a week I will be out of here! Finally have the chance to make some friends who don't run away as soon as I tell them my name.

Mum was trying her best to impress the guests with her trout and tomato rolls. I heard some people whispering over by the fried spider stand that Malakai might be making an appearance at the party. My heart froze, he better not be, otherwise I am off.

I watched from my new hiding spot, just inside an alcove in the wall hidden by shadow, and observed these *evil* people, who, in some way or another were kind of ugly. I recognised quite a lot of faces from the Malakai meetings. There were Warlords and Warlocks, Pig-people, loads of Wicked Witches with their black cats and broomsticks, (yes, the stories are correct).

Then my brothers found me. Creeping up on me by disguising themselves as the wall, they think they are so clever with their Magic. I knew they were up to something as soon as I saw them, they had that evil glint in their eye - too much rotten apple punch for a start.

"What do you want?" I said.

"Oh Avis," said Rory, the oldest. "That's no way to talk to your beloved brothers."

"Yeah, we just want some fun," said Gary smiling malevolently, he was known for his evil smile.

Rory, Ross and Gary held my shoulder and stood me up while Larry and Stan chuckled behind.

Rory winked at me. "Were gonna make you *evil* Avis…"

I sighed, there was no use getting out of this. There were six of them who could all do Magic, against one of me, who couldn't.

They stood with me at the food table, Rory stayed close, whispering in my ear. "Right, grab that big bowl of trifle."

I did, too weary not to comply.

"And…" Rory chuckled then signalled to the others.

With a flick of their fingers, the bowl left my hands and flew into the air. It sailed right across the room to where Wendice stood. The trifle splattered all the way up her back as the crowd went stony silent. I turned, heart in my mouth, but my brothers had resumed to being a grey shade of wall. All eyes fell on me.

The scream from Wendice sailed around the castle louder than a clan of banshee. Mum jumped in front of her, for she looked like she might murder me.

Rory suddenly appeared from nowhere. "Avis, how *could you*?!" he called.

"Yeah!" said Gary and Ross. "To your own *Sister*?!"

Rory grabbed me by the collar. "Think you need to be punished!"

They marched me to centre of the crowd. Before I knew it, my trousers and pants were round my ankles, in front of anyone who was anyone in Happendance. My face went more scarlet than the cherry punch. In a scramble, I tried to pull my trousers back up, but couldn't, they were stuck! They had been Spelled to the floor... so everyone just stood, three hundred odd people, watching me flounder around on the floor with all my bits and bobs out. It's safe to say, if I wasn't a laughing stock before, then I was the definition of laughing stock now.

Wendice seemed reasonably revenged and laughed heartily along with the crowd. Mum and Dad undid the Spells and marched me away from the hall. Mum yelled at me for crying, then Dad told her he would "*handle it*". Dad didn't look at me, he was ashamed, I knew it. Silently he walked me the servants quarters, handing me over to Butler Kilkenny, telling him to find me a locked room where I wouldn't be found (which is partly what I wanted originally).

Clunk went the door lock. There was no way out. I paced my new room in a complete foul mood. I should be used to it by now, getting treated like that for being the outcast, but the truth is I'm not. Not at all. I hate them all so much, with their smug faces and nasty, vindictive personalities. My brothers will all be patting each other on the back now and plotting their next prank on me. None of them care though, because well, they are evil… they are raised to be evil and follow perfectly in my parent's footsteps. All will one day, be working for Malakai. I didn't want that.

I summoned all my stuff to this new room, a Spell which I have used far too often. I have to change rooms a lot to avoid being harassed by people. The Spell doesn't work as well as I'd like, I have to do it about ten times until all my stuff actually comes. Butler Kilkenny had put me in high turret, with a view of the deepest cavern below our castle. He did that on purpose. He knows I hate heights. I blocked the window with my dilapidated old wardrobe, it was falling to bits because of the amount of times I moved it around with the summoning Spell.

If only I had some friends. I could move out of here and go live with them. I could plot against my horrible family. Make them look stupid, make them know what it feels like to be the laughing stock for once.

After I calmed down I started to get all my stuff ready for Hailing Hall. This put me in a better mood, Hailing Hall was my way out of this damp, cold castle with incremental visits from various evil people. Hailing Hall would be my salvation. Every time I thought about it a little butterfly did jumps in my stomach.

Enclosed in the letter from school I had a list of stuff I needed to get. I found my big green bag with wooden toggles and started to pile clothes in.

Socks. *Check*.

Pants. *Check*.

Trousers and Jeans. *Check*.

Shirts. *Check*.

Jackets. *Check*.

Jumpers. *Check*.

Once that was suitably full I got another bag for my books. This bag was square, perfect for books, and made of Hubris leather so it could handle a lot. I piled in as many as I could fit, which sadly, was only about thirty. I hope they have a library at this school. My best friend and fluffy rabbit teddy Sedrick went in a third bag along with all my wash bits - Beatle Bit's Toothpaste, Newt Eye Underarm Spray, Moss Moisturiser and Spider Leg Shower Gel.

I am afraid I piled it all in rather haphazardly, as I was in a such a foul mood, that something rather smelly began leaking. I left them in a corner and sat on my bed for a long sulk about the gits downstairs. It's then, that I noticed writing on the other side of the letter. The list continued on the back! I scanned it and was horrified as it read:

Channeller: a Ring, Amulet or Pendant.

Cauldron.

Ever-changing long robes.

Ever-changing tie.

Then below that:

No teddy bears or animals, alive or not, are permitted, nor are any books or reading matter.

I huffed and stared at the letter. No books?! No Sedrick?! I charged back across my room and pulled all the non-permitted stuff out again. I put the books back on the shelf, and Sedrick back on my bed, brushing off whatever had leaked in the bag. I would have to hide him while I was away, so that no one would come looking for him to rip his head off or something.

This left me with one bag, I returned to the list.

A channeller? I had nagged Mum and Dad all summer that they needed to get me one, but obviously they had forgotten! A channeller is a thing that you wear that channels Magic, everyone has one. You can't really do proper Magic without one. Everyone in our family has the Blackthorn ring, it's a silver ring with the Blackthorn family crest intertwining all through it. I was fascinated as a kid and couldn't wait to get mine. I sort of gave up that dream when I was old enough to realise that I was useless at Magic and a burden to the family.

So what on earth was I supposed to do without a channeller? Would I be turned away from the school? Perish the thought! There's no way I was spending another day here longer than I had to. I returned to the list.

A cauldron? We had loads of them lying about I could pilfer. Dad had a load of rusty ones in the garden.

Ever-changing long robes? Now that's difficult. Ever-changing clothes are basically clothes that change colour. I am guessing it's based on what year or class you are in. Ross is going into his last year at Hailing, his long robes were navy, but yesterday they turned dark green. And his tie is red, I know they both mean different things, I just have no idea what, he won't tell me. I just know that they change by themselves.

There was no way Mum or Dad was going to take me shopping now, not after what just happened downstairs. Even though it wasn't my fault.

**

Over the coming days, I had no idea what was happening at the castle. Malakai could have killed my entire family for all I knew. Dad had put so much Magic around these turrets that the only noise I heard was Butler

Kilkenny's old man boots and stiff creaky knees as he climbed the stairs and bent down to push another sandwich through the door flap. They were mostly all dry and horrible by the time he got up here.

This time, however, I was ready for him. As the corn beef sandwich rattled through the mini door flap, I reached out and grabbed his wrinkly old arm.

"AH! Gerrof!" he cried.

But I wouldn't. I had been crying and screaming for my family to let me out for the last two days and this was the last straw. I was due to be at Hailing TODAY, and I was pretty sure they had forgotten.

"What you playing at boy!" he rasped at me.

"You need to let me out! I'm supposed to be going to my new school today! You need to take me!"

"No chance!" he spat. "Your parent's orders are to keep you up here out of trouble," he croaked.

"Tell them, I am starting school and I will be out their hair for good." Butler Kilkenny paused, he knew this might please my parents, he's such a suck-up.

"Fine," he said, wrenching his hand back. "I will go and tell them."

The tiny flap shut and sealed again. I paced the room, listening painfully to the creaking knees. I resisted the urge to tell him to hurry up.

Twenty minutes later, the key turned in the lock and the door opened. Butler Kilkenny stood glum and indicated for me to follow.

"Well?" I said. "What did they say?"

"Not much."

I had hoped they would be a little melancholy that their youngest son was off to big school, perhaps give me a teary goodbye, like they had all the others. I remember when Ross left six years ago, Mum and Dad held a leaving party and escorted him to the school in the ceremonial carriage.

I grabbed my bag, said a quick goodbye to Sedrick, who I had hidden in a crevice under a wonky stone, and left.

"So, erm, who's taking me?" I said, suddenly realising I didn't know where Hailing Hall was.

"I take you to the station, you go from there. Map is on the letter."

I just had chance to grab a cauldron from a pile of rusty ones by Dad's greenhouse before jumping into the carriage and flying off. Away from the castle, my home for twelve years. There were no teary goodbyes, I didn't see my parents, or anyone else. The house was as quiet as a fart in Farkingham. The carriage soared high above the cavern and over the Forest of Trill, which I used to play in as a child with the leprechauns, until they turned nasty, so I try to stay away if I can. The horses pulling the carriage were Dave and Henry, both looked very indignant as always. They hated flying.

CHAPTER TWO

The Boy from 'Yorkshire'

Butler Kilkenny flies like a maniac. I tried to tell him it was not Trill station I needed but the next one - Unverdown. That's what my letter said anyway. I stuck my head out the carriage window and screamed at him to turn around because Unverdown was *"back there!"* The stupid old deaf git didn't hear, or chose not to.

I didn't have chance to tell him what a dozy pratt he was, because as soon as I got out the carriage outside Trill station to tell him to go back to Unverdown, he flew off! One of the horses nearly took my head off, I think it meant to.

I sighed. Approaching the station I saw my worst nightmare. A small sign stood with bad news.

"Unfortunately due to not enough people wanting to travel today, we are closing the station as we can't be bothered."

Not even an apology. Brilliant. Unverdown was only a couple of stops from Trill, but god knows how long it was to walk.

Not wanting to waste any time, I hitched up my bag - cursed how much I'd packed, and began to hike off in the general direction of Unverdown station.

Guess what, as soon I started walking, this huge black cloud came overhead and started pelting it down. It was the kind of rain that hurts when it hits you in the face. I trudged, soaking wet all through, with no coat, along paths that became more like mud baths. I walked through Trill village, with its suburban brick cottages and carriages outside. I thought about stealing one, but the guilt would overcome me. Anyone in my family would do it in a heartbeat. But me, I just couldn't.

At the end of the village was a sign to Unverdown. I continued to trudge along this country lane, using my bag as a kind of crap umbrella. If I could do Magic this rain would not be a problem, but, well I couldn't do much Magic so I had to settle for being wet and miserable. I walked alongside Trill forest and these Gnomes came out to watch me. They all pointed and laughed. I was being mocked by a gang of Gnomes, my life really just continued to plummet.

Eventually I did make it to Unverdown station. Even though I had to ask a suspicious looking old man where it actually was. He pointed to a house. When I looked blankly at him, he told me to open the front door of number 42. Anyway I left him as he continued doing what ever he was doing, staring at the ground looking old and weird, he'd probably used too much Magic, let it rot his brain. That happens apparently.

So I opened the big red door of number 42, an end of terrace and expected to see a cosy living room, yet, it led straight out onto a small platform. Unverdown station at last. I breathed a sigh of relief, I might make it to school yet. Standing in the driving rain for what seemed like days, waiting for the train to arrive, was not ideal. When it finally arrived, I was soaked to the skin, with my bag of clothes now wetter than a drowned fish. But, I finally boarded the packed train. It was full of OAP Witches and Wizards, three warlocks, a sneezing Norse, a grumpy egg-man, and a wolf dressed as a nanny and whatever else (I tried not to make eye contact).

The train was hot, too hot. I steamed up the whole carriage then consulted the letter again to see how many stops it was until we got to Hailing, but the letter didn't say. I scoured the carriage to see if there was a map or station list, but there wasn't. Why on earth not? If I was a train manager, that's the first thing I would do!

The train shot forwards, the trains in Happendance run themselves, they don't have drivers. Just Magic I think. I'm not too sure.

The conductor appeared next to me in a flash, he was tall and dressed in a navy moccasin, when he turned I saw it was Mr. Wolfe - the half-man, half wolf, descended from the one and only (the fairytale about the wolf and the pigs, 'I'll huff and puff and blow your house down' type thing.)

He looked awful, mind you it's not natural for him to be in a suit taking tickets on a hot stuffy train. The pigs in the corner cowered, I reckon they were trying to dodge their fare - they're notorious for that.

"Have. You. Got. A. Ticket?" he said, in his wolfy voice.

I bought one off him, three gold pieces! It goes up every week! Lucky I had enough gold stashed away in my room.

I asked him when we would be arriving at Hailing Hall.

"About Two. Hours…"

I thanked Mr. Wolfe as genuinely as I could, without repulsing at the slime dripping from his jaw. I did feel sorry for him, I really did.

Two hours wasn't that bad, the letter said as long as we arrived before sundown then we would be there in time for the induction. I couldn't wait, excitement coursed through me, something I hadn't felt for a long time. All I had to do now was stay awake. On this hot… Stuffy…Train…Oh dear…

Zzzzz…

***

"Hello?" said the snake's voice. "Hello? Hello?" It circled round me, then in a flash jumped and bit me on the arm.

"AHH!" I cried.

14

My eyes opened. I was on the train. It was just a dream! Thank goodness for that, I hated snakes. But there was someone standing over me and prodding my arm.

"Hello?" he said again.

I rubbed my eyes and looked around. The boy was tall, wire thin and spoke with this funny accent from your world - the north of England somewhere, I saw a programme about it.

"Erm, hi?" I said, noticing I was still on the train and it was nearly dark! "Oh no! I haven't missed Hailing Station have I?"

"What? Naa, that's why I was waking ya…" he said, his little beady eyes blinking nervously behind thick glass frames. "To ask if you were going to Hailing Hall school too?"

"What?" I was genuinely surprised, somehow I didn't expect to see anyone else going to Hailing Hall on the train. His beady little eyes looked down at me through the comical little circular spectacles. "Yeah I am, are you?"

"Yeah, the stop's soon, thought I'd let ya know. Don't wanna sleep through and miss ya' first day o' school."

"No exactly."

I stood and stretched, the carriage now empty. My pockets felt oddly empty too. With a sinking feeling, I put my hands in them to check, all my gold pieces had gone! I would have cried if that boy resembling a lamppost wasn't standing there. I made sure I had enough gold for the entire year, but now I had nothing. I shouldn't have left it in my pocket, that was so stupid. If I found out who stole my gold I would do something… *evil* to them.

I sighed. Who was I kidding?

"I'm sorry I woke you," said the boy, he seemed to think he was the one who'd upset me.

"No it's not you, it's me. I've lost all my gold."

"Oh… bummer. Well I haven't got any money here either if it makes ya feel any better… me Dad couldn't get to the exchange place. I am from the normal world, I mean, I am from York, in England, in the other world…" he pointed. "Where are you from?"

I eyed him up, he was a nervous sort of lad who tried not to make eye contact. He had a big leather suitcase with wheels on it. The train jumped and shuddered and I nearly fell and smashed my face into the perplex glass window, but luckily I caught the seat just in time.

"I am from Happendance, the fourth Magical Kingdom… I'm Avis, Avis Blackthorn." It was safe to tell him my name, he was an Outsider. I stuck my hand out to shake, something my family would never do.

"Robin, Robin Wilson…" he said as we shook.

If I told most people my name, especially the second name, they would either run a mile or tell me what an evil family I had. But this kid Robin was from the Outside and, well, he hadn't a clue. Which meant, I had probably just made my first friend.

CHAPTER THREE

The Condor Form

I lugged my backpack off the train and set after Robin who pulling his bag along on wheels! I'd never seen anything like it. A large sign in front of us read *'Hailing Hall that way'* with an arrow. Mind you, as I regained my full consciousness, shaking off the sleepy daze, I saw that there were now lots of other people, our sort of age getting off with suitcases and backpacks. The platform was long, lots of conductors now stood and directed the flow of children up the hill ahead.

Me and Robin followed the chattering crowd. Falling in line behind three older boys who were laughing and joking about, they were slightly older and seemed excited to see each other again. We followed, I huffed and puffed, as the joking threesome walked purposefully out of the station and up a hill. Robin kept trying to make conversation with me and I could tell he was nervous because his tiny eyes were open terribly wide. I couldn't reply to him though because I was so puffed out lugging my stuff up the hill.

Soon enough the hill levelled and we came to these huge iron gates emblazoned with *'HH'* in fanciful metal writing. Following the current of people, we walked into the grounds of our new school - my new home for the next year. Even though I was knackered, I smiled, I was finally free!

Hailing Hall stood huge before us. It was very wide and perhaps five stories tall with a centre spire shooting so high up into the air it was surrounded by it's own formation of clouds. It looked like a monumentally huge manor house, with white brick and mullioned windows. It had taste, I'd give it that. Much better than the cold, grey, sprawling mess that we called our home. In the walk up to the school, along this yellow stone path, we got to see the grounds. Living in a dark castle with no life in it whatsoever, the only plants being some dead bracken, I was gobsmacked at the life in this place. I could feel the Magic in it, which made me feel kind of warm and cosy. There were long green hedges encircling the grounds, which bowed us. Large white stone statues and fountains of animals and strange creatures that stood to attention. They looked happy and playful, watching us enter. There were these strange colourful bird things wondering about, with huge purple fans on their back. I thought it was some strange Magical creature I'd never seen before, but when I pointed this out to Robin, he laughed at me.

"No, they're not Magical. They are just peacocks."

These peacocks strutted around and made an awful racket, but I liked them. I had never seen anything of the sort before. The sun shone across the garden, and it felt awfully nice. I am not used to sun you see, the only sun I ever get is when I manage to escape the castle and go for a walk in the forest.

Suddenly I heard a *NEIGH*!

And then Robin shouted. "Duck!"

We both jumped to the floor as a flipping great carriage came zooming in over our heads.

"Cor, that was close!" said Robin, dusting himself off.

"Yeah…" I said, annoyed. My parents would have sent a hundred Spells at that carriage, but me? I just got angry and carried on walking. The carriage landed some way off, where a landing bay filled with hundreds of carriages sat. People were getting out and marching into the school, their luggage floating just behind their head. I wish I could have done that up that poxy hill.

Then I spotted Ross, my brother, the git had just got out

of Mum's special work carriage. It's completely black, she loves black. Flash git, some girls nearby were crooning over him as he got out.

We waited for ages near the main entrance. This batty looking old woman was lingering near the front — she looked far too mad to be a teacher. A large collection of new years were already there, sitting on their luggage and looking nervous. The sun was going down behind the castle and it started getting nippy. I sat on my bag next to Robin and we watched on in silence, as all the existing years of the school made their way in with curious, devilish glances towards us. Someone nearby kept trumping, I could smell it. To be fair, I was a bit nervous myself but I held in any gaseous give-aways. I wondered how many people here had come from the Outside, where Robin was from. It's hard to tell though, we all look so similar. Looking around at the crowd of new years, there was around fifty of us, but the next moment their must have been a *mega-carridge*, because another forty or so nervous looking first years joined us, sitting down, looking like they might pass out and probably trying not to trump.

The old women at the front put down her papers and, with a flick of her hand, the papers, chair and desk she was sat at all disappeared. I heard a few more trumps. She stood quite still for a moment gazing off into the darkening sky. I couldn't make out her exact age, she looked old, but the way she moved indicated someone much younger. Her hair was greying, long and platted at the back, which is strange for an old person.

"Hello and welcome to Hailing Hall. My name is Magisteer Dodaline. Pick up your stuff and follow me..." she called turning with a flash of her tweed brown robes, and marching off towards the entrance.

Me and Robin sort of stayed close, and followed the line

inside the school. We went through these giant wooden doors and into this great big entrance hall. It was kind of plain, but charming. Stone floor, velvet drapes and hundreds of sheets of paper, pinned to the wall containing a multitude of information. To the left was a great big carpeted staircase. It was hot as well, with fire in brackets going all the way around illuminating the high, beamed ceilings.

"Woah…" we all chorused as we entered.

"Leave your stuff here, they will be taken to your rooms." We all dumped our bags and, as I let go, it slid across the floor to the wall, where they all now stood in neat rows. A name tag popped into life above each bag and wrapped it self around the handles. Wow, this was an awesome place.

Magisteer Dodaline turned to us and waited for absolute quiet. "Shortly, you will be taken in to the Chamber. All the remaining years are already awaiting your arrival. As is the Headmaster, who we address as *The Lily*. You will announce your name and something vaguely interesting about yourself. You will be put into forms and later you will be taken to your allotted rooms. Lessons start tomorrow at 7am, lunch time is at 12pm, lessons finish around 5.30pm and dinner is at 6pm. We have lessons six days a week. Sundays are for homework. Toilets are signposted on the walls. Any questions? Good," she said curtly. "Follow me."

I was suddenly really nervous about having to stand up in front of the whole school, I could see everyone trying to think of some interesting fact. What on earth could I say? I belong to an evil family? I have a birth mark on my left buttock? I had no idea. Magisteer Dodaline walked quickly to the corner of the room. We all frowned, confused. Then, the wall suddenly gave way to a large descending staircase. She beckoned us to follow and shortly, we were stood in a long, tall, underground corridor facing another set of big wooden doors. I could hear a lot of people the other side of these doors. And I'm not afraid to say I cowered behind Robin, who seemed to shrink as far as he could into his green pullover, until he resembled a turtle. The cacophony of noise that hit us when the doors opened was deafening. And I felt this hot draft blow across me. As well as the smells of varnished wood, old stone, burning coals and a strange flowery incense. At once, all eyes in the room turned to look at us.

I looked around at this huge room so as to avoid any eye contact. The huge, long room was stone walled and I see why they called it the Chamber - there were no windows and the stone walls curved round into roof, creating a dome effect. It felt like standing in a huge stone fish tank. The noise reverberated deafeningly around the curved walls which were fit to bursting with stuff. Swords, armour shields, flags and quotes, pictures of famous Wizards and a picture of every form. All the way around the outside of the walls were fire brackets, with the fire changing colour. All through the chamber were these dark oak circle tables where the existing years were now stood. There were ten tables in the middle that were empty. Ours I guessed. At least I didn't have to sit with the existing years, could you imagine if I had to share a table with my brother Ross? I shuddered at the thought.

Magisteer Dodaline led us through the crowd, everyone wore different coloured robes and ties. There was a huge mix, creating this rainbow effect of colours. The oldest and tallest ones were wearing bottle green robes, and what looked like the year just above us were all in red. And in the middle were blues, purples, browns, yellows and oranges. The teachers, or that's who I presumed they were, had their own round table to the left, raised up a little to survey the

Chamber. They all wore brown, black and grey, except one man, who was stood and dressed all in a brilliant, pristine white. When we reached the front of the Chamber we were turned around to face everyone. My heart suddenly began beating a million knots an hour.

"Welcome, welcome!" bellowed the man in white who stood and smiled wide. "I am The Lily, your Headmaster here at Hailing Hall." He began to walk slowly round the staff table. He was an old man, but he had this... aura, I suppose you call it, no one in the Chamber spoke or made any movement when he was speaking. He glided towards us and walked along the line, looking at each and every one of us. He was completely bald, but his white robes were so dazzling to the eye I couldn't look directly at them.

When he got to me, it felt as if time slowed down. My hammering heart stopped racing, I felt calm. Then, I felt as if he had just scanned my entire soul. And I saw this small smile dance across his face. He knew who I was, I didn't even need to tell him my name. His face was kind, his nose large, his eyes grey and spotted, but twinkling as they scanned his subjects. I was already fascinated by this man who was called The Lily.

When he finished, he moved around the room, between the tables doing the same with everyone else who had returned. "At this school we pride ourselves on our ability to learn the most sacred art of Magic. Something denied to ninety-nine per cent of the world. You are the privileged ones. And I needn't remind you of the great power that comes with these abilities. You are all very powerful people, in your own right, and together even more so. Therefore the fate of humanity is in your hands, whether you like it or not. Many have assumed this meant they had the power over those less fortunate, but others know this is not correct. The true nature of man, is not his ability to rule others, but their ability to treat others less fortunate exactly as themselves."

His words echoed around the chamber, no one spoke. Ross and his friends didn't look as receptive. The Lily turned to us.

"We all welcome you here as part of the Hailing Hall family. We have a long tradition of good and able Wizards. To use their skills learnt here to help and improve the lives of others. But also to help sow the seeds to help everyone realise their innate Magical abilities. The lessons here are tough, long, arduous but rewarding. Our Magisteers are the most experienced, practical Wizards you will find anywhere in the Seven Magical Kingdoms. You will shortly, be placed in forms. This form will consist of seven girls and seven boys. They will be like your family. Get to know them well. We have not put them together by random, but in the hope that your qualities will complement each other. You will be given a form tutor each. This Magisteer will be more like a parent. Treat them as such. As for me, I encourage you to come and ask me anything, if you feel the pressing need. So without further ado, lets commence!"

A bong clapped out of nowhere and made me jump. Then, this small pedestal grew out of the ground. The Lily indicated one of the new years to step up. Poor girl, she looked terrified. I was glad it wasn't me first.

"H-h-hello… my name is Ursula Herrald and erm… an interesting fact about me is… erm…"

"Come on," said Magister Dodaline impatiently.

"Erm, erm, is that my great-great-great-great Granddad was the founder of the Herrald newspaper…"

The crowd crooned. That was a good one, I don't know why she hesitated. The Herrald is very popular Magical newspaper. Mum and Dad don't get it, as it's biased against Malakai. But I sometimes saw Butler Kilkenny reading it in the servant's quarters.

Ominously the line trickled down. I felt a ball of gas that needed to be expelled swell violently in my lower colon. I held onto it. Robin was next, and looking more like a turtle peeping out from under a shell, he took to the podium.

"Ello. My name's Robin Wilson, I am from the outside, a place called Yorkshire in England. And an interesting fact about me is that... I won the spelling championship of England aged seven." Robin looked kind of sheepish, he said his interesting fact kind of apologetically as if he felt boasting was sinful.

And then, it was me. My legs like jelly as I walked up to the podium. In my nervousness I think I looked a bit sour. It's not my fault, it's just what my face does when I'm nervous, goes all sour and superior. The Chamber of people looking at me was quite surreal, for I was used to this many people laughing or making fun of me. All I had to do was not muck this up and I'd be fine. I could see Ross's face smiling devilishly, whispering to his friends.

"H-hi. My..." I cleared my throat, because my voice kept cracking. I didn't want to look weak. "My name is Avis Blackthorn." I announced. There was a kind of groan, some people tutted and looked away. Some of the people nearest Ross nudged him. I was losing them already, I didn't want to be associated with my brother, or any Blackthorns, I wanted to be my own person...

"And the interesting fact about me is..." While we were queuing, I decided that my fact would be that I had a birthmark of the number seven on my bottom, it would be sure to raise to a laugh. But, after the initial reaction to my name, I stupidly, trying to win the crowd back announced: "And I am nothing like my family in any way, they are all evil, I am not..."

There was a wave of *Oooing*, as eyes started to sway

towards my brother. He played it cool of course, his dark eyes fixed on me. I felt a wave of dread, I knew what those eyes meant. He was really angry. I swallowed. Some people, I think, looked kind of pleased that I had denounced myself from my family, others didn't look convinced, perhaps they thought it was a Blackthorn trick. I hobbled from the podium in silence and joined Robin at the other side of the Chamber.

The next boy up caused a wail of laughter as he tripped headfirst into the podium, which rocked on the spot. The lad was quite large and got up not looking fazed at all. He laughed at himself with this big booming laugh which made the crowd laugh harder still.

Then he said, causing more laughter. "My name's Hunter. My interesting fact, is that I am not a hunter." He hopped away to join us and nearly head butted me, clearly Hunter was quite accident prone.

We were swiftly given our form name and table. Through sheer luck and good fortune, myself, Robin and Hunter were all in the same form, we were *The Condors*. We sat at this large round table in the middle of the Chamber. Also joining our table, one by one were: Graham, a "Scottish" boy from the Outside. Jess, this red lipped, pure white faced girl who looked like she might break if you dropped her. Florence, a girl with loads of freckles. Dennis, a short funny looking lad who spoke so quickly it was hard to understand him. Ellen, this shy girl with large glasses and long poker straight hair. Jake and his twin sister Grettle, I'd never seen identical twins before, especially not a boy and girl one. They were both blond, with green eyes and this kind of naughty, mischievous look. I wasn't sure if I liked it, they sat side by side laughing intermittently as if passing each other telepathic messages. The last four were, Simon, a plain looking boy from Happendance like me. Joanna, a girl who looked like she belonged more in the woods as her flyaway bushy brown hair would otherwise indicate. Then Dawn, a very large girl who was munching on a box of chocolate raisons.

Apparently the last girl who was supposed to be in our form hadn't made it, or had decided not to come… so we were a form of thirteen.

We all sort of sat there at the table not looking at each other or saying anything. When everyone was seated, The Lily stood and clapped his hands. Suddenly the tables exploded with food! Plates and saucers of all kinds of stuff just appeared. There was so much to look at my eyes kind of went all funny. The food was barely on the table for a second before Hunter picked up his plate and started spooning great clumps of mash, mini pies, peas, peppers, cabbage, this weird sausage looking thing, all sorts. I took a little while longer, before commencing tentatively.

"Weird innit…" said Hunter, he was speaking with his mouth full. I hated that, but I didn't say anything. "There's only three black boys including me in this year."

"Oh," I said, I didn't know what to follow this up with so I kind of looked around and nodded. "I suppose there is."

"Yeah, there's thirty in the year above."

"Oh right." I said, again not knowing what to say.

"Anyway, it's not about how many or what colour is it? We're all the same, we're all Magic!" he shouted and this pea flew across the table and hit Ellen on her glasses, it left a nasty smudge on the front and she just kind of looked at it.

"Sorry," said Hunter.

"It's fine," she said wiping them with her sleeve. "Just eat them with your mouth closed next time."

Hunter did.

I had more pressing issues however. I enquired gently of

the people round the table, as if I was just making idle chit chat, if they had all brought their Ever-changing robes and channellers. Every single one of them said that of course they had. I felt a stone drop in my chest. What if the school chucked me out because I didn't come with the right stuff?

After I finished my jam tart and custard the table fell into a getting to know each other chat. *Where are you from? What's your name again? Are you an Outsider or a born Wizard? Predictions about what we would be doing at school.* All that kind of stuff.

The girl called Jess started speaking to me. "So Avis, you have an older brother here?" I nodded. "So you, out of all of us, must know what will be happening over the coming weeks?"

They all looked at me. "No, well, my brother hasn't told me anything, he wouldn't, we don't get on. He's evil, like my family…"

"I've heard about you *Blackthorns*…" said Dawn, through a mouthful of cake. "You all work for *Malakai.*"

I didn't like Dawn's tone. "No. I don't. My family does."

"Same thing," She said.

"No, it's about as similar as a Dragon and a gecko."

"They're related, both reptiles." She said, crumbs falling everywhere. Her and Hunter really were made for each other.

"You know what I mean." I could tell me and this Dawn were going to have a problem with each other.

"Who's Malakai?" said Robin.

Dawn got there before I did. "Oh, well you wouldn't know would you being an Outsider. He's the most evil man in all the Seven Magical Kingdoms, a Sorcerer, he's killed more Wizards than I've had hot dinners…" I reframed from saying out loud the insult I had in mind. "And he rules with black Magic and evil dark powers. Some say his evil

27

Magic turned him into this horned beast with blackened skeletal hands."

"Nothing wrong with that," said Hunter.

"No! But charred, long clawed hands."

Most people round the table shuddered at her waffle. She wasn't wrong. He was all of those things and more. But it's how she said it that grinded on me.

Graham, Ellen, Hunter and Robin were all Outsiders, like you, and the rest were from the surrounding seven Magical Kingdoms. Jake and Grettle were from Golandria, English was there second language, they were quite good at it but definitely needed work. They kept getting *'hello'* mixed up with *'how are you'*.

Mind you, I would never be able to speak Golandrian.

Soon after that and quite late into the evening the older years took themselves off to their rooms. Then one by one, each new years' table was escorted by a Magisteers to our rooms. Apparently the dorms were all over the school. Ours was out of the Chamber, back into the hall, up the large staircase, then along about fifty hallways, left, right, left, right, left again, I would never remember this! Then along a dark third floor hallway complete with turquoise carpets, oak panelled walls, large hanging chandeliers and strange ghoulish pictures, and finally we were at the entrance to the Condor boys dorm room.

The Magisteer leading us wore all grey and was stooped with no expression whatsoever. He didn't even introduce himself, or even say a word for the entire walk through the castle. He unlocked the thick oak door and pushed. We all traipsed in and looked around. So this was our room for the next year. Seven beds lay spaced around a large open room. It had a three leather sofas facing a grand fireplace, the same turquoise carpet as the hallways, and two tall mullioned windows looking out across the back courtyard.

It was dark by now of course, but in the distance I could just make out the lights from Unverdown.

"Your suitcases are next to your beds," said the Magisteer with no expression. "Bathrooms are along the hallway, turn right, left and right again. Your form tutor will arrive tomorrow morning to pick you up for classes. Goodnight."

We all sort of looked at each other nervously as the door slammed shut. Hunter jumped on the nearest bed and lay down, before we had even searched the beds for our bags. My bag was on a bed was in the middle, facing the windows. Either side of me was Dennis and Graham. Robin was opposite, with Jake, Hunter and Simon in the other corners. The beds all sort of faced each other and it was smaller than the one I had at home. But boy, when I got on it… it was the comfiest bed I'd ever lay on! Must of been made with clouds, or Unicorn feathers. Somehow the mattress seemed to take all the stress out of my body from this monumentally tiring day. Either side of ours beds was a wardrobe, and a desk. I put all my clothes away and stashed my bag under the bed. I lined my pens and paper out on my writing desk. Then, we all sort of collected together by the door to go and get washed. Bit sad really, but if we got lost together it wouldn't be as harrowing. I collected my wash bag and off we went.

We found it ok. The Bathroom was long, with thirty sinks and mirrors all a line, with a large walk in shower and toilet cubicles the other end. Past the long line of sinks were these huge white steel bathtubs, with their equally huge metal taps. Along the wall nearest them was a selection, in glass decanters, of special bath foams, shampoos and soaps. They had some for born-wizards and others for the Outsiders who were a bit squeamish of spider soap and slug juice shampoo.

Robin looked particular grossed out by the selection in my wash bag. He nearly feinted when I started brushing my teeth. Mind you, he began using this white minty stuff, it stank! Hunter, oblivious, was already using some of the stuff in the jars to wash his face. I don't think he looked, because he was using *Worry-free Worm Juice Bubble Bath* to wash his face. He was a strange boy.

I walked back to our dorm with Robin. The girls' dorm was on the other side of school, for this I was glad, as I don't think I could have stood trying to share a room with Dawn.

"What do you think of the place?" I said to Robin, who looked shell shocked, with big bags under his eyes.

"I didn't know Magic existed until last week, now I find myself in a Magic school… it kinda feels like some strange dream."

As soon as my head hit that soft pillow I was out like a light. Strange dreams flew round my head. Like they do when you first go to a new and strange place. I was sure I kept waking up, confused as to where I was. Someone was snoring awfully loud. My bets were on Hunter.

Then, at some god awful time in the night, I had the fright of my life. I had just heard something. So I sat up slowly and peered round in the darkness, snores reverberating around the room. When suddenly, out of the blue this glowing white, monstrous faced entity shot out from under my bad and stared at me. His eyes were black, his mouth gaping wide, his skin crawling with a thousand maggots.

"AHHHH!" I screamed.

The glowing white face screamed back at me, it's gaping mouth opening wider than a black hole. The others woke.

"What's the matter?" said Robin half asleep. I pointed up at the thing, which floated up near the ceiling, a large pot in it's arms. Robin took one look and dived beneath his sheets, trembling. Simon and Jake began laughing.

"Ha, ha," said Jake. "Why 'ar you gettching sca'red of the work ghosts?"

"Work ghosts?" I said, trying to stop my bedsheets from trembling.

"Yeah," said Simon. "They do all the crappy jobs in this place, didn't you know that?"

I didn't say anything, but turned over. Ashamed of myself that I should have screamed out loud because of a ghost. We had loads at home.

"Such rudeness!" The ghost cried fleeing through the wall, dropping the chamber pot with a crash (thank goodness it was empty).

Well, no one told me about ghosts working at the school. As I tried to get back to sleep again, my poor heart hammering in my chest, I could hear Jake and Simon still laughing to each other.

CHAPTER FOUR

The Lost Channeller

It wasn't long before we were all awake. I woke when I heard the bedroom door creak open. Through the curtains I could see it was still dark outside. But now someone with a gas lamp was creeping inside.

"Good morning..." said the voice softly. I pretended to still be asleep. "Boys? *Boys*?"

No one stirred, the man sighed softly. "Oh well..." He clicked his fingers and a second later an ear splitting *BONG!* erupted across the room. There were a few thuds as Hunter and Graham fell out of bed. It shocked me too and I was already awake!

As my eyes adjusted to the small light, I saw a man dressed in a browny-green tweed suit, with a strange triangular hat, large round glasses, and a soft demeanour.

"Up we get boys, up we get..." He began to walk around the room slowly. "My name is Magisteer Partington and I am your new form tutor. Now, get dressed, as we will go and get the girls up and then go for a walk. I'll be outside in the hallway, you have three minutes."

As he shut the door, fire in brackets started to light up around the room, casting a warm, cosy orange glow. I hopped out of bed and pulled some clothes out of my wardrobe. Hunter was still so sleepy he put his trousers on back to front. We all joined Magisteer Partington in the hallway outside.

"Ah well done boys, two minutes and fifty-four seconds. Right, lets go and get the girls up." As we followed him along the corridors, I rubbed the sleep from my eyes. Fire in brackets popped on as we walked, lighting the hallways a fiery orange. I wondered what time it was. It had to be early.

None of us were sure why our new form tutor had chosen to take us out now, for none of the other new years were up, we heard them snoring as we passed.

After waiting nearly five minutes for the girl's, they finally emerged looking bleary eyed and confused. Magisteer Partington took us down a long winding staircase to the main hall, where he stopped and turned. In the new light I saw he had a face like an owl. A long beaky nose with round spectacles and a thin, almost non-existent mouth.

"Now, I do this every year, take my new form on an explore of the school, then we will go and have breakfast in our classroom." he pushed the door wide and stepped out into the dark morning.

I mean, this could have been anyone, how did we know this was our form tutor?

We walked along this tiny stone path around the school grounds. After a few minutes Simon sidled up to me and muttered. "That was you getting scared by the chamber pot ghost wasn't it?" I nodded stiffly, hoping no one else heard. Simon just sort of laughed. What was he getting at?

"I thought you Blackthorns were supposed to be... I dunno... *hard*."

"Yeah well, took me by surprise." I wanted to say something clever, but couldn't. It was too early. Simon sneered, clearly he thought he was better than me, just because he wasn't scared by a ghost.

Magisteer Partington breathed in the cool morning air. "Ahh, I love early mornings, the quiet, the serene beauty. When it gets warmer, we will be able to do some lessons outside." He said, then jumped as a small tree nearest him stretched, yawning wide.

We walked all the way around the huge school grounds.

Robin was counting the windows under his breath, I don't know why. As the sun started rising, Dawn began speaking. How strange, that Dawn should come alive at dawn.

"Oh wow, there's a huge greenhouse. What do we do in there, Magisteer Partyton?"

"Well, Magical studies stretch to more than just waving our hands around and saying funny words," he laughed. "And… it's err… Partington actually."

"And!" she carried on. "I heard that the sycamores gather when it's someone's birthday and sing the ancient songs of birthday cycles. Is that true?"

"Yes, if they like you…"

"Oh!" she burst. "How do you make them like you?"

"Well, just like people, they get a *feeling* for someone."

I didn't know the sycamore trees but I had a feeling that they would find Dawn very annoying. Robin raised his eyebrows at me, he was thinking the same, I just knew it.

The grounds were huge. Magisteer Partington pointed to a place just off the horizon where the grounds ended. It was a mix of forest and open green land separated by large green hedge that moved. Beyond the hedge was a cliff edge and by all accounts a very long drop. Off to the left and down the hill was a stadium with a big chequered pitch, I was going to ask what it was for, but Dawn was asking a rather exasperated Partington whether sycamores liked being hugged or stroked.

As we started walking back round the back of the school, the sun began streaming over the horizon. In some of the windows I could see some people moving around, the rest of the school was rising.

"Right off to form," announced Partington.

He led us back into the school, through the huge main doors then up and up and up, to our form classroom. We started walking up this circling staircase and I had a small feeling we were going up the large centre spire. I was going a little dizzy with the amount of circles we did and the air felt thinner up here. I cursed, if we had a classroom with a long drop I wouldn't be happy. I hated heights.

"Here we are," he led us out of the staircase (finally), into another small hallway. Everything in this place was stone. But the floors were lined with rugs, all higglede-pigglede, with thick drapes covering the walls. Our form room was on the left through the first door. There were a couple of other doors, but they looked empty and unused. We all piled into our new classroom, it smelt dusty and there was a faint whiff of mould, but it was cosy and these great big, dark oak tables with high backed intricately carved chairs. There were windows, at the back, and when I looked out I went a little dizzy, but it wasn't as high as I thought. Perhaps five or six floors. I could just about handle that. Hunter immediately stuck his head out the window and looked up.

"Woah! There's clouds up there!"

"Get in child!" called Partington. "*Jeez*... Right, breakfast!" Partington clapped his hands and a huge platter of food burst into existence on the desks.

We all stood around chatting and eating, the food was really good! All around the outside of the room were these strange objects, most of them with large dusty cloths over them. On the walls were display boards of previous years work: above the blackboard was a display about the *Phonetics of Spellwork*, to the left, near another window was a display of magical artwork based on the famous Wizard Jermain, and behind us were examples of A star written work essays.

Partington made us go around and say our names again. Taking some paper he stretched out his hand, a pen zoomed into it and he started writing all our names down.

Rather informally we kind of stood around and said where we were from and stuff. When I said I was a Blackthorn, he kind of looked at me with half a smile.

"Ah yes, you're the Blackthorn who isn't evil? I remember you from the introduction."

"Yeah, he isn't evil alright, he screamed at the chamber pot ghost last night," said Simon and everyone laughed, I could have punched him.

"They do take a bit of getting used to," said Partington democratically, then asked us if we had any questions for him, so we stood and tried to think of some. "I will be taking you for most of your lessons in the first year, teaching you the basics and what not, but you will have specialised lessons with other Magisteers around the school, only one at first but then others…"

"Is it true that we start at 7am?" said Jess. I couldn't help staring at her red lips, they were so red it was ridiculous.

"Yes. But from 7am to 8am you will be in here doing homework or such like, we call it the *warm up hour.*"

"What is that pitch over there?" I said pointing out the window to the chequered pitch in the distance.

"That's the Riptide pitch, we will be playing a match on there at some stage."

"What's Riptide?" said Hunter.

"It's the Magic sport of course…" said Dawn as if it was blindingly obvious, Hunter shrugged.

"Right, any more questions?" said Partington. "I will get you your timetables…"

I needed to ask him about not having half the right equipment, a channeller and robes but I didn't want to look stupid. He must have noticed because he looked at me. "Avis?"

"Yeah," I said. "Erm… I don't have any Ever-changing robes, tie, or channeller." Everyone in the room frowned, maybe thinking I was joking.

"Right," said Partington confused, then said delicately. "Did you lose them?"

"No," I said looking at the floor, wishing they'd all look away. I should have approached Partington on his own.

"Well… ok… we'll have to sort some out then, won't we? May I ask *why* you didn't get any?" he said softly.

Everyone looked at me and my face went and burned all bright red, which was even more embarrassing. "Erm… well, my parents… they didn't… I never erm… they didn't get me any…" I mumbled.

The silence was horrible. They were all judging me, I could sense it.

"Did you say your name was Avis… Avis *Blackthorn?*"

"Yes," I said curtly, because I could sense what he was thinking - Blackthorn's had a reputation, we had gold and influence so he was clearly wondering why my parents hadn't got me anything ready for school.

"They kind of hate me," I said, trying to offer him an answer. "They are all evil and I am not."

"I see…" he smiled a bit, pleased, I think. "Okay, go with one of the ghosts to the lost property room and get the stuff you need. I am sure you parents will sort out what you need in time…"

Simon sniggered. "I'm not sure that's a good idea sending Avis off with a ghost sir…" some of the girls laughed now, and I tell you I could have chucked him clean out that window, if I wasn't so nice.

Partington had a funny little device on his desk that looked halfway between a little bell and a pepper pot. He shook the little thing and inside this white mist began to form, then it shot out into the room. This transparent man, all haughty and dead looking, said impatiently.

"*Yeaass?*"

"Impkus, can you take Avis here to lost property and see if we can find him some Ever-changing robes, tie, and channeller?"

Impkus, the ghost, nodded slowly then floated off through the door. Partington indicated for me to follow. I sighed, glad of a reason to leave the room and had to run to keep up with the ghost who sailed off down the winding staircase. I followed as best I could as he darted into a main corridor, then straight through a large tapestry. I went under it and followed the glowing white light down three flights of stairs. It was cold down here.

"These are the dungeons…" said Impkus. "Don't make a habit of coming down here too often, unless you want to end up like me."

I didn't know what he meant, it was dark and damp but I couldn't see any danger or way of being murdered.

He zapped through a big metal door to the left, then pushed it open for me from the inside. The lost property room was bigger than I thought and full to the brim with stuff piled up as high as the eye could see. The smell was an overpowering aroma of centuries old dust, something dead and rotten, mixed with a fifty year old broken bottle of Butterfly perfume.

"So you need some Ever-changing robes?" said Impkus chucking an enormous cardboard box to the ground in front of me. I had a short coughing fit as the plumes of dust went up my nose. Inside the box was a mass of tangled silky black ever-changing robes. He made me search through them and boy they stank! I found a few that fitted ok, but they just smelt so bad I had to put them back. Eventually I picked out the only one that didn't smell of mouldy feet and put it on. It was miles too big and the bottom trailed on the floor behind me, but it didn't smell.

"This one will do," I said as the colours changed. The

black faded into this horrible bright turquoise just like the carpet in our dorm room.

"Here's a tie," said Impkus, handing me this thing that looked like a chewed up and, very dead, snakeskin. He noticed my hesitation and huffed. "A tie's a tie's a tie." I took it and stuffed it in my robe's pocket, glancing around to see if there were any others I could quickly take, but there were none in sight. There were lots of old rusty cauldrons, dented kettles and *things* floating in jars but no spare ties.

Next, he chucked me this clear plastic box that jangled as it slid towards my feet. Inside was the biggest collection of dirty, broken, or discarded channellers I had ever seen.

"Which one would you like?"

"One that works preferably." I felt really depressed as I stood there. I had one of the most influential families in all the Seven Magical Kingdom's and here I was, in a dungeon with a ghost, choosing, not even a second hand, but a discarded channeller. Channellers are supposed to be sacred to the user. In our culture it's like a ceremony that you go and you try all these channellers on. Rings, amulets and pendants are all presented to you depending on your personality, star sign and numerological value of your name. The one that's right for you kind of... feels right, sometimes it heats up, other times it does something else. When Wendice got her channeller from *Mardies* (this posh channeller shop) this ring she put on spouted a vision of a man's face who told her that this was the ring for her. (I think it was a scam, because it cost loads). Ross's channeller was a pendant that my Granddad gave him, Ross was his favourite somehow, but when Ross put it on the whole room lit up. Frankly, I wasn't expecting the same thing to happen to me here in this dank dungeon with this impatient ghost. Still, I took my time and lay out my final three choices:

- A gold ring with a picture of a skull on it.
- A sticky pendant with a glass circle inside the pewter.
- This dirty, thick silver amulet, with all these dark markings.

Impkus looked at my choices, and immediately said — "Don't put that ring on!" he promptly took it and threw it somewhere down the bottom of the room. That left two.

"This pendant looks ok," said Impkus. "Oh no… you see this sticky substance? That's channeller blood, when the owner blew his spark using too much Magic it killed the channeller too."

So that left me with the grubby silver amulet. I gave it a polish with my robes and slipped it on my wrist. I don't know what I was expecting; fireworks, trumpets and a marching band maybe? Needless to say, none of that happened. Not even close. There was a rather loud puffing noise and the amulet blew out a circle of smoke. Like a tired out man, breathing out a lung full of stale cigar smoke.

That was it. I waited, Impkus waited. But nothing else happened. They do say if the channeller doesn't like you, then the Magic you do will be ineffectual. I thought about having another root around in the box, but Impkus picked it up and threw it before I had chance. It sailed over a shelf and landed with a crash. He pushed me out the room and led the way back to the classroom, I followed nearly tripping on my new robes.

When I got back to class, everyone else had their robes, ties and channellers on and were all comparing. They laughed at me when I walked in. Their robes all fitted perfectly, stopping just before the ankles. As I was shorter than everyone else in the room anyway, I now looked like a leprechaun.

Partington was admiring Ellen's channeller, which was a

rather extravagant pendant of silver-gold entwined with a polished pearl face. Grettle asked her how the Outsiders get their Channellers.

"Well it was strange," said Ellen, who was coming out of her shell. "The day after we replied to the letter saying I would be attending, this funny man turned up on the doorstep with a brown suitcase full of channellers. We sat down with him in the living room and he proceeded to show me all these different types. Anyway, when I put this pendant on, the TV blew up! And he said I should take that one."

The whole room *Ooooed*. I didn't. It wasn't that impressive. To tell you the truth, I think I was a bit jealous. Out there somewhere in a shop, or a man's suitcase, was my true channeller.

Robin had this thin bracelet kind of thing, made of bronze. Hunter had a signet ring which he proudly waved around at every opportunity. Simon was slightly embarrassed of his and didn't want to show it off much. When I looked closer I had to laugh. He was wearing a thick pearl necklace. I sniggered as he kept it hidden as best he could under his top.

"And er…" said Simon, sidling up to Partington and whispering. "What do we do if our channeller probably isn't what we were expecting? Can we get another?"

"Oh no, not very likely," said Partington.

I laughed, then realised that I had a Channeller that was probably useless. At least his worked.

Jess, Dawn, Grettle, Joanna and Dennis were in one corner inspecting Florence's beautiful ring. I could hear Dennis exclaiming "Oh isn't it beautiful… it's so lovely, your hand fits it perfectly."

I helped myself to another apricot croissant and sat down on my own. After a minute, listening to them all rabbiting on about their channellers, Partington approached.

"Here, you'll need these," he handed me a smart white shirt and a sheet of parchment with my timetable on it.

"Thank you Sir."

Partington turned to the class again. "Oh, I forgot to say, house rules… at night, leave your dirty washing in the dirty washing cotton bags that will appear on the end of your bed. The laundry ghosts will collect them at some point in the night." Simon was about to say something, but I raised my eyebrows and smiled, stroking my neck softly. I think he knew what I was about to say, because he promptly shut his mouth, tucking his pearl necklace further under his shirt.

I was a little concerned that all the other guys had made quite good friends with each other already. Robin left the table where I was sat and went over to Graham and they started laughing and talking together, like two people that had always been friends. I made a bit of effort, I went over and tried to mingle, at the same time wondering how long this *free time* was going to last. I approached Jess and Florence who were talking about their timetable.

"Hiya," I said.

"Hey," they chorused.

"Did you get your channeller then?" said Jess.

"I got *a* channeller yeah," I smiled, they both sort of nodded and no one said anything.

Jess turned back to Florence. "So… what classes did you put in for?" and they began talking to each other about how exciting it was to be doing Practical Magic at last. I stood, awkwardly for a minute, then kind of backed out. I was getting that sinking feeling again. I thought this place would be different, I wasn't expecting to be popular exactly, but just not so wildly unpopular as I had been before.

After this free time, where I mainly tried to enter

conversations and failed, I sat on my own, staring at my timetable as if it would provide me with some thrilling conversation. Partington said we were to go down to the Chamber where we would be able to mingle with other years and forms.

Ergh, more of this? Really?

He told us to dress smartly, so I pulled the tie out of my pocket and put it on. It hang loose, crumpled, and turned a pale, grubby turquoise. The new white shirt Partington gave me was also a little big and the collar left a huge gap. I didn't look, or feel smart as Partington had asked, in fact I'd have felt smarter wearing a gnome costume.

"Remember, we are the Condors!" said Partington trying to gee us up as he led us down to the Chamber.

It was packed full again. Partington led us to our table, but we weren't sat for long. Everyone sort of got up and introduced themselves from other forms and other years. Robin and Graham were walking round together. I sighed, just when I thought I'd made a friend. Perhaps he thought I was too tragic. Hunter had made loads of friends, he seemed to be able to make people laugh, just by laughing, his big booming laugh carrying across the whole chamber. Try sleeping in the same room as him, I thought, then we'll see if you still find him funny. I sat at the table feeling tired and glum. There was more food, spread across the tables, nibbles and drinks littered them like this was a wedding or something. No trifle though.

The Magisteers were sat chatting and observing. The Lily in conversation with a very tall, wide and stern looking… woman? She had one thick black eyebrow, and a tight black bun on her head. Remind me never to cross her. Magisteer Dodaline was talking glumly to the expressionless Magisteer, but broke off, looking thankful as Partington took the seat next to her. Everyone else around me was a stranger, I knew, nor recognised anyone. I felt shy and embarrassed, and anxious that I might end up friendless.

Then I spotted Ross, who, soon as he saw me, came over with his tall, intelligent looking friends and sat next to me.

"Alright little brother?" he said grinning. His friends Hamish and Gascoigne sat to my left giggling like hyenas. "Settling in ok?"

He was up to something. I spotted it immediately. When you live in a house full of evil people, you are always on the lookout for trouble and my alarm bells were ringing straight away.

"Fine thanks…"

"Yeah, listen I forgive you for what you said yesterday. Thankfully most people think you were joking about not being evil," he laughed.

"But I'm not ev-"

He held up his hands. "You don't have to say anything, I told you, you are forgiven," he said softly, too softly. "That's right, isn't it lads?"

His friends, still giggling, nodded. Perhaps he was being genuine? I couldn't tell.

"What are you up to?" I said, I looked behind me to see if there was anyone waiting to trap me in a Magic net or something. Ross held his hands up.

"Oh little brother, this is Hailing Hall, I would never be nasty to you here. We're brothers, and brothers stick together. And hey, I like your new robes and… oh a new channeller, where dya get it?" he actually sounded genuinely interested.

"… lost property," I said. "Mum and Dad didn't get me anything, so this ghost took me."

"Yeah. Mum and Dad they can be… heartless sometimes. Too busy for us, aren't they?" He sighed.

I nodded, still frowning.

"Anyway, take care little brother, see you around. If you want or need anything, just give me a bell. My dorm is on W wing," he touched me on the shoulder and left.

"Sure," I said. "Erm… thanks."

I sat there feeling a little stunned, feeling my body all over to make sure he hadn't done anything to me. Perhaps he was just acting evil when he was at home, perhaps this was the real him at school? Feeling a little better I stood and went to mingle, hopefully this time would be a little more successful.

Robin and Graham were talking to two girls, they all looked really awkward. I saw a large group of people I could join, Hunter was standing there too. They were sort of in a circle and consisting of four girls: two snooty ones, a pretty one and a plain one. Simon was there too, as well as three other boys. One tall bullish lad was regaling them all on a previous victory of some kind. I walked up slowly, feeling stupidly nervous.

"And then, I mean I had to duck," said the bullish lad. "Otherwise the Wolf-raptor would have had my head off." They all applauded, even Hunter who looked transfixed.

"What's a Wolf-raptor?" he said.

"You don't know what a Wolf-raptor is?" said the bullish lad, as if Hunter was a bit special.

"He's from the *Outside*," said one of the snooty girls, she was dressed in a red skirt, which looked pretty silly with her new turquoise robes. I snuck into the circle next to Hunter who didn't acknowledge me at all.

"And then," said the bullish lad, he had a really nasal voice, which I didn't like, he sounded like Ross. "I drew my fathers carving knife and showed the Wolf-raptor who was boss!"

I couldn't help but frown with suspicion, he must have been talking about a dream he'd once had. Then he spotted me and my frown. "Oh hi," he said. "Who are you?"

"Avis Blackthorn," I saw him recoil instantly at the sound of my name. I stuck my hand out, he checked my hand and shook suspiciously.

"Hi, I'm… David Starlight."

I waved at everyone else in the circle, they all nodded back, friendly enough. "Sorry, please carry on… What was that you were saying before?" I said, urging him to carry on. It may have come out a little sarcastically.

"Yeah…" he looked unnerved now. "I was just talking about the time I defeated an army of Wolf-raptors." He said smarting. I think my presence had spooked him and for once I was glad I was a Blackthorn. "And I…" then he stopped speaking, looking directly at my chest.

"HAHAHA!" He burst out laughing, pointing at my chest. Then, the rest of the circle began laughing, except Hunter who looked around the room. I looked around with him, what were they laughing at? I followed their eyes down, down to my robes. Which were flashing up pictures… of me! I went bright red as a picture of me crying flashed up, with *"cry baby"* written next to it, from three years ago when one of my brothers, I don't know which one, ripped off my teddy Sedrick's head. More embarrassing pictures began to flash all across my clothes. Behind me I heard more laughs at this impromptu presentation of my most embarrassing moments.

Me on the toilet. Me naked in the bath. Me hanging upside down by the ankle with my brothers standing around laughing. Me hanging out of the window from the topmost tower of the castle by my pants. The horses eating my ice cream, and an assortment of these kind of horrible memories I'd locked away hoping no one would ever reveal again - let alone to people I was trying desperately to impress.

I tried in vain, to cover it up, but the images showed through no matter what I did. This could have only been one person... Ross! The sly git almost had me convinced. I saw him now, watching with glee from across the room giggling and slapping his friends. Then the whole Chamber was laughing. You should have seen it, honestly, a whole room full of people you want to impress, all in hysterics laughing at your most barest moments from your past, all laid out in front of you, unable to get rid of it. Hot tears welled up in my eyes, and a large lump in my throat. I swallowed. I couldn't and wouldn't cry in front of all these people.

One of the Magisteers came over. I didn't hear what she said, but escorted me by the shoulders out of the Chamber. I stared at the ground so I didn't have to see any more laughing faces. I could still hear the laughing as the Chamber doors shut.

"Are you ok?" she said. I felt so numb I honestly didn't know so I just nodded. She put a hand on my shoulder as the images kept flashing. Hold on, this wasn't a Magisteer. I looked up and saw the most beautiful girl I've ever seen. My sad watery eyes met these big, brown, saucer shaped eyes that sparkled back at me. She had skin like golden sunshine and a perfect, symmetrical face full of freckles. Her hair, a silky, shiny brown, swished around behind her.

"I thought, y-you were a Magisteer..." I stammered.

She laughed. "'Fraid not," we stood there in silence, the picture of me in the bath flashed up again. "My name's Tina by the way. Tina P."

"Nice to meet you Tina. I'm er... Avis... Avis B," she laughed, she knew what my last name was really.

"You a new year too?" she said.

"Yeap."

"It's tough the first few weeks isn't it?"

"It is when you have an evil brother who's determined to make you look like a fool, and it's… so hard to make friends."

"Well you've made one," she grinned and these shining, bright white teeth dazzled my eyes. Honestly, she was a walking model for Toad-Eye Toothpaste. "And, what I find used to work for me was, if you laugh with them, make a joke out of yourself, then they can't laugh *at* you, they have to laugh *with* you."

She was bloody right, you know. This angel had to just walked into my life and saved me. As I watched her walk off back to the Chamber, I half expected her to flap a pair of white angel wings as she waved goodbye.

At midday, lessons official started. We had Partington all day, except the last hour when we had Practical Magic, which everyone was very excited about.

Partington returned ten minutes before the rest of the class, I was already sat waiting, he said he would remove the *photo illusion* for me, it was kind of fading by now anyway. He waved his hands a couple of times and it completely vanished. Thank god for that.

The rest of the class came up together talking about all the cool new people they had met. Jess, Jake, Grettle and Dennis and even flipping Ellen had a giggle as they saw me. I could see Simon gearing up for his ultimate put down and as soon as Partington went outside the room to get something he was off—"Hey Avis, I hope you're not wearing the same pants as the ones you were dangling out of the window on…" On cue, they all laughed.

I remembered what Tina said and smiled. It really hurt.

"Pants? I don't wear pants Simon…" Ok, so it wasn't the best comeback in the world or whatever, and most of the girls grimaced. But I could work on that.

"Right!" announced Partington as he launched into the

room. "Let's learn Magic!"

He gave us each some of this Magic parchment stuff. I was more fascinated with that than the lesson to be honest. Robin, who was sitting to my left and Hunter on my right, were as fascinated as me. What you had to do was write on this sheet of parchment and when you got to the bottom, the text would vanish. But it would appear on another sheet inside your *Main Book*, as Partington called it. He had all our Main Books laid out in front of him, on his desk, so he could check what we were writing all at once. Clever huh?

The pens were simply fountain pens with ink pots. Robin said he preferred it. Hunter however, was getting in a right mess, he would have been better with one of those automatic pens I've seen some of the Outsiders with.

Partington stood regally, fingering his lapels and began to teach. "Magic is a difficult thing to teach because it's an abstract art. We can split Magic up into many different categories, to do with everything in our physical and non-physical worlds. Everything you look at can be affected by Magic, if you learn how. As Wizards, you have a responsibility to stand up for good and challenge the darkness of our worlds. We are the ones who rebalance. I am not expecting you all to choose now what category you want to go into and be a specialist in, but you should keep it in mind. There are specialists working with plants, animals, with minerals even. We have seers who can read the future, or necromancer capable of taming the most difficult of demon. You can be a spirit raiser, a defence specialist, a charmer, a hexer, a dragon tamer, an elemental worker, a weather worker, a builder, a traveller, or a master of black Magic - although I would advise against the latter. Or you can be all of these things. There's so many things to do and be in Magic you can never be bored, yes it's hard work, but fortune in Magic favours the hard working."

After this introduction, we wrote down all the categories of Magic that we could think of.

"Hunter," said Partington frowning and looking down his nose at Hunter's Main Book. "Do you think you can write, perhaps, a little more neatly. Your Main Book is full of blotches and ink spills, it's leaking onto my desk."

"Sorry sir, it's just I'm not used to this pen."

"Well, use one of these automatic pens of mine," he handed Hunter this strange clear pen. "It's a *Biro*. One of my last form, an Outsider, gave me a box full as a present, she knew I liked them."

Partington would, occasionally, add another category to the board, which appeared with a wave of his hand. We went through, one by one, putting a description of what we thought a person who did that job would entail. It kept us busy and I liked it. I felt quite at home here, doing work, so much so that I nearly felt all better after this mornings incident. I looked up at everyone else working hard, the view out of the window was pretty cool now I'd got used to it. The clouds looked like they were playing as they chased each other through the sky. One of the clouds started to mould and change in front of my eyes. I blinked and looked closer as it changed into Tina's face.

"You ok Avis?" I jumped, watching Partington frown at me. "You haven't finished already have you?"

"What? No... I mean, yes, I'm fine... No, I haven't finished"

I looked back at the cloud, but it had vanished. Strange.

At the end of that lesson we had our first external class. Everyone was buzzing as Partington escorted us across the school and down many stairs to this dark, underground corridor lit by fire brackets. A very tall man stood in the gloom and watched his own form leave. David Starlight brought up the rear. I kept my head low, but he still spotted me.

"Hey cry-baby-Avis..." he whispered loud enough for all to hear. I gritted my teeth.

"Yeah," I said as cheerily as I could muster. "Boo hoo, that's me..." it sounded a bit forced, but... success, no one laughed. This was major progress. Or perhaps they were just bored of it? I don't know.

This Magisteer who watched his form leave looked kind of strict. Partington nodded at him then scurried away.

"I am Magisteer Straker, you will address me as Sir. Enter..." He had a barky, short voice and looked really miserable. He wore a grey corset type thing that did up all the way up to his neck, as if his head needed suspending. His robes was as grey as his personality.

We had all been really pumped for Practical Magic lessons, but now that joy had just been sucked out by this fun sponge Straker. His eyes followed us as we entered, but he didn't move his neck at all, and I didn't see him blink once, like a lizard. We trudged into this large dark room with no windows and the cold... *brrrrr*, it was like taking a dip in a frozen lake, soon as you walked into the room, the ice slid into your bones and wouldn't leave.

Magisteer Straker made us line up in alphabetical order, which was harder than it sounds. I was first. Then he looked at us one by one to choose who would sit next to whom. I had to grind my teeth to stop them from chattering as he pointed me to a seat. The room was strange, it was big and split in two. Desks and chairs one side and a open hollow the other, with nothing in it. The only light in the room was coming from these gas lamps that admittedly supplied zero heat. I had Joanna on my left and Dennis on my right. The table we were on was just one long desk facing Magisteer Straker who stood with his hands pressed tightly together, as if in prayer.

The joy that had been sucked out of the room, remained sucked out. Magisteer Straker proved to be an immediately dislikable Magisteer and person. He spent most of the first lesson telling us about the numerous rules that we must abide, if we didn't, it was Magical punishment. However, the rules were so convoluted and confusing and numerous that I, for one, lost track. I got the impression that it boiled down to: don't do anything, unless Magisteer Straker tells you to. Instead of putting our hands up to answer a question, he would just randomly point.

"Most people who start these lessons with me, think they would be jumping straight into some practical Magic. Well, you are gravely mistaken," he said with great pleasure. "In these classes we will be learning the foundation for your studies of practical Magic... and if I don't pass you, hec, you might never get to do any," he smiled, his teeth were all brown in the cracks - he needed whatever toothpaste Tina used. He had, I noticed, long fingernails too. I didn't like that on a man. It looks kind of strange, like he was a part time mole. "You boy!"

Hunter, who was staring off into space, jumped and fell of his seat. "What was rule 37b? ... Always look at me, unless I expressly tell you not to."

"Right Sir, sorry Sir..." said Hunter getting back on his seat.

Straker was scanning a list of paper that he made jump from the desk to his hand. "Ahh," he said the most active I'd seen him all lesson. "We have a Blackthorn."

I swallowed and cowered a little. I couldn't tell if he sounded impressed or wanted to take the mick. "Which one of you is the Blackthorn?"

All their eyes turned to me. I raised my hand slowly. "*Me* Sir."

"Oh," he said as his black disappointed eyes rested on

me. "You weren't the one snivelling in the Chamber earlier were you?" I felt that stone drop again in my stomach.

"Erm, yeah, kind of… my brother Ross he—"

"Great boy! Great boy Ross Blackthorn, real eye for Magic he has, just like his parents." I was starting to get a picture of who and what this man was, and it certainly meant trouble for me. I kept my head down and stayed as quiet as possible for the rest of the lesson.

That night, I stayed up. All the other boys were asleep by half past nine. I put a few more logs on the fire and poked it a bit, trying to get the last bit of cold out of my bones from Straker's room. I went over and sat on the window seat and stared out. Hunter was snoring softly, he sort of sounded like bear choking to death. The moon was bright tonight, and it seemed bigger from the grounds of Hailing Hall. I felt cosy sitting there, with the fire crackling, my pyjamas and dressing gown on and the glow from the moonlight streaming in. And then I thought how grateful I was, that I was here and not at home. No matter how bad it got here at Hailing Hall at least I was not at home. I thought about my first couple of days at school: meeting Tina was the highlight, every time I thought about her, my stomach went all fuzzy, it was such a strange feeling, I wondered if it was love.

Rory once told me that when you fall in love these demons grow inside you and tear your insides out, I believed him for ages. Outside I was sure I could see a tall, dark shape moving in the shade of the hedges. I slid back against the wall hiding behind a tree. The moonlight shimmered on this thing's back, I say thing, because whatever it was, it gave me the shivers. It looked like a tall man, with a long head and small horns and… long blackened, charred hands.

It was Malakai!

The evil high lord of darkness, his form horribly disfigured due to workings of dark Magic, was strolling across the moonlit lawn into the school!

I jumped away from the window. I didn't want to scream again, but I had to tell people that Malakai was here. "Robin… Robin!" I shook him, and he shot up. "What is it?"

"Wake the others, quietly. Malakai's here!" Then I realised he didn't know who Malakai was. "The evil lord of darkness… he's here." I think Robin got the urgency from the tone of my voice.

"What does youw' mean Malakai is 'ere?" said Jake rubbing his eyes.

"Over here," I said. "Look out the window!"

All of them, except Hunter, sleepily trudged over to the window. "Careful," I said. "Keep to the sides…"

"I see nothing," said Graham.

"What are we looking at?" said Dennis. I scoured the darkness where moments before Malakai had been. But now I couldn't see him anywhere.

"He was there, right there!" I whispered, it only took a minute to wake them up, he couldn't have walked all the way up the courtyard in under a minute. Mind you, this was Malakai. "I saw him, bold as brass, head like a goat, hands like a… dragon."

Jake sighed deeply. "I think, per'aps you were 'avin a bad dream."

"No I wasn't asleep, honestly!" They all began to groan and moan that I'd woke them as they drifted off back to their beds.

"Even if he is here," said Simon. "Nothing we can do about it is there? Might as well be tucked up in bed while he murders us. Oh and put that fire out."

I trudged off to my bed. Sick of it. I had definitely seen

Malakai. Or had I? I was sure I had. Perhaps it was someone doing an illusion? I lay there for ages, even the comfy bed couldn't send me to sleep. I lay for ages and ages and ages until the clock above the mantelpiece showed half past three. Then, I felt a twang in my bladder, I needed the toilet. And knowing my bladder, I couldn't wait - but I didn't want to go on my own. I only just about knew the way and it would be dark. And I didn't have a chamber pot, not after that ghost smashed it. But imagine the embarrassment if I wet the bed! Oh jeez, that would just cap it all off.

That made me get up. I put my dressing gown and slippers on and crept out of the room as quietly as I could, there was this floorboard right near the door that squeaked loudly. I made a mental note to avoid that next time. Out into the corridor the fire brackets were on the lowest setting, I could barely see my own feet. I kept my head down as I was frightened silly. Left, right, left, right, I recalled... then the toilets are on the right. Yes, success!

I did the business and sighed happily, ahhhh, that was better. I washed, glancing at my haggard, tired face in the mirror. And I tell you the next second, my bowel's nearly dropped. A face appeared in the mirror behind me, out of nowhere! Scaring the living bejeezus out of me. "*AHHHHHH*!" I yelled turning quickly, ready to attack.

"Ah! Don't hurt me!" said the tall cowering frame of Robin. I dropped my fists, breathing hard. "Sorry, didn't mean to scare you," he said. "I just heard you leave and realised I needed a widdle. Just about remembered the route."

I clutched my chest and leaned against the sink. "Christ, don't do that to me... I thought you were... Never mind."

After he finished we walked back together, my heart coming to rest. "Warn me next time, you could have said something, instead of creeping up behind me."

"Yeah well, I was kinda sleepy."

I berated Robin some more, I was never gonna be able to sleep now! Not after that shock. Then, as we turned out of the bathrooms I saw something out of the corner of my eye — I was sure I had just seen someone dart behind a suit of armour just a way off down the corridor.

"You're not dreaming again are you?" said Robin.

"No, I wasn't before... just down there. I'm sure I saw someone. Come on."

Robin protested but soon followed. I was sure I had seen a person dash behind a suit of armour to the right. We tip toed along the corridor. And then, I knew I was right because I could see them, illuminated by the fire bracket above.

"Hello?" I said quietly. "I know there's someone behind that armour."

"Go away," said the voice.

I looked at Robin who wanted to take it's advice, but I was curious.

"It's alright, we're not Magisteers or anything."

I heard the person sigh then step out. The gas lamp above illuminated the golden skinned, sparkling eyes and brilliant white teeth of, "Tina?"

"Avis?" she looked like she had been prepared to give me a mouthful of verbal abuse, but she completely softened when she saw me. "What are you doing here?"

"I could ask you the same," I said.

"Who's lanky?"

"That's Robin," I said, as Robin waved awkwardly.

"We just went to the toilets," said Robin. "Not together, well together but..." he stopped.

"Right," said Tina eyeing him suspiciously.

"So what are you doing out here, creeping around?" I

said.

"None of your business," she said curtly, then sighed again. "Oh fine, look, you both better promise not to say a *word*!"

I swore, sealing my mouth. Tina looked all flustered, her brilliant white teeth glowing in the darkness, her eyes perpetually scanning the hallways all around us. "I was trying to get into this door. I have a skeleton key but it doesn't seem to be working."

"A what key?" said Robin.

"A skeleton key," she said impatiently, holding it out. Robin was fascinated, he said he'd never seen a key made out of bone before. "It's supposed to open any lock, but it won't," she said.

The door looked pretty plain to me. "What's in there?"

She flicked her hair back, she was wearing her pyjamas too. "Well... that's kind of a secret I'm not willing to divulge."

"What if someone catches you?" I said.

"I'll just pretend I'm sleepwalking," she said matter of factly. "I'm in my jim-jams already... I shouldn't be telling you this... Let's just say, someone close to me, whom isn't with us anymore left me a quest, a big quest..." She turned away and fiddled with the key. "He was my older brother, he went to this school a few years ago. But he died and no one knew why... and then I found this note in his room with my name on. I've been trying to figure it out from then on," she didn't say anything else and after a few goes of the door each, we gave up. We walked back to our dorm, at the entrance to our corridor she gave me a rib cracking hug.

"Promise you won't say anything?"

"I promise," she waved goodbye to Robin and went, back into the darkness towards her dorm.

In bed, I continued to not sleep, but now for different

reasons. After an hour Robin sat up and whispered through the darkness.

"Avis? You awake?"

I sat up slowly, "Yeah."

"What do you think was behind that door?" he sounded like he had been thinking the same as me.

"No idea. It's a complete mystery…" I was thinking more about the hug that Tina gave me than what was behind the door, but still.

"It is… I wish she'd tell us. Wow, imagine being left a quest."

I nodded in the darkness, then realised he couldn't see me. "Yeah, I know." I lay back and wondered what she was up to, did she even know? She certainly had guts to be creeping round the castle on her own at night, all alone on a quest left by her dead brother. How did he die?

Then I thought about seeing Malakai earlier, I know I saw him. But what would he come to Hailing Hall for? Perhaps he was after the same thing that Tina was. I laughed and finally slipped into sleep.

CHAPTER FIVE

An Evil Humiliation

The next few weeks were ok. I coasted along quite nicely. Me and Robin became good friends again, the incident with Tina seemed to bond us together. Anyway, Graham and Simon seemed to strike up a pretty good friendship. We sat together in all our lessons, which at the moment were just with Partington and Straker. The lessons with Partington increased in interest, as we learnt more and more theory, and he started setting us homework all about Spells which I worked through each night, next to the fire with great gusto. Robin next to me, would say things like:

"Is a Solvent-Spell under the Law of Richardson, or is it an Unrestricted?"

I'd scoff and say, "Unrestricted of course! Says it right here…" But, if I was honest, he was much cleverer than me. He picked up Magic a lot quicker seeing as he was an Outsider and I had already done five or six years of basic theory at my last school.

The first Sunday was a full day off, my god that was a sweet day off. It was a gloriously sunny day and I woke up really early, lit the fire then went down to breakfast with Robin who had toothpaste all round his mouth. When I told him he went mad.

"Why didn't ya tell me earlier, instead of letting me walk round like a berk?"

We were pretty much the only ones in the Chamber that early, which was quite nice actually, sometimes it can get too crowded and because there are no windows, you can get a build up of condensation on the roof which periodically drips on you. I sat down as food burst onto the table, I loaded my plate with bacon and sausages and eggs and fried bread. Robin tucked into some porridge, orange juice, tea, then a full breakfast like mine, and some croissants for afters. He could certainly put food away, but I wasn't sure where it went. He was so skinny you could almost see his heart beating through his skin, like a transparent fish. Newspapers popped into life on the table in front of us too now. Two copies of the Herrald. On the front page at the bottom was a small headline about Hailing Hall:

"New Pupils Start a New Year of Magical Studies."

"Wow," said Robin. "We're famous!"

The front page of the Herrald was pretty boring, something about Sorcerers refusing to pay tax, and the leprechauns scrounging off the Magical Council. I never really read newspapers before, but I felt quite civilised as I sat there nibbling a croissant, sipping my tea and thumbing through the Herrald. There was some good stuff too, this is what I learnt:

- The pig people who are in charge of all the gold want to go on strike because they are not allowed massive gold bonus's.
- Mr. Wolfe, the conductor on my train is up in court, responsible for biting a piggy banker (the consensus seemed to be that he was more of a hero than a villain, even though the judge was a piggy.)
- Malakai and his supporters had stormed a local council in Gilliggan and taken it over, (so that's what my parents had been up to).

Robin was very interested about anything Magical and asked me constant questions whenever they popped into his head. He was fascinated with that fact that I was born into the Magical world. Over breakfast he seemed to think of more questions, perhaps the newspaper had sparked a few more ideas.

"So do you have different races or species in your

Magical Kingdoms?"

"Yes," I said sagely, folding the newspaper. "There's the pig people, leprechauns, fauns, Imps, Gnomes, erm… loads really."

"Cor, in my world, we were always taught that those things were made up, myths and fairytales."

"Yeah, course you were," I laughed. "Who do you think wants you to think there a myth?" He looked at me blankly. "We do of course, there's more of you than there are of us."

When me and Robin went back up to our dorm the others were just rising and milling about like zombies. Me and Robin had just started a game of backgammon, before there was a knock at the door. It was some of the girls. I was quite glad because Robin was beating me and I didn't like losing.

"Do you boys want to go for a walk around the grounds?" said Jess, who was joined at the doorway by Gret, Ellen, Joanna and Florence, who winced at the apparent smell that emanated from our room.

"Sure," I said grateful for a reason to abandon the game. Hunter grunted something and turned back over to sleep, Jake nodded at his sister and Simon snored louder, which I guessed was a no.

So we all went for a lovely stroll. The grounds of Hailing Hall are truly spectacular. We went down these big stone steps in the hill, that wound down to the forests. Far ahead lay the cliff edge and a huge canyon. Floating just above the cliff edge was an island. A great big lump of rock, covered with a wonderful, heavenly garden floating on a bed of cloud. A long drawbridge hung across shrouded in cloud. The floating island had a big fountain in the middle with a stone angel statue fluttering her wings, the water from the fountain went off in a stream and fell off the edge of the island in a long, white waterfall down into the canyon. There were benches, vines and little rabbits running all over it.

"We must go to that at some point," said Robin.

"Hmmm…" I said, I wasn't too sure. I especially wouldn't be crossing it with Hunter, he was too accident prone.

"Oh yes, we must!" Florence said, clapping her hands together.

The rest of the gardens were like some horticultural heaven. The statues all spoke to each other gracefully, and the trees sometimes decided that they didn't much like where they were rooted, so pulled their roots out with this weird snapping noise and re-rooted themselves somewhere else. The forest to the left was lit up by the morning sun and you could see all the way through it. I could see some of the older years messing about and chasing each other. Now and again they would do a Spell and someone would be launched into the air by their backside, where they hung limp, robe over their heads.

"Apparently," said Jake, whose English was getting much better. "Dat game 'dey are playin' is called Riptide… you have to work in teams to get as many of 'de other team in the air…" It actually looked really fun.

The path led down through the forest and on the stroll, we met many more people. A lot were just sitting in the sun, in the large grassy open land near the floating adventure play area. Some were doing work where they sat, others leaning against a tree and reading, or sleeping. Surrounding the forest and grassy expanse was a great river, big and wide with a gentle current. We all sat and watched it for a while. It was so relaxing. Some older years were sailing past on this handmade raft, we were surprised because there wasn't much wind. One of them, at the back, was sitting there with his hands outstretched muttering something. The sail on the front was caught, as if by huge gusts of wind.

"He must be a weather worker," said Joanna fascinated.

Some part of me really hoped that Tina would walk past and join us. Only once had I seen her, on the way to a lesson with Straker as we came out, but she didn't see me. She was deep in thought and not paying much attention to what was around her, I am sure she would have said hello, had she seen me. Robin wondered if she had been caught sneaking around yet. I imagined saving her from Straker's icy grip as he interrogates her about the quest, then she hugs me and calls me her saviour.

She was very mysterious. I didn't know what form she was in or anything. Over the coming weeks me and Robin caught a little more sight of her. She would eat lunch and dinner at funny times, often when we were just leaving late. But when she did eat with her form, who we couldn't distinguish, she ate without talking and would be the first to leave.

Me and Robin, whose interest was caught by her... and her quest, wanted to find out more. So, during free time on Saturday we went in search of her dorm room, hoping she would be in there. We searched high and lo, but couldn't find anything.

I had seen a rather haggard ghost float through a wall towards us near the numerology rooms. Bloody thing was deaf as a stone. I had to shout at it to stop, then when we asked it (loudly) where Tina's dorm might be, it just looked haughty and said: "*Boys* are not allowed anywhere near girl's dorms!" Then it floated off back through the wall in a huff.

Our attention with Tina's quest (and Tina herself) was all but abolished by Partington in one fell swoop the next afternoon, when he announced the most terrifying news ever.

He ran into the room two minutes late, skidding on the stone, sweating at the temples and looking round at us with a terrified expression.

"Now, there has been a slight… oversight in this area and… it's not my decision," He said, polishing his glasses, wiping his brow and pacing up and down. "But because of Magisteer Grenadine's illness, her form will not be taking part in the friendly Riptide match tomorrow afternoon. Which means one form had to take their place, and er… well, *we* were chosen."

There was a horrible intake of breath and much farting. "What?…" called Simon. "But we don't even know how to play!"

"I know," said Partington. "If I would have known our first game was tomorrow, we would have been out on that pitch the very first day practicing! Our first match was not supposed meant to be played until the second year!"

Call me naive, but I didn't know we had to do any type of sports or activities at Hailing Hall. I just assumed that we studied Magic and it would be a quiet boys utopia, but this was beyond my coping mechanism and I felt a full blown meltdown ready to exude at any moment.

Partington carried on rather hurriedly. "So today's lesson is cancelled, instead we will be learning the rules of Riptide." Partington carried on in this rather rushed tone, before Graham and Dawn managed to convince him to take ten minutes to himself and come back. He said that was a good idea, and that he would return with the rule book.

When he went, we all burst into terrified shouts.

Jess: "How can this be happening!?"

Simon: "I want to go home!"

Graham: "You're all a bunch of pansies!"

Dawn: "In front of the whole school? You lot better be good!"

Florence: "Is the field muddy?"

Robin: "I hate Sports!"

Jake and Gret: "We love Riptide!"

Ellen: "It sounds scary!"

Joanna: "Oh my god."

Hunter: "What the hec is Riptide?"

I didn't say anything but let out a huge long moan. How could they do this to us? Ten minutes later and after much moaning, Partington appeared looking slightly calmer, but still fraught.

"I have a book with the rules, and I managed to find out the location of the Condor's Riptide Shirts. They all come with your names on."

Oh god, this was all becoming so real! Surely Partington would turn around in a second and laugh at his brilliant joke? But he didn't. He began with a big swig of coffee (or something), and he was off, like an information machine gun... "Right, Riptide... is a game... that's been played here at Hailing Hall since day zed. It's a simple game yet complicated at first, with twelve players and two substitutions. The aim of the game is to get your *flounder*, or coloured ball, into the other team's goal. Yet there is more to it. The main points awarded are for getting your ball into the other team's bolt-hole, or goal. At the same time, they are trying to do the same with their flounder. So you have to attack and defend simultaneously."

This picture of a chequered pitch drew itself on the board behind Partington. Twelve dots moved around on the pitch, throwing a blue and a red ball to each other. "When you get your ball in the other team's bolt hole, you score a point..." this jet of red light shot into the air from the bolt hole. "And light shoots out into the sky. The goal which we

65

call a bolt-hole is a magical stone, looks like a stone fountain, you must get the ball in there." I was taking notes and trying to keep up furiously with what he was saying. "But… you can also score points by stealing the other teams ball and putting in their own goal." Everyone was scribbling down notes now.

"There are seven allowed Spells in Riptide, which is more like twenty-three if you include Counter-Spells. These seven Spells are for offence, defence, effecting your ball and changing yourself or the environment. The main two you will want to use are…" Partington counted on his fingers. "Raising an opponent into the air and the Spell for breaking the Spell that raises you into the air. We will cover these shortly. When you raise an opponent into the air, if they are airborne for longer than *three seconds*, then they are out of the game. If you escape within three seconds, you're safe. It's all governed by Magic, so there's no cheating. When you are eliminated, you will shoot off, back to the game bench.

"Now, the pitch. The Riptide pitch looks chequered, but it's actually what we call an *illusory-habitat*, write that down. It means that the pitch will change into a variety of set environments. So it might fill up with large rocks, good for hiding behind, or with long grass, or with trees, or with historical buildings which make for the best entertainment. It could be anything and you won't know what until you step out there and the whistle goes."

"The flounders are always red and blue. You can throw them, hide them, do whatever you want with them, as long as you get it to that bolt-hole in time. The games run for twelve minutes and there are five games a match. Extra points are earned for getting the entire opposing team into the air, no matter how many points the other team has, you win that game. But don't worry about this too much for now.

"Now, the environment has other tricks up its sleeve. Hidden around it are what we call Ornaments. It might be a vase on a fireplace in a Venetian fourteenth century setting, or a locket in a tree stump… these Ornaments have special powers that last the entirety of a game. The powers are too numerous to name, but could include - making you invisible to the opposite team, they make your ball invisible, give you flight, it could be a Spell shield… literally anything you can think of…"

The whole time he was talking, I was trying to think of a way out of this. These thoughts tripled when I found out the whole school would be there to watch! Fancy that, the first game of the season between two teams who have no idea what they were doing. When Partington finished talking all our stomachs were rumbling, so he sent for food, not that we could eat. I just sat nibbling an egg sandwich.

"Sir?" said Graham. "Who will we be playing tomorrow?"

"Oh…" said Partington. "You know, I never looked."

Suddenly and without warning, Straker appeared at the door without so much as a sound. It scared the absolute bejesus out of me!

"And I thought I was expecting you *all* at my lessons?" he said, voice aimed at Partington. Straker's eyes drifted to the board. "*Oh…* I see we have some new opponents tomorrow?"

"What?" said Partington, sounding like he might break down at any moment. "We're playing… we're playing *you*?"

"Oh yes… my form is the *Eagles* isn't it? And you are the Condors?" he said with a sneer. "Therefore we are playing tomorrow at noon, good luck to you all. Oh, I nearly forgot," he said, turning looking vicious. "You have homework, in for tomorrow from today's class. It will be on your form table at midnight. Anyone who doesn't do it, will get my dungeon detention." He sailed out of the room chuckling.

"Git…" muttered Partington under his breath.

We stood facing our partner. Partington had written seven Spells on the board with a flick. They floated up in shaky white chalk.

Pasanthedine
Kadriepop
Goaternut
Sevhurton
Nouchous
Zxanbatters
Returious

Sounded like gobbledegook to me.

"Make the words big in your mouth as you say them." said Partington. We repeated them over and over, until everyone in the room remembered them without having to look - we *all*, however, had to wait for Hunter who couldn't remember *Zxanbatters* - God, it was painful.

But, everyone pulled together and we did it. I think it was the fact that we were against Straker's form that spurned us on that little bit extra. Once we all remembered the Spells, Partington asked us to put our channellers on and hold our arms out in the correct position, which he demonstrated.

"It doesn't hurt!" he assured us.

I put my amulet channeller on, which felt big and heavy on my wrist, then raised my right hand at Robin.

"On three say the first Spell," said Partington. "One, two… THREE!"

The room echoed with — "*Pasanthedine!*"

As soon as I said it, I felt the channeller grow red hot on my wrist. Then this translucent swirling wind like a tornado expelled from my hand. In fact a whole line of swirling tornadoes flew across the room, hitting our partners square in the chest... but no one moved. Robin just stared back at me through his fingers.

"Ok, try again..." said Partington. "Let's call that one a practice."

We all repeated the Spell again, the tornadoes flying across the room. This time, it worked! Simon, went straight up into the air and dangled by his foot like a bag of shopping caught in the wind. Hunter proceeded to do this dance around the classroom until Partington told him off. Robin, who I was spelling didn't move, he twitched a bit but, disappointingly, that was all. Robin didn't look confident when it was his go, but as soon as he said the Spell, I felt the tornado flap around my robe, before I was yanked unceremoniously into the air. I felt my face grow red as the blood rushed downwards to my robe covered face.

"Yes! *Yes*!" called Robin.

"Well done!" said Partington.

This carried on for hours. I kept trying the Spell but nothing would happen, followed by Robin lifting me into the air. He'd done it so many times now even he was getting bored of it. Finally, with me and Jess, the only two having not mastered the first Spell, it happened.

"Yes!" I cried, as Robin, all nearly 6 foot of him, was yanked up and he floated upside down.

"I see now," he said. "It is rather unpleasant isn't it."

Partington proceeded. "Now you know how to launch each other in the air, it's now time for the second Spell, getting down again. Expect in a match for this to be used as much as Pasanthedine. You must know your *Kadriepop*."

We did the same again, this time launching our partner in the air and watching them flounder around recalling the

Spell…

"Kadriepop! *Kadriepop!*" Robin cried as I bent over laughing with Graham.

"No, no Robin," said Partington as Florence and Dawn floated back down looking red in the face. "You have to move your arms in the circular motion around your body…"

Eventually Robin got it. I didn't get it so fast, I now languished in mid air going a little dizzy waving my arms around reciting the Spell over and over. When I did get it, that was it. There was no going back. The atmosphere in the class got better and better with each success. We all applauded one another whenever someone completed another Spell. The other Spells were not as important as the first two, but still played a big part in Riptide.

Goaternut - made you kind of blend into the background like a chameleon, but it weighed you down to walking pace.

Sevhurton - froze a patch of ground making it skiddy.

Nouchous - created a temporary wall of fire.

Zxanbatters - that gave you a magnetic grip of the ball.

Returious - is kind of a complicated Spell, because its a bridge to other more complicated Spells, like growing the grass taller, or cutting through it, or raising the water levels or being able to see through buildings. So you'd have to say '*Returious* - ____' then the other Spell.

"Ideally…" Partington was saying. "You will want to use all these Spells to become the biggest bad-ass team in all of Hailing Hall! But for now just concentrate on the main two."

In the afternoon Partington took us to the Riptide pitch. He made us run up and down to see who was fastest. The stands were huge and stretched all around in a hexagonal formation of oak stands and red seats. I imagined it full of people, then regretted it as I immediately felt sick.

When we sprinted to the end of the pitch, I beat everyone! I was always fast as a kid, you have to be if you have lots of evil siblings chasing after you. Robin and Hunter were really slow, as too were Dawn and Ellen, who ran with her hands in her pockets.

We practiced our Spells some more as we ran around. Partington said it was harder to aim at a moving target. It was too, you had to really aim your arm right. I managed to get Simon, who I had been aiming for all afternoon, he was scooped up in the air and hung, robes over his face, whimpering. I smiled. The girls were much better than I thought they would be, that's not sexist or anything, it's just my sisters never played any sports, mind you, exercise is not their strong point. Eating cake is though.

Gret, Jess and Joanna were naturals. When Partington got the flounders out, which were blue and red, he chucked them to us. They were both biggish but able to be held in one hand, squishy but hard and made of Hubris leather and it had these tiny sparks all over it.

"Now remember, the Spells we learnt earlier can be applied to the flounder too. So, you can freeze it, disguise it and hide it, put a wall of fire around it, or anything else via Returius... but also you must learn how to throw and catch, kick and control... When the ball is in the air you can use Kadiepop to guide it towards you. When it's on the ground you can use Pasanthedine to shoot it into the air. But *communication* is the key."

We threw the flounder around to each other and ran around attempting Spells on them, all were moderately unsuccessful. Then it started getting dark and cold. In the school were warm orange glows of fire as people retired to their common room for the night, or perhaps had some dinner in the lovely warm chamber. We, carried on all night, running around the pitch with those blue and red founders. How ridiculous we must have looked.

"This is how we will line up tomorrow," said Partington holding a large sheet of paper with the ink moving around. "Hunter, you're *Guardian,* that means you keep back near our bolt-hole at all times and protect it. Robin, far left, Avis far right…" I didn't know if this was good or not so just nodded. "Jess and Florence down the middle attack, and Jake and Gret centre…"

We had no idea really, I think he put Joanna at the front because she's kind of wild. Jake and Gret together in the middle because they are pretty tough. Hunter at the back because he's useless. And me on the right because I'm kinda quick? I don't know. Literally, I had no idea how tomorrow would pan out.

We all trudged to the Chamber, grabbed a plate of dinner and took it to our dorm room. I saw David Starlight grinning at me, bloody idiot.

We all sat around the fire in silence. I nearly fell asleep with a sandwich in my mouth, thinking about the game tomorrow just made me feel sick. I already had a thumping headache and needed a shower. Then, on the table, this pile of sheets appeared.

"Oh no!" cried Robin. "It's the bloody homework from Straker!"

I'd forgotten, we all had! The clock chimed for midnight, and we all moaned.

"Let's just do it as quick as possible, even if it's rubbish at least we can say we did it." I said and they all kind of agreed, although I think they would have preferred to go straight to sleep.

The questions Straker had set us were so hard! He'd done it on purpose of course, but what a sneaky guy! My eyes were drooping as I wrote the last sentence. Hunter was already asleep on the sofa, and Graham's handwriting was barely legible. Just as I was about to get undressed and climb into bed, there was a tiny knock at the door. The other guys were asleep and Robin was nodding off, his ink pot dangerously close to spilling all over him. Tina poked her head round the door, saw me and grinned. My stomach did a strange flip, I rubbed my eyes for fear I was dreaming.

"Fancy joining me?" she said grinning her perfect grin.

I couldn't say no could I? Not to Tina, this brilliant girl that had occupied my thoughts almost entirely for the last three weeks, so I cranked myself out of the seat and tapped Robin. He looked around with big bloodshot eyes, saw Tina at the door and stood instantly like a soldier standing to attention.

At the door she inspected us. "Are you sure you're ok? You both look knackered!"

"We're fine..." I said smiling. "Where are we joining you?"

"You'll see..." me and Robin followed her sleepily along the corridors, I kept stumbling, my legs felt like jelly and Robin nearly walked into a suit of armour. "What's up with you two?" she said, pulling Robin upright.

"We've been playing Riptide all day... shattered..." said Robin.

"Oh, well, if you would prefer to go back to bed that's fine."

"No!" me and Robin chorused.

"We want to be here, believe me," I said. Some part of me had wished that she'd have picked a better day to go off gallivanting round the school at night. But this was Tina.

Robin began peering through his glasses as we went deeper into corridors. "Where are we going?" he said.

"Aha, here we are..." she said, as we stopped outside these large wooden, double doors.

"The Library?" said Robin sounding disappointed that

he was missing out on sleep to go to the Library.

"Yes, the Library. It has books and things, first years aren't allowed in without supervision, but... I am sure there is a book in here which has all the information I need about..." She looked around, then leaned in closer. "...*my quest*. It's just finding it that's difficult, so you guys need to help me look."

"But..." I said. "We're not allowed in the Library, what if they catch us?"

"What if, what if. Do you want to help me or not?" she said with a stern look.

Me and Robin nodded. Tina put her hand to the lock and whispered something that sounded like *Percival*. The door swung open silently and we trotted inside. Moonlight lit the dark, dusty room. I say room, it was more of a cathedral in size. As long and far as you could possibly see. In the middle of the room was a small river, with bridges going over all the way along. I'd never seen a Library with a river in it before. Tina clicked the door shut behind us and marched in. The bookcases were so high there were ladders a hundred feet tall, if not bigger. You wouldn't get me up one of them.

"Oh bums, this is a lot bigger than I thought it would be..." said Tina, marching around.

The hunt was unsuccessful, Tina grew increasingly frustrated as we all searched for this mystery book. Me and Robin were searching blind. We had no idea what we were looking for.

Robin began leafing through one book and said. "Wow, this books got Spells in it. There's a Spell here that blocks Magic attacks!"

"What?" I said. "Pass me that book."

Robin chucked it down to me and I read. It said this Spell would block most basic Magic, including Illusions,

Hexes and Spells.

Dancidios was the Spell-blocker.

"Robin, Spell me!" I said. "Let's try it out."

Robin raised his hands at me. "Pasanthedine!"

The tornado swirled towards me. "*Dancidios*!" I said. And as it tried to yank my leg up, this giant black paw batted the tornado away, as if it was an annoying gnat.

"Woah!" we both said.

"OI!" called Tina from a long way off. "You didn't just do what I think you did, did you?" She said, suddenly appearing stony faced. "Because this Library has Anti-Spell alarms after hours…"

"Whoops…" I said.

Tina swore loudly. We didn't know that did we? She hadn't told us. "But you Spelled the lock on the door?" I said as she began marching to the river in the middle of the Library.

"That was outside! You idiots! Bloody idiots! You've ruined it!" She climbed into one of the little boats and unhooked it from the side. "Get in!" There was a rumbling and echoing of running footsteps outside. People were coming. I stepped into the boat as fast as my jelly legs would allow. "HURRY!" she pulled me into the boat and shoved an oar in my arms.

"Row!" she said.

Me and Robin rowed, the boat cut through the water silently and under three bridges before we sailed into what looked like a big, round, black hole. Underneath the corridors of the school. I, to tell you the truth, was terrified. As we went into the pitch darkness and out of the moonlit Library, we heard these deep voices echoing round in the cavernous room behind us.

- "Intruders, in the Library!"

- "Spells and Magic has been done."

- "Send for the Magisteers and Ghosts, we need to do a head count, see who is out of bed."

Tina leaned across to us in the impending darkness and whispered. "Row faster, we need to get back to our beds before they do."

We did, we rowed and rowed hard. My heart was beating fast, the adrenaline pushing my arms forwards. If I was sleepy before then I was fully awake now. Robin was panting hard next to me. The roof above us was low and dripped water, or whatever it was, on my head.

"Ouch!" Robin yelped as his head made a crunching sound as it collided with the low roof.

"Quiet!" Tina snapped. We had no idea where the boat was going, only Tina seemed to know.

"Stop here," she said. "You two get out, touch the wall, there should be an opening." Robin fumbled around, with Tina tutting, and managed to find these slippery stone steps. I was really wobbly getting out of the boat, but with Tina's sharp hisses giving directions, my feet found solid ground.

"Where are you going?" I said as she began rowing off.

"That's the nearest entrance to your dorm. Mine's up here. Speak later *idiots*."

And that was it, she disappeared into the blackness. Robin began slipping up the dark steps, he nearly bloody slipped and fell in that water too. I wouldn't have been able to even save him because I could see nothing. God knows what was in that water! But when we walked up through that cold, pressing darkness Robin only walked ten steps before whispering:

"Found it…" He was looking through a small grate. Through it, I could see sinks and cubicles. It was the boys bathroom, right near our dorm! Tina sure knew what she was doing. Robin pushed the metal grate away and we squeezed out of the gap as quickly as we could, pushing the heavy grate back into place.

Then we legged it back to our dorm. As we rounded the corner, I could hear footsteps and voices coming quickly from behind. We jumped into our room, closed the door and got back into bed, with all our wet clothes on, just in time. Because as soon as my head hit the pillow, we heard voices outside the door. Then it opened. A dull glowing bluish light fell into the room.

"That's all my lot accounted for…" said Partington's soft sleepy voice. Then the ghost that must have been with him muttered in suspicious agreement.

And then, I fell into a blissful, yet short sleep.

When we awoke the next morning, big yellow and black shirts with names on, hung at the end of our beds. For one glorious second I thought it was Christmas and a big stocking awaited me filled with glorious goodies. But then, as the sleepiness slid away I came back to reality and realised what they were. I heard some of the boys talking, I just wanted ten more minutes sleep.

"Do we wear them down to breakfast?" said Graham.

"No," said Jake. "If we win then we will wear them to dinner."

I sat up bleary eyed about twenty minutes later feeling no better. Robin sat up and we exchanged sympathetic looks. The others had gone down to breakfast already.

"We were that close to being caught," I said, going over to poke the fire. My legs and sides were burning.

"That was too close for comfort," Robin said before chewing his lip anxiously. "Hey, are you a bit nervous about today?" he was fumbling with the yellow shirt on his bed.

"Yeah," I said, usually I would never admit my weakness as my parents would always tell me, but I was petrified.

Butterflies were multiplying and churning somewhere deep in my stomach.

"Me too," said Robin, looking a deep shade of green.

Partington was so nervous about the Riptide game we had to calm *him* down. Our classroom was full of nervous pacing, and farty noises. At eleven-thirty it was time to make our way down to the pitch. The whole school was already in the stadium. We had watched them making their way over there. We got dressed into our shirts, mine was overlarge as usual and resembled a baggy nighty. Hunters didn't fit at all and threatened to burst at the seams, and Robin's was so baggy and small he looked like a stick insect in a dress.

"They could have took our sizes!" said Dawn, who looked to be struggling to breath.

"Mine fits beautifully," said Dennis, doing a pirouette.

Partington led us out of the safety of the classroom, through the deserted school and towards the pitch. I felt like my innards could fall out at any moment and I hadn't eaten anything. I just couldn't. The girls were really quiet and huddled together like cold penguins. And then, sooner than possible, we were standing in this long, dark tunnel waiting to go out. I could hear the crowd roaring. I felt like crying. Robin's face was a darker shade of green than the pitch. Graham and Simon looked grave, and both starred at the ground. Gret and Jake had their heads together in a baying silent prayer or something. Hunter was trying to crack jokes but no one was listening.

A tall thickset woman dressed all in black, came up and began searching us one by one with a long probe.

"I'm Magisteer Underwood, the referee. I'm just searching you all for restricted weapons and Spells," she announced, running her hands all over the place, which felt quite undignified.

Then, she signalled for us to go out. This was it. Butterflies in my stomach doubled, tripled, then flapped around at a furious pace. And I needed the toilet. Again. But it was too late now. Joanna was at the front and began leading us out onto that chequered pitch to a tumultuous roar. The sound was deafening, it kind of hit you making your ears squeal. All around us were faces and eyes. Some part of me felt like this was some massive trick and at some point they would say *'hold up guys, it's only a joke your not really playing… that would horrible and mean of us… go back inside in the warm.'* But that didn't happen. The sky was dark and cloudy and moisture hung in the air. The crowd were wrapped up warm in robes and scarves as I stood, jealous, in a baggy yellow dress with my teeth chattering against the cold.

Partington was waiting for us at the side of the pitch and began yelling to us over the noise. "Take your positions… and ready yourselves."

What positions? This was really happening. And none of us really knew what to do or expect. I walked over to the right side of the pitch, over the chequered squares. I could hear a section of the crowd calling my name.

"Avis… Avis… Are you really a Blackthorn Avis?" I didn't look up, but it sounded like my brother and all his friends, before large swathes of the crowd began to join in. The Stadium looked bigger now it was full of people, eyes from everywhere watched and judged, almost sensing our ineptitude before we'd even started.

Then, Straker appeared, with his form the Eagles, dressed all in red. Leading them out was none other than David Starlight. Straker stood next to Partington, who ignored him.

"Okay…" called Underwood, who had a whistle floating just in front of her mouth. "Take your positions. As we let the Habitat *change!*" Then she gave a gigantic blow on it.

There was a great roar from the crowd and I had to shield my eyes as a blinding white light lit up the green pitch., Suddenly we were standing on this sandy desert with small mud huts and cactus plants. It was surreal, all at once we were in the wild west. The cactus plants were huge and spiky. The tall mud hills steep, and the sand was hot.

"Ooo, a nasty one for this match," said Underwood. "Your flounders will appear in your bold-hole in five... four... three..."

I wheeled around to look at Hunter, the ball would be appearing right next to him. "Two... One... *PLAY*!"

Twelve shots of fizzing Spells went straight for us. One hit me in the face and I felt my body swell into the air. What was the bloody Spell called!

"Kady... Kadie... *Kadriepop*!" I cried, falling to the floor. As I wheeled round surveying the scene as time seemed to slow: Hunter hadn't spotted the blue flounder in our bolt-hole, but that was the least of my worries. Robin, Jess, Dennis, Florence, Ellen and Simon were hanging in the air, then all at once a streak of blue light zapped them off the pitch. Oh no. Now it was only me, Gret, Jake, Graham, Joanna and Hunter left. The Eagles began running full pelt across the sand towards us. I ducked behind a mud mound and saw this red ball go flying through the air towards our bolt-hole. Hunter finally realised, with Joanna screaming at him, where the ball was. He picked it up and threw it, but not before a fizzing Spell flew through the air and smacked him in the face, raising him into the air. What's worse, our blue flounder stopped in the air and flew back towards our own goal! David Starlight burst past me hiding behind a mud mound, kicked off a cactus, launched himself into the air, caught it and smashed it into our bolt hole. A shot of blue light erupted into the sky.

I could have Spelled him, that was my chance! But he

was so quick I had no time to think. We had to get the other ball. I looked up round the mound. The other ball was…

"*AHH!*" I cried as I was launched into the air. I hung upside down with David Starlight's face grinning at me.

Then the git laughed. "Did you really think I didn't spot you?"

Before I knew it, this blinding light took hold of me and yanked me by the toes towards our team bench, which was quite full already. I sat breathing heavily, and took in my surroundings. That could not have been any more humiliating. Robin was on my left looking green still. We were sat in a line, on a long bench, set just away from the crowd near the pitch. It was a humiliating position to be in as everyone could see you. This was more brutal than we imagined and the crowd was laughing!

Gret and Jake soon zapped back, so poor Joanna was the only one out there now. We couldn't even see her. The Eagles had found our other ball and scored, but now, with eight minutes left they could Spell Joanna and receive full points.

It didn't last much longer than a minute, somehow Joanna had found an Ornament which turned her invisible, but one of the team spotted her footprints creeping through the sand and they got her.

The announcer suddenly called out, nearly scaring me half to death — "AND THATS THE END OF GAME ONE! 5 POINTS TO THE EAGLES!"

Straker smiled smugly. The worst bit about this was — we still had four games left.

The second game was another white wash, they won 4-0. Only because Hunter managed to throw our ball out of the stadium! I think it caught a charmed tree on the Habitat, which this time resembled a thin dead forest, and was belted away by it. The games were getting rougher too. As we ran through Robin got an elbow to the jaw and hung in mid air while blood dripped all over our ball.

By the third game, I lasted two full minutes! The habitat was this grey rocky plane with hidey holes, cracks and tunnels. One of the Eagles ran straight past me. I lifted my hand and aimed for him.

"*Pasanthedine!*" I called. The tornado zapped straight for him as my channeller burned red hot. He shot into the air and dangled helplessly. Zapping back to his bench. God that felt good. The crowd who had taken to laughing at our ineptitude were quiet for about thirty seconds. Jess had the ball and had managed to make it invisible. Robin, Graham and Joanna stumbled upon us, and together we charged towards their bold hole… only to *all* fall down a large crater in the rock. I grazed my knees and the Eagles almost didn't Spell us in time, they were laughing so much. Partington had his head in his hands.

By the forth game, there was this long grass, surrounded by bracken, and we lost 2-0. We still hadn't even scored! It took until the final game for us to actually score a point! The Habitat was a terraced house street from the Outside world. Florence found an Ornament in one of the houses that gave her flight. When the Eagles tried to Spell her they all missed as she circled above the pitch Spelling all the Eagles. Joanna ran clean through as they were all looking up and scored! The crowd didn't clap or celebrate though, only a few ironic cheers greeted us.

"WELL DONE TO ALL WHO PLAYED TODAY. TO THE EAGLES…" there was a massive cheer. "AND THE CONDORS…" There was nothing, except maybe laughing. "NEXT TIME… IT'S THE MANTICORES AGAINST THE CENTAURS IN HAILING HALLS RIPTIDE!"

So that was it. Our first venture as The Condors into the world of competitive Riptide. And we were awful. I mean, absolutely rubbish. We were laughed off the pitch. Partington couldn't get out of the stadium quick enough. We tried to keep our heads down as we mooched away down the tunnel and back towards our form class. We all huddled together. I had cuts and bruises all over me and my shirt was torn in several places.

David Starlight had made sure to clatter into me at every opportunity and my knees were grazed and sore. Robin was all but crying, he had scraped all his palms and couldn't move his jaw. Jess and Florence looked disgusted with themselves as they waddled back, caked in mud. Gret and Jake whispered conspiratorially in their own Golandrian. And Dennis was actually sobbing because his shirt sleeve was ripped. Ellen put her broken glasses back on and Simon bemoaned to Graham the lack of training.

As we walked back, some people were pointing and laughing. I heard people saying:

— "He's a *Blackthorn*? You must be kidding me!"

— "A Blackthorn? He's got about as much Magical talent as a gnome!" followed by cackles of laughter.

"Hey little brother," said this ominous voice that sent shivers down my spine. Bloody Ross with more of his goofy strange friends, sidled up to me. Some of the faces around us turned to look. I carried on walking, climbing the stone stairs back to the school. He was going to Spell me, I knew it, after years of him at home I could read him like a book.

"So you're not signing up for the Riptide All-Star team at the end of the year then?" he cackled in his best impression of Mum. I ignored him. "I cheered you on, you have to stick up for one of your own don't you? But the thing about Riptide is, you really need to THINK FAST! *Aperincho*!" He called. A whizzing red and purple ball of wind shot at my face.

"*Dancidios*!" I had it ready in my mind. And miraculously, his ball of thorny light fell to the floor leaving only a scorch mark. His face dropped. I've never seen it do that. The people around us who had stopped to watch, crooned.

"Looks like little Avis has learnt a thing or two at school," he spat.

"Not enough..." said another voice behind me. "*Parsanthedine*!" Yanked up by my toes, I dangled helplessly in mid air as David flipping Starlight grinned at me again. Again! Blood boiled in my veins.

"You bloody coward!" I called. "That was from behind!" The crowd carried on walking. David and Ross high-fived, and walked off together.

"Kadriepop... *Kadriepop*!" I must have been there for an hour, I had no strength left to wave my arms round. Fortunately, Partington spotted me out of his window, Spelled me down again and walked off without a word.

I was fuming. I thought this school was supposed to all be about being nice to each other, helping one another out and cheering each other on? The crowd had just laughed at us playing Riptide, did they not know that we had less than a days training? I know we were awful, but still. I couldn't help this burning cauldron of fury burn inside me all the way back to the dorm. I wasn't going back to the classroom, no way. I stomped mud all the way back up the corridors, several ghosts chased after me and shouted at my dirty insolence. So I returned some choice words for them and they soon disappeared.

I was sick of it. The humiliation, the teasing, the bare faced bullying, the not being good enough, the lack of respect from everyone. I couldn't face it anymore. As the blood rushed back to my head, I decided...

I would make them all regret the time they crossed Avis Blackthorn. It was time I did what my family had always wanted, and got my revenge. Time I became a real Blackthorn... it was time that I became *evil*.

***

I didn't really speak to anyone for the next week, keeping to myself. I had been making copious notes about how to be evil and what I could do to get my own back on:

- David Starlight and the Eagles, (the image of them laughing at us in the crater still echoing through my mind).
- My git brother Ross.
- Anyone else who had crossed me.

What was even more unfortunate was the fact that we, the Condors, were kind of infamous now for being '*The worst Riptide team in Hailing Hall's history*' — even though it wasn't true.

Everywhere we went as a form, people would point and laugh and remind us of our 'huge loss' or remark on the awful Spell I did or something else that was equally appalling in their eyes. I would try and ignore it, but it just made me more fired up about being evil and making a note of each git face who laughed at me in the corridors.

Hunter was so upset about being continually teased as he walked the corridors that he took to being late for lessons so he could walk the corridors alone and in peace. Add that to the fact that he'd been sleepwalking. Me and Jake saw him, the night before. He got up to dress, but then put his trousers on his head and proceeded to crawl around the floor searching for the door. The stress had got to all of us. In class, an argument had erupted between the girls. Dawn and Florence began tearing each other's hair out and had to be separated by Partington.

One night, sitting by the fire, me and some of the boys were doing *more* Straker homework, the git had given us an assignment on *the rules of Riptide*. None of us had properly spoken since that day.

Robin, who was rubbing his jaw, looked up. "Do you think we'll ever be like… cool?"

Graham sniffed. "Not while we're at this school, not unless we modify *everyone's* memories."

Hunter, who had a right sour face, said. "We're the *losers* aren't we?"

I wasn't listening too much, concentrating on my evil plans which I was brainstorming, having finished my homework. I put my ink pot and pen down and looked up at them, trying to be cool and mysterious.

"We're not losers," I said. "We're just not… *respected*, yet. We cannot blame ourselves, we had one day to learn Riptide. Straker's form had a month," they all nodded, I had them onside. "What we need to do now, is show everyone, that we are not to be *messed* with…"

Some of them scoffed. "And how?" said Simon. "Do we do that?"

"My parents are evil. I've learnt a lot from them over the years. Whenever they think that someone has disrespected them, they show them how mistaken they were. They scare the living daylights out of them." They were all looking at me with wide eyes. "We do something *evil*… Something that will make people so scared of us, that they daren't say anything else."

***

I had the formation of a plan. A plan to resurrect what dignity we and I, had left. To be honest with you, this plan benefited me more than the others but they knew it would only work with me. Anyway, if we pulled this off, no one would ever say or do anything to us again.

Over the coming weeks, me, Robin and Hunter talked non stop about the plan. Graham occasionally came over to join us, but I don't think he could decide if he was wanted in or not. Jake refused point blank when I told him the plan and Simon shrugged and sat on the window seat in silence. Dennis spent so much time in the girls dorm, that we hardly had chance to tell him.

"We ought to tell the girls you know," said Hunter. "They might want to join in, get some girl power back!"

We laughed at him, he was funny. "Yeah, they have been a bit... what's the word?"

"Hormonal?" Hunter offered.

"No, no..." I said. "Just depressed. Joanna sits on her own in the lunch hall, Jess has come out in Hubris stress spots, Florence and Dawn try and rip each others throats out at every opportunity, Ellen has retreated firmly back in her shell and Gret..."

"Gret is fine," said Jake. "She a tough cookie, like you say."

"Fine, Gret is fine..." I said. "But this has torn all our form up, least we can do is ask them."

Jake led the way to the girls dorm. We had to walk through three tapestries and up five flights of stairs until finally, along this well decorated hallway with lots of pictures of famous Witches lining the walls, we knocked on the door. None of us, apart from Dennis, who slept in there most of the time, had ever been in the girls dorm. When Dawn opened the door and let us in, we were shocked. I mean, we didn't say anything, but it was a complete mess. Clothes and stuff just chucked all over the floor. There was even a ghost in here which lit the room up a silvery glow (as the curtains were drawn), it was aimless picking stuff up and putting it into piles looking stressed.

"Oh hey boys," said Florence looking uninterested. She had a crush on a boy the year above, since then, she didn't really like to talk to any other boys. Girls are weird.

"We need to ask you something," I said.

Needless to say, their apathy was contagious. They were not interested. You couldn't blame me for trying. Ellen thought the plan was good, but had a few flaws — our ineptitude for Magic for a start. Jess, who was applying copious amounts of *Beatle Bum Gel* to her face, thought it was an awful idea and Dawn, who was really quiet, just sat and poked the fire.

This, if anything, made me more determined. I wanted to raise the morale of the girls, and the boys for that matter. In fact, I would be the saviour of the Condors!

CHAPTER SIX

Malakai

"*Severton...*" I said. There was a sealing noise as the black river froze.

"It's way too dark under here!" said Graham, as Robin shushed him. We were in the tiny passage, facing the black river leading to the Library. We'd all just climbed down through the grate in the boys' bathroom. It was my idea, I kind of thought it would be the only way back in the Library as I couldn't remember the door unlocking Spell that Tina did. The freezing Spell was Robin's idea.

"Come on..." I said, putting my foot onto the ice, crouching and moving along the frozen river gingerly. Surprisingly, it didn't crack or anything.

"This is crazy," said Graham who quite possibly, was right.

"Just space out," I said as Hunter stepped onto the ice and there was an ominous splitting sound. We stumbled and slipped through the blackness, crouching all the way along the river, until we stepped into the light of the locked Library.

"Woah..." Graham and Hunter echoed.

"Off the ice now," I said. "Up here..." I climbed up the small stone staircase out of the river and looked around. Moonlight streamed in through large cathedral like windows, casting red and yellow amongst the silvery blue across the teetering oak bookcases.

This was my plan... find some books with evil Spells and plans in. Make ourselves known so that no one messes with us again. And, perchance find the book that Tina wanted for her quest and regain her friendship.

"I am going back," Graham whispered, halfway up the

steps.

I turned on him. "You can't!"

He frowned. "Yes, I can!" with that he turned, walking back out of the Library, down the frozen river and away. Stupid idiot.

"We need to look for a book," I said.

"You don't say," said Hunter gazing around.

For four hours we searched, Hunter was surprisingly diligent, the embarrassment of being the *'losers of the school'*, as he kept repeating, had seemed to spur him on. We grabbed books from all corners of the Library that looked like they might be of interest and laid them out on the table and one by one and leafed through them.

"There's a Spell here," said Robin. "That seals up someone's mouth!"

"Err nasty," said Hunter. "Might be useful though. Hey, I've got an evil plan. What we do is: ask the Eagles form to join us in the grounds on Sunday for a kind of rematch, but then somehow take them to that floating island, cut the ropes and leave them there!" he laughed.

"Yeah," I said slowly. "I can see a slight hole in that plan."

I was leafing through a book about demons, which sent chills down my spine. It was a horrible, nasty old book, something that my parents would love. In fact, when I was young I always had this nightmare, except, I later found out, it wasn't a nightmare at all. It was real.

In this nightmare I am in the dungeons at home, hanging onto my Dad's leg. He and Mum were raising demons in this salt circle. And then this thing, horrible, transparent and black, rose up from the ground like drooping tar or an waxwork melting upwards. Then it emitted this piercing scream that went through me. It stared at me with no eyes. Then I wake up sweating. Still gives me the shivers.

"Why don't we raise a demon?" I said, joking and shivering a little as I tried to imagine it.

"No!" said Robin. "Straker told us about them, you never interfere with their world, they are dangerous and unpredictable."

The contours of a plan were enfolding around my mind, but to do it would take serious guts. I wasn't sure if I had those guts. Also, I didn't know who I was maddest at, my brother Ross, or David Starlight. My secondary mission of finding Tina's book had failed completely, I mean, it would help if I had any idea what I was looking for.

Hunter was asleep on the table and snoring loudly by three in the morning. I was knackered as well, but I still hadn't found what I was looking for. We'd found loads of Spells but none that were particularly useful to what we wanted to do. But then, a breakthrough...

"Look, I think this will work," Robin passed me this dusty old book. After I read I smiled and nodded.

***

It took me, Robin and Hunter a week to prepare and collect the relevant bits that we needed. In Straker's boring-ass lesson, in which he continually teased us about our huge loss, Hunter found an old suit of armour head, covered in a dirty cloth that had gone all rusty.

But, even better... after leaving that lesson I spotted something on the wall. The corridors down in the dungeons always had something frightening, but this was another level. Me, Robin and Hunter had walked another way out of Straker's lesson to avoid being rumbled as we made away with the suit of armour head, hidden under Hunter's jumper.

"Stop," I said, standing back. "Look at that…"

Robin and Hunter turned. "Woah…"

On the wall around us was the biggest skeleton I've ever seen. I didn't know what it was, but it's spine curved around the ceiling and down. Robin and Hunter didn't know what I was so impressed with it, until they saw me pull off two long, charred, skeletal hands.

"Ahh, I see…" they chorused.

Robin took three large bedsheets from the Ghosts' laundry cupboard and, panicking when they asked why, he said he wet himself in the night.

"Next time, use the chamber pot we provide!" called the Ghost.

Robin returned to the dorm very embarrassed. "The ghosts better not say nothing!" he spat.

"Hey," said Hunter. "We're already a laughing stock. Don't think it'll make much difference."

While the dorm was free during lunch the next day, I had a scout around the room. I needed something blue and reflective. But I couldn't find a thing! Then, it hit me. I was wearing it! Taking out a pair of scissors on my desk, I cut off two squares from the bottom of my robes, and cut them into circles. My robes looked even shabbier now, but at least they didn't trail on the floor anymore. Pleased with myself, I returned to lunch to tell Robin and Hunter what I'd done.

It felt strangely exciting, standing in the boys bathroom, in the dead of night, over our collection of props and objects. Robin had a list of Spells to perform individually on each object so it most resembled what we were after. We practiced all night in that bathroom, trying out different Spells for this and that, arguing which was best.

"I think that will do now, I need my bed," said Hunter yawning.

"It has to be perfect Hunter!" I said, rubbing my eyes

and scanning the list of Spells for an alternative.

Robin took off the armour head, "I agree with Hunter, for once, Avis it's really late, I'm really tired. Honestly what we've got looks good…" Robin backtracked as I gave him a funny look. "You know what I mean… not *good*… terrifying."

"Okay fine…" I said smiling, as we stashed the objects away under the grate. For once, this plan felt like it might really work!

After a few more days of planning, the plan finally came to a head - we were finally ready for the first stage of being evil.

The target, was David Starlight…

Me, Robin and Hunter prepared ourself down a dark, empty corridor lined with animal skulls. We couldn't use the boys bathroom as it was in use. A small grandfather clock on the wall chimed for ten o'clock, lights went out in five minutes.

"It's time…" I said.

Robin climbed on top of Hunter's shoulders and I threw the huge grey sheet over them. I passed Robin the armour mask, the shiny blue eyes and the long skeletal claws. Together, we said the Spells that transformed the collection of objects into a terrifying effigy. Small horns poked out of the armour head, which now looked like a long skull. The blue robe patches now shined bright beneath the skulled face. The long grey sheets, now a seamless black cape covering them in shadow. And the long skeletal, charred hands needed no Spellwork.

The person who now stood over me was not Robin and Hunter… it was Malakai.

They looked pretty dam terrifying in the darkness as they stood over me. Robin had found this Spell that deepens your voice and when he spoke it made the floor rumble. Hunter wore these big, thick black boots that he said didn't make a noise, a gift from Partington who grew impatient with Hunter's flat footed stomping. But, as Hunter said, *"Wearing these will make it seem like we're gliding along..."*

Moving was a little trickier, Robin wobbled around on Hunters shoulders.

"Hold tighter!" I said. "Right, come on, let's do this." We walked slowly, through the darkness until we reached our destination. Outside the Eagle form's dorm room. We waited, breath held, hearts beating. Any minute now David Starlight and the other Eagle boys would turn round that corner and see us. We had tracked them all week, found out where their dorm was, what time they use the bathrooms, everything.

Then at last, the sound of footsteps. I drew myself up to my full height and glanced one more time, up at the huge cloaked, skeletal face and blue glowing eyes of Malakai.

I heard the boys laughing jovially, light from the fire brackets illuminating the path ahead of them. But then, as they turned the corner the lights went out. Four of them stood there in the darkness looking about.

"That's strange..." one of them said.

They didn't see us at first... but then, with a click of my fingers, one fire bracket nearest us sparked blue flame. Slowly their eyes all moved as one towards us. Their faces froze, eyes wide, petrified to the floor. I recognised all of them from the Riptide match, their faces were the ones that laughed at us on the floor. You could have cut the silence with a blunt blade.

I looked down at my nails, inspecting them thoroughly. "Oh..." I said gently. "Hello boys."

It was then, that David Starlights voice echoed along the corridor.

"Oi Jason! … Jason? Steve? What are you guys looking at?" he called in his bullish manor.

As he came round in his spotted pyjama's, he circled his frozen friends, then caught their gaze and followed it. He saw me, grinned then as quick as lightning, his whole mouth dropped. Wiped from his face in one swipe. His eyes rolling upwards at the fake Malakai.

I stepped forward and spoke slowly. "Not so *confident* now are we boys?" Taking a moment to enjoy myself and mentally photographing their terrified faces, I did my best Blackthorn act. "Did I not mention it? I'm Malakai's apprentice…"

David's mouth twitched, his eyes gazing at the immense Malakai. "*You?* Why you?" He said it in a small voice, clearly some bravado remained.

"I'm a *Blackthorn*. This is who we are and believe me, the Spells he's already shown me… *Reptlylidiulis*!"

From the ends of my hands grew a green and brown light that morphed into a giant snake. Giant neon fangs snapped the air in the front of them.

"*AHHHH!*" they all cried, stepping back.

"Please Avis," gibbered one of them, hiding behind David. "We'll do anything, please!"

I smiled. "Yes you will. If I hear you say anything nasty to anyone in my form, then something much worse than a *snake* will be after you…" My eyes rolled upwards to Malakai and with a loud *poof* of green smoke, the snake disappeared.

David was breathing heavily, his eyes darting around. "I'm not scared… you can't do anything to us. We haven't done anything wrong!"

I tried to smile confidently, but it was rather weak. David seemed confident all of a sudden.

"…YOU…" said Robin in the deep rumbling voice.

"WILL OBEY AVIS BLACKTHORN."

David backed away. "Yes… yes…" he said in small voice. "Anything…" The voice had scared him into submission! For once, Hunter had actually come up with an idea that worked!

But then, the worse possible thing happened. I was about to tell the Eagles to go, to run away and tell everyone that Avis Blackthorn is Malakai's new apprentice, when… I… we all… heard this muffled… *ACHOO!*

"What was that?" said David looking around.

Impossibly, Hunter must have sneezed, because our fake Malakai began swaying. Hunter began flailing around. Robin lost his balance on top. Then, just as I aimed a balance correcting Spell at them - Hunter fell, tipping Robin backwards into the wall. With a sickening crunch Robin hit the floor. The grey cloak flying off over his head. Hunter and Robin lay in a tangled heap. The metal armour head now rolling away down the corridor. Both lay groaning.

What on earth did I do now?

David and the rest of the Eagles realised they'd been duped. I thought it was all over. That they'd call for the Lily and I'd be expelled or something. But no, it got a lot worse than that…

The five Eagle boys looked livid. David's face went a puce purple colour with rage. His golden pendant lit up a fiery orange. I covered myself ahead of a tirade of Spells. But then, they looked away from me, into the darkness of the corridor. Then, they scarpered. As fast as they possibly could back the way they had come.

"What the hec?" I said, watching them run. What could have possibly made them run like that?

I felt this icy cold tingle run down my spine. Like someone had placed an ice cube down my shirt. I recognised that feeling. It was one I'd had nightmares about. One I never cared to have again. I turned slowly. Standing in the shadows, eight feet tall, skulled face hidden by shadow and gliding towards us with blue glowing eyes and long skeletal fingers... was the *real Malakai*. I couldn't speak, my breath caught somewhere in my stomach. Robin was tangled under the grey cloak, and Hunter lay panting on the floor, both oblivious to the impending danger. A voice echoed round my head, deep and awful.

"*You* could never be *my* apprentice. This insults me. Malakai does not employ dirty *seventh sons!*" spat the voice that resembled splitting wood. My heart was beating, I couldn't even run, my feet were frozen to the spot. "You are a *disgrace* to the Blackthorn name."

This horrible whistling noise lit the air. The hair on the back of my neck stood up. An inky black substance rose from the cracks in the floor like a waxwork melting upwards. It looked straight at me with no eyes. Time stood still. My heart beating petrified. All at once it shot at Hunter. The demon leapt on top of him, screaming with joy as it began attacking him.

"AHH! Ahhhhhwwwwwwwwoooo!" Hunter cried as the Demon ripped into him.

I jumped back against the wall. "HELP! *HEEEEELP!*" I called at the top of my lungs. Robin pulled the sheets off, and watched horrified, scrambling back against the wall. The awful gurgling screams from Hunter shot into every possible crevice. It seemed like an age before our calls of help were answered. Poor Hunter writhed around on the ground, the demon's sharp black teeth like knives ripping through the air at every available space on his body.

Straker appeared, out of breath by the corridor entrance, flanked by another Magisteer. When he saw the mess his pallid face dropped like a penny in a well. He marched forcibly towards the demon, hands outstretched, saying something impossibly difficult. It began to crawl off Hunter, desperately trying to get away from Straker. But Hunter wasn't moving. The pool of blood touched my shoe and I had to turn away, the sight of it... Magisteer Dodaline crouched over Hunter then raised him above the ground, suspending him on an invisible bed.

"Get him to the Healer's Room!" Straker cried waving his hands at the faceless Demon, which shrank back into the ground with a pop. Straker wiped his sweaty face as Dodaline ran off fast with Hunter floating next to her, hanging limp. It all happened so quickly. Robin was curled into a ball crying. I stood frozen to the wall, feeling like I was about to puke any second. I heard doors slowly open around us to see what was happening. With one click of Straker's fingers all the doors shut and a lock clicked consecutively in each. Straker's dark face turned to us. His voice soft as his eyes went from the huge pool of blood to me and Robin. "Who did this?"

No one spoke. Straker looked at Robin who's eyes lifted. His hand outstretched and finger slowly uncurled... coming to point... at me.

I swallowed hard as Straker's head swivelled. "What?" I said, my voice croaky. "Robin what are you talking about? You think *I* would, could, ever do that?"

Robin sobbed into his arm.

"Sir, it was *Malakai* Sir. I saw him, over there. It was him." I had never seen Straker's face say so much, and it wasn't good — he certainly did not believe me.

***

Everything that happened next seemed like a dream. It passed me by in some numb strange place where time sped up and I was just led along. Inside though, I was thinking *how? why?* To go from a stage where you are almost victorious, to being accused of attempting to murder somebody was too much for my mind to handle. Hunter's gurgling screams echoing through every pore of my body, as Straker led me to a dark turret high up in the school, locking me behind a thick metal door.

After a few days I came back to earth. Perhaps when things get too hard, your mind goes on a little holiday?

I couldn't hear anyone, or see anything. My stuff from the dorm was in a bundle in the corner where Straker had dumped it. I suppose you could call the room a cell. There was no bed, just a kind of hard rug. There were no windows. The room was small and the roof pitched up into a cone shape, with lots of dark wooden rafters. The floor was cold and dusty and a draft seeped through the cracks round the bottom of the wall. I sat in the middle of the floor and didn't move for three days. A plate of bread, cheese and water appeared three times a day in front of me. I didn't eat it. I hated cheese. Anyway, I couldn't eat.

Hunter had just been attacked and probably killed. And Robin thought it was me. Everyone now thought it was me. I didn't want to think about it, I felt sorry for myself as I lay in the dirt. The only sound was the whistling wind and the scurry of one lone rat.

None of this made sense. I felt guilt, even though I hadn't done anything, I felt pain, anger, despair and a sick feeling in the pit of my stomach.

Why hadn't Malakai attacked me? Did he mean to? And why did he attack Hunter? One minute, we were scaring the living daylights out of David Starlight and the Eagles pretending to be Malakai, the next minute the real Malakai turns up and… well, does the most awful thing imaginable.

And Robin accused me. For the last three days I was

cursing him, but then, when I thought about it, that would be the accusation I would come to.

- I mentioned (as a joke) that we should set a demon on the Eagles after reading that awful book.
- He perhaps thought I was angry at Hunter for sneezing and messing up the plan.
- Robin and Hunter did not see or hear Malakai.

Yes, David Starlight and the Eagles had seen Malakai, but would they tell the truth? Or did he wipe their memories? I know my parents have done it before, so Malakai must be able to. The evidence was firmly stacked against me and I didn't want to go to Magic jail.

***

A week later I was kind of settled in my dusty old turret, it reminded me of home. I hung my clothes on a low wooden rafter, turned my bedsheets into a half comfortable bed-come-nest and got on with some homework. It was hard to see, because the only light came from the cracks in the roof. Soon enough I had lost track of days and the passing of day to night, my circadian rhythms were proper messed up.

Then, after maybe a week, I was lying on the floor trying to peel back a roof slate to get more light in, when suddenly a shaft of glowing blue light lit up the room. I was puzzled, but when I turned I saw where the light was coming from. It was a ghost. It had just come up through the floor.

"Hello pal," it said, cheery for a ghost but in a *I feel sorry for you* voice. "How you keeping?"

"Erm, fine." I said, my voice croaky as I hadn't spoke for a week.

"Good... for a week or so you and me are gonna do some work. Magisteer Partington sends his warmest regards and gave me some sheets from his classes that we can get on with…"

"Okay…" I said. "How's Hunter?"

The ghost looked at me and smiled weakly. "He'll be ok."

"Ah, thank god!" I cried, unable to help tears welling up in my eyes. "I thought he was dead!"

"Well…" said the ghost, floating across and inspecting my raggy bed. "He was as good as dead for some time."

I swallowed. "They do know it wasn't me don't they?"

He didn't need to say anything, the look was enough — a sorry tilt of the head and a wry look away.

I found the ghost, who told me his name was Ernie, pleasurable and handy as I now had enough light to work with. It was like having a full moon sitting cross legged opposite me. His features were very defined, he was a young ghost, perhaps early twenties, dressed in a smart suit with a smooth, kind face, longish fair hair tucked behind his ears and a warm, likeable personality, which is strange for a ghost - most of the ones I'd met were horrible. Everyday Ernie woke me up at 7am sharp and brought handfuls of work sheets to go through that Partington had sent up. And… he sneaked me some food from the Chamber! Each day became an excitement, to see what luxury he would bring me.

After a few days I got so used to him being there and didn't want him to go. I was nibbling on a butter candy cake, and he was reading my notes back to me about Hexes and Wolves, as I was wondering about everyone back in the school. What were they doing? Would I ever see them again?

"Does everyone in the school think it was me?" I said.

"*And the Hex*… What?" said Ernie peering over my essay, then sighing. "I am sure that… the truth will come out in the end," he said diplomatically then carried on reading my essay. They were probably burning an effigy of me right now, led by my brother Ross. Mind you he and my family had finally got their wish. I had finally done something catastrophically evil.

A few days later and Ernie appeared looking immensely cheerful. "You are allowed out!" he called. "Someone will be up in about…" he looked down and through the floor. "… ten minutes!"

"Allowed out?" I said feeling a huge sense of dread. I had got so used to this little room that I was comfortable here now. "But, but…"

"It's ok," said Ernie bobbing up and down. "The Lily is obviously not convinced that it was you, that's why he's letting you out."

"The Lily?" I mumbled. "But what about Hunter? Is he ok?"

"He's awake in the Healer's Room, but I wouldn't go there just yet, not until everything is smoothed over."

"No, yeah," I said. "And am I going back to lessons? Back to my form?"

Ernie laughed. "Don't make yourself so stressed about things that might not happen kiddo. Let's see what the man says. See ya around," he winked.

"Wait! Will I see you again?"

Ernie's head floated just above the floor. "Of course!" he laughed before vanishing.

Ernie was right, just ten minutes later the door opened. The tall frightening Magisteer stared down at me with distain. I'd heard about her - Magisteer Simone, the Lily's assistant. I'd heard people refer to her as Scary Simone. She was about seven foot, with a tight bun of hair fastened to her head, an angry leathery face and only one bristly eyebrow.

"Well *hello* Avis Blackthorn, proving to live up to your family's name at last?"

I didn't bother trying to tell her I was innocent. So I just weakly agreed. "Yeah…"

"On order of the Lily you are being allowed out, however you will not return to your dorm, this is your room now. You will return to lessons, but only with the ghosts in the East Dungeon's. However, you are free to *do as you please* in the school again…" she spat the last sentence as if it pained her to say it. Obviously she would have me locked up here forever, innocent or not.

I was worried that having my freedom back would cause people to, I don't know, come and get me. Magisteer Simone held her hand out. On it, was a tiny shrivelled head on a string.

"You will be accompanied by a Shrunken Head to protect you from Spells, Hexes, Curses and bullish behaviour from others while we ascertain what *really happened*…" She chucked the head to me. It was small, with flaky skin and rough hair, it's eyes and mouth sealed by thread. "Put it round your neck, then make your way down to Lunch." This had to go round my neck? Ergh.

"What happens?" I said. "If someone does attack me or whatever?" I saw her smile as if imagining it.

"You're a Blackthorn? And you don't know about Shrunken Heads? Dear, oh dear…" she tutted and vanished from the room leaving me standing, stranded in a prison cell I didn't want to leave.

I put the horrible Shrunken Head around my neck. It hung limp for a bit, then the thread in its eyes and mouth disappeared with a *poof.* It groaned and began mumbling strange words to itself. The string around my neck disappeared in a short blaze of orange as the head floated up just behind my left shoulder, where it stayed muttering to itself.

"Hello?" I said. But it ignored me, eyes shut.

I felt like a newborn animal tip toeing into the dangerous jungle for the first time. I discovered how far up in the tower I was. All I could see through the thin slitted windows around the staircase was dark clouds and mist. But also it took ten minutes to walk down all the stairs and make it back, finally, to the main school again. The Shrunken Head bobbed along next to me, awkwardly. I felt naked, hoping no one would see me as I scurried along the corridors, blinking at the immensely bright light that stung my eyes.

I was in the main building now, with all its glorious, garish portraits lining the walls, and long tapestries hanging down like dirty waterfalls. My eyes had been so used to darkness and nothing, that they buzzed and were very sore. I desperately needed a shower too. I hadn't changed my clothes in a week. Then I saw people, up ahead, in plain clothes (it must have been Sunday) milling around in the corridors. There were three boys in dark red robes from the second year, who were playing some Magical card game. I scuttled past them as quickly as possible. When they looked up and saw me, they cowered back against the wall, eyes following me as if I was Malakai himself.

It wasn't far to the Chamber, but it felt like I was running some emotional marathon. I entered the hall with trepidation, for I could hear lots of voices. I kept my head low as possible, avoiding the eyes that now fell on me. After ten steps or so, I felt the conversation change as group by group, person by person, they saw me. Hushed whispers now reverberated around me. I didn't look up, didn't say anything, I just kept moving and moving quickly. The solitude and lack of noise had caused the whispers to sound like shouts. All around me, hisses and spits split my ears with accusations.

Here comes the boy who raises demons. Who attacks his friends. Who nearly killed a boy. Who pretends to be an evil Wizard. Well he is a Blackthorn! Why is he still in the school? How can he stand there knowing what he did?! To one of his own form!

Well *I* didn't!

I was relived to finally be standing in front of the Chamber doors to escape the whispers. Thankfully, the Chamber was not very full, a smattering of people eating, some doing homework with a few Magisteers at their table. All, however, noticed me when I walked in. Everyone stopped talking. Magisteer Dodaline who had taken Hunter to the Healer's room looked affronted. Others looked terrified and began scribbling away at their homework, amongst dropped glances of barely concealed contempt.

I could see the accusations in their eyes, they thought I did it. I was so hungry I dived for the food. And ate my first proper meal for weeks, the bobbing head beside me silent and watching. It felt like more of a beacon than a helpful tool to stop me becoming a victim of vengeance.

***

Over the coming month, things didn't change much. Hunter left the Healer's room and went home for a few weeks. When he returned, the whole Chamber burst into a tumultuous roar, one by one they shook his hand and stroked his scars which were horrific. He seemed pleased with them. I was sitting at a table on my own, in a shadowy corner of the Chamber. I didn't know how he would respond to me, so I stayed where I was.

I found out the hard way that I wasn't allowed anywhere near my dorm, Partington's classroom or the Eagles dorm, as a barrage of ghosts would appear, hurling abuse at me if I stepped one foot over their invisible boundaries. That really had scared the living daylights out of me.

I returned to my new favourite place, the clock tower. It was set up high in the spire. And no one came up here, ever, they couldn't anyway. I only found it by accident when having a hunt around near the dark turret room. Both clock faces are see-through so I can see everything that happens from both sides of the courtyard and the gardens. It's weird watching people because I get sad that I can't join them. I found it hidden behind a large tapestry in one of the long corridors near my turret. The first night I sat still listening to the satisfying clicks of the metal clockwork and watching the sun setting over the horizon. Then I couldn't stand going back to the small, dank turret, so I collected all my stuff and moved into the clock tower. At least here I had a view, some light and no Magisteers coming to check up on me every other day unannounced. I mean, it wasn't perfect, the bells rang deafening loud at certain times, there was a flock of pigeons up in the rafters that pooed all the time and it was incredibly dusty, but it sure felt homely.

Things moved slowly on the '*innocent campaign*' however. I decided, through a motivational talk from Ernie who pops by each day, that I should do my best to clear my name. Seeing as no one else was prepared to do anything about it. I had not heard anything, except a rumour from Ernie that the Lily was waiting for Hunter to be completely better before asking him what happened. Straker had already been having long discussions with apparent witnesses. For definite I knew he must have spoken to: Robin, David Starlight including Straker's own form… so if they told the truth, surely Straker would have to profess my innocence?

But as yet, I heard nothing.

Spurred on however by Ernie's motivation that I would clear my name, I attempted to speak to Robin.

It was lunch about two weeks ago. I saw him sitting with

the Condor boys, he and Graham were talking about something, I couldn't hear what. I walked over slowly and sat next to him. When he saw me, he nearly jumped into the air.

"I just want to talk…" I whispered.

"I don't… don't wanna talk to you!" he said trembling, loud enough for the whole Chamber to hear.

Five third years in orange robes near us stood and eyed me up. The Shrunken Head on my shoulder eyeing them back. I stood and sighed as eyes all around the Chamber followed the proceedings.

"You really think," I whispered. "That I, would do *that* to Hunter? I am telling you it was… *him*…"

"You're not right in the head," said Robin tapping his temple. "I saw you."

"Right come on," said the fifth year. "Leave now."

"I just wanted to…" more people around me on tables stood now, their hands ready to Spell. What did they think I was? "Fine, fine…" I managed.

That was as far as I got. I left the Chamber and returned to the Clock tower where I stayed.

Tina's face floated through my dreams constantly. She had probably forgotten all about me, or thought I was a nasty disease like all the others. I wondered how far she'd got with her quest. I still didn't know what it was about. As I lay in the dusty clock tower, moonlight shining in through the large oval face, I lay wondering about what she was doing right now. Perhaps she was in the Library looking for that book. Who knows, perhaps Robin was helping her.

Lessons with the ghosts were so boring. I had two teachers, three if you included Ernie. Magisteer Hungerford, who was a right evil cow, stuck up and with an attitude problem of some sort because she wouldn't let me answer anything, just droned on asking rhetorical questions.

It was really annoying.

Mr. Jenkinson was really boring too. He said everything as if I was five years old and sometimes he'd just fall asleep half way through talking. And if I woke him up he began the lesson from the beginning, so mostly I didn't bother. The dungeon where I had my lessons with the ghosts was drab, dank and cold. It was a long walk from my room in the tower to the dungeons every day, past the offensive looks in the corridors, down into icy cold, damp dripping rooms with less light than a lit matchstick. It was only me in the lessons too. At least, I think it was.

Ernie taught me too, still bringing me up bits of work from Partington. He would relay things to me he had picked up as he flew around the castle hearing titbits. Lately he had taken to hiding in suits of armour near the Eagle boys dorm, but didn't hear anything of value.

Spurned on again by Ernie's talks in the clock tower about retribution, I gee'd myself up to go and talk to certain people. Like he said, I didn't have anything to lose. I'd already decided that if I was kicked out of Hailing Hall, I wouldn't be going home - I was never going back there.

On Sunday morning I spotted Hunter walking alone in the courtyard. I made my way down as quick as I could into the blistering sun, which I was not used to at the moment. Zooming out of the back entrance, my heart beating fast, I walked quickly to catch up with him. Expecting him to run away I slowed and tried to make myself small and unthreatening. I could see his scars properly now. He had two deep gashes across his face, on his left cheek, stretching up to his forehead. Like a giant sideways smile.

I swallowed. "Hunter, it's me, Avis."

He didn't stop walking, but smiled. "I know," he said smiling.

"Right... erm... god, this is so hard but I want you to

know... I would never do anything to harm you, and I swear on my limited life, it was not me who did that to you."

"I know," he said.

I frowned. "What do you mean? Everyone thinks it's me. Straker, Dodaline, the whole school..."

Hunter stopped and shook his head. "Even if it was you, I would forgive you. I've... seen things now that made me realise that life is too short for holding grudges, or worrying about being a loser. And I got a month in this sweet ass Healer's room, take me back there any day! And a couple of weeks at home with the family. Ok, the demon was scary as hell... but I know that could never have been you. I know you Avis." He looked at me, his left eye partially shut because of the scar. "You aint got it in ya' to do something like that!"

He smiled, and something inside me breathed a huge sigh of relief.

"Anyway, I saw him..."

"Saw who?"

"*Malakai*. Big shiny blue eyes, long fingers... saw him in the reflection of the armour mask. Not for long, but I saw him."

"But... " I was on the verge of tears. "Everyone hates me, they think I did it."

"It was a stupid plan, we are all accountable in some way. But I agree, you should not be blamed for this." He said pointing at his face.

I swallowed the tears. "Has anyone asked you about it?"

"Yeah," he said as we crossed the grassy field towards the floating island. "The Lily asked me and Straker. I told them it was Malakai. They asked me not to tell anyone else in the school. Made me swear..."

And then it dawned on me why everyone still thought it

was me - the Lily didn't want people to think that Malakai was coming into the school! I was the scapegoat!

"Don't worry Avis, the Lily assured me this would all be sorted out and you'll be fine," he gave me a tap on on the shoulder and walked across the bridge to the floating island, leaving me standing there in disbelief. That was not how I expected the conversation to go. The Shrunken Head was shielding itself from the sun behind my shoulder so I made my way back indoors.

Resuming my place, cross legged behind the clock face, I stared out across the courtyard watching everyone playing and frolicking in the sun. I couldn't help the tears, the despair too much — I felt appalling sorry for myself and lay in a ball cursing this crappy world! I cursed the Lily, Straker and the Eagles. They all knew I was innocent, but were using me as the scapegoat, so no one else in the school would become terrified that Malakai could just waltz in whenever he liked. I was sad that my experience of this Magical school had been robbed of me, unjustly.

Ernie appeared and sat opposite me, bringing food from Sunday dinner. I wasn't hungry. I just wanted to sit and listen to the clock ticking it's loud satisfying clunks.

"It's not healthy to trap yourself up here. You have to be brave and face the world."

I sniffed. "Yeah, not right now." I told him what Hunter said and Ernie nodded along and hugged me. He was cold, but it felt... comforting to feel the touch of someone, even someone dead.

I didn't leave the clock tower for a few days, I just lay and stared out across the landscape. I bet the ghost Magisteers hadn't even noticed my lack of appearance. Hec, probably no one did.

Ernie brought me food which sat in an uneaten pile in the corner. I continued to sit and watch the sun chase the moon into night and day. Warm, hot days replaced overnight with falling white snowflakes and frosty cold winds. The black clouds rolled in, bringing winter with them. Christmas was just around the corner. Ernie gave me a Spell to make a contained fire. It sat behind me providing this modicum of heat, yet I could still see my breath in front of me. Some people went home for Christmas. I watched them, with their new levitating Spells carrying their bags and cases across the courtyard, into carriages and flying home. For a moment, I couldn't decide where I would rather be… here, or home.

***

Lying in my pit, staring out at the familiar view across Hailing Hall, moonlight streaming across soft white snow, blue flames unable to melt the ice that had settled in my bones, I slipped in and out of dreams. One, was a wonderful dream that I was intent on trying to prolong. I was with Tina, down by the lake, swimming… then we were running in the sun and Spelling each other for fun… then she kissed me. It ended just before our lips met. And I woke to the cold, shivering between my blankets.

Something outside caught my attention. A shape was moving through the snow, along the side of the hedge. It was tall, with long skeletal hands and blue glowing eyes… Malakai was walking towards the castle. Cloak hiding his skeletal head. I rubbed my eyes, making sure I wasn't still dreaming. He was the one who had done this to me. But why was he coming into the school?

For five consecutive nights, at one thirty in the morning, I saw him making his way into the school. It could not have been a dream. I stayed awake watching. On the sixth night, I sat up and made a decision, I had to find out what he was up to. I reasoned for a long time, but in the end I thought *I have nothing to lose.* Once I decide on something its pretty hard to persuade me otherwise. And I had decided on something major. I would find out why Malakai was coming into the school, and I would do everything I could to stop him and his evil plans. Avis Blackthorn would get his revenge!

I felt reinvigorated. And Ernie seemed perkier at my renewed vigour, for I had a mission. I was trying to think of a way to follow Malakai without being spotted. I needed to get to the Library and hunt for invisibility Spells. Resuming my spot at the clock face, cross legged as if in prayer, I sat and thought about Malakai night after night, contemplating what he was and what he could be doing. I didn't know much about him. Not much at all. How old was he? Where was he from? What was his favourite dinner? Strange thoughts indeed, but necessary, for he was just a man.

All of a sudden I heard this charging noise. Streams of people came pilling out into the courtyard below for a snowball fight, it looked amazing. Graham and Simon led the charge, with their ties around their head. Hang on, had their ties changed colour? They had! Turquoise blue when we started, their's were now maroon! That must have meant that they had gone up a level in Magic!

A jealous pot of rage suddenly burned white hot inside me. They were steaming ahead with their Magical training and I was being left behind, being taught by some shoddy ghosts. All because I was being made a scapegoat. Well, I would show them. I didn't need a tie to tell me how good at Magic I was.

"Go and join in," said Ernie watching them play.

"Naa…" Can you imagine? They'd all run back in as soon as they saw me running towards them.

I could tell Christmas day wasn't far off, perhaps a day

or two. Decorations littered the outside of the school and a huge Christmas tree stood proudly in the centre of the courtyard. I was woken each morning by the flipping bells, which rang out this deafening Christmas song for about ten flipping minutes.

It seems I would be spending Christmas alone. At least, not with anyone who was alive.

***

In the dead of night on Christmas eve I made my way down through the school. Tiptoeing quietly along the corridors I hadn't trod for weeks, into the boys' bathroom. I pulled the metal grate away and eased into the small passage. Descending the stairs, I iced the river as I had done before, and entered the dim cathedral-like Library. I was searching for: a Spell, or an idea that would enable me to follow Malakai without him spotting me. And, maybe some information on the man himself. It occurred to me that if I could find a Spell that copied books I could take some back with me to the clock tower. I almost knew how to levitate now, but it was hit and miss.

Searching books in the Library is a long and arduous process. Magic books are unnecessarily big with too much information. Wizards, I know, like to waffle on. Some of the ladders were wobbly too... I wish Ernie was here, he would be good company, and give me a bit of light.

I laid some interesting looking books out on the table and began reading, taking notes on my ink and parchment.

After an hour, the page was full of tiny Spells, ideas and thoughts that the books had given me. I felt alive, standing over these brilliant books hunting for clues. A lot of Spells and passages in the books had been black marked, but eventually I found a Spell that didn't quite give you invisibility as such, but damn near close. It made whoever looked at you avert their gaze and forget what they saw, your image drawn away from their retina like a magnet. Combine that with Spells for making no noise when you walk and you're near enough impossible to be noticed. But did Malakai have retinas? I wondered.

I searched for ages for a book about Malakai but searching the *M* section for books entitled *Malakai* revealed nothing. I suppose finding a Malakai autobiography was a bit of a long shot. There were, however, certain passages and paragraphs written about him, but nothing I didn't already know.

Footsteps tapped softly along the icy river. I ducked under the table instinctively. Someone else was coming! My heart beat hard, breath short. Eyes scanning under the table where I could see someone emerge slowly. Their eyes scanning the vicinity, looking for the person who had frozen the river. Who was this? It was too dark to tell, probably a Magisteer.

"Who iced this river?" called the voice. It was a voice I hadn't heard in a long time, but one which I dreamed of hearing for a long time.

I stood. "Tina?" Her hands raised automatically through the gloom. "It's me, Avis." She didn't drop them straight away, stepping forward slowly until she got a good sight of me.

"Avis!" she stared at me for ages, as if I perhaps wasn't real. "Where the HELL have you been?! I've been looking for you everywhere you dopy git!"

It was not the reaction I was expecting. "Er... the..." I stammered, not knowing what to say first. "Clock tower... looking for *me*?"

"Yeah, Partington too, said you weren't in your room, he keeps checking. Said you disappeared, or were hiding.

You're a good hider."

"I am. Years of practice."

"Clock tower ayh, good find." She said climbing out of the river. I just stared at her trying to remind myself this was not a dream. "I came to find you weeks ago, but you just went off radar… I wanted to tell you that I believe you are innocent, always did. When people started saying it was you, I thought, something doesn't stick here… Anyway, you're still a git, I wondered who iced the river. I couldn't get the boat up here, had to *walk* it," she tutted then looked at me suspiciously. "Anyway, what are you doing here? It's Christmas Eve silly."

"I was…" Did I tell her about my plan to follow Malakai? "Just looking for stuff, bored, and er…" I shrugged feeling uncomfortable, my cheeks hot.

She eyed me again and frowned, then sat down at the table. I tucked my parchment away. "Ahh, nice to sit down. Sit down Avis, don't be so nervous. No one's gonna come in, it's Christmas Eve!" She winked.

"What are you doing here then?" I said, sitting.

"Came to look for more books, in my *quest*, which I am no further through." She tilted her head back and stared up into the immense domed Library ceiling. I tried to look cool, even though months of solitude had made me forget social etiquette and had to stop myself staring.

"You never told me what your quest was," I said.

"No… I didn't did I. Wasn't sure I could trust you to be honest, but, I think I can *now*."

She was still looking up into the roof, smiling. "Why now?" I said.

"Because you've seen *him* haven't you… Malakai? He was the one who set the demon on Hunter. Even Hunter said as much. The Lily is scared to admit that Malakai is coming into the school so he let you take the blame."

I nodded. She'd got it in one, but I didn't know what that had to do with her quest.

"That's why I can trust you Avis, you've seen him. He did something horrible, knowing you would get blamed for it. Do you know why?" She was leaning across the table looking intently at me now with her twinkling eyes, my mind flickered back to the dream I had.

"I have an idea," I said but truth was, I didn't, just a best guess. "I'm a Blackthorn, not a very evil Blackthorn, we are expected to be evil and join him as soon as we leave school. He knows I will just be a liability?"

Tina juggled her head, she wasn't satisfied with the answer, but I was on the right track.

"Well, I mean, he did say something about me being a *seventh son*?"

Her eyes flashed. "You're a what?" she said terrified.

I sat back. "What? Yeah, I'm a seventh son, he spoke to me telepathically, said he never wanted a seventh son to work for him."

Tina blinked fast. "He *kills* seventh sons."

I frowned and giggled a little. Perhaps it was the solitude again. "What? Why?"

"You really know nothing about Magic do you?" I didn't answer. "Seventh son is a myth, but it could be real. Seventh son's have a power that no one else has. That's why Malakai doesn't like you. You're a threat to him. Yes, yes, that's why he didn't just kill you, he got you in trouble instead."

"I think maybe my parents have something to do with the fact that he didn't kill me?" I said hopefully, wishing that perhaps they had, for once, stuck up for me.

"I can't remember the myth, need to look it up! Not now, too late. My *quest*..." she said leaning forward even closer until I could feel her breath on my face. "Listen...

116

My quest is to find the source of Malakai's power..." she said. "My brother, he died trying to find and destroy it. Wish he'd just not have bothered. He was the nicest person you could ever meet, tall, handsome... but anyway, he got close, but I think he anticipated what was coming because he wrote all these instructions and Spells, and his notes up for the next person to take up the quest and eliminate Malakai."

"How did you find it?"

"He left some notes in his desk at home, in a letter for me." As starlight twinkled into the room, I saw a tiny tear in her glassy eyes. "I think..." she said wiping them. "Malakai has *The Book Of Names*... You must have heard of that?" When she saw my blank expression she carried on. "Fine. Let me explain... The Book Of Names is this huge, ancient book that's recorded the name of every Wizard that's ever been born. Their *given name* appears in the columns next to their *true name*..." I gasped. I had heard about this. "So my given name is Tina, but my true Magical name, which I don't know, is in that book. When you know someone's true name you have complete power over them! Most people don't even know their true name, its too dangerous to know it in case someone tortures it out of you. But if you have the Book Of Names, you have power over everyone! Now, you are different... because seventh son's true names are not in the Book Of Names!"

"*Ohh...*" I said, as the revelation finally dawned on me. "So, what your saying is, Malakai can't control me, like he does others because he can't know my true name?"

"Exactly," she said sitting back.

"So that's the book you were looking for... the Book Of Names, is it in here?"

"No," she laughed. "It's not going to be here... Why don't you show me where you've been living these past months Avis Blackthorn."

We crept up to my clock tower and I showed her round. She danced around the huge bells, and sung Christmas carols.

She laughed. "It was Christmas day two hours ago…" she said, looking at the giant clock face. "It's cold up here! However have you managed?"

I said my fire Spell and in a column of blue light, fire lit up inside the glass cabinet.

"*Oooo* very impressive," she said warming her hands. "And you *sleep* here?"

She got into my bed, well I say bed, it was a collection of cushions, pillows, sheets, rugs and clothes.

"I prefer to think of it as a nest," I said.

"I like it…" she said laying down and patting the space next to her. I joined her in my bed. This was like some awesome dream, but somehow it felt so normal. I wrapped all the blankets over us, and we simply lay there watching the stars through the clock face. At last, I had someone to share Christmas with.

"Merry Christmas Avis."

"Merry Christmas Tina."

Zzzzz…

***

The bells for Christmas day rang out, nearly deafening us both. "What the hec!" Tina called above the racket, her hair everywhere. When it ended she flopped back down.

"Merry Christmas," I said smiling.

She rolled her head to the side and looked at me smirking. This filled my stomach with butterflies. "Got me a present?" I swallowed, "I'm only joking," she laughed.

When I looked around I realised my Shrunken Head

which I had grown so used to, had vanished. How strange. It was with me when I left last night to go to the Library. Oh well, I was glad to be rid of it.

Tina stretched. "You better not think this makes us *an item*."

I went a little red. "What? No, no way," I scoffed.

Would I ever?

"Come on," she said, dressing quickly. "Let's go and get breakfast."

It was early, really early. I wasn't sure how much sleep I'd had but with Tina I didn't feel tired at all. We walked together through the school, which was alive and brimming with noise and activity. People were running down the halls, knocking on friends dorms. Fireworks blazed overhead, crackling Christmas songs. Snowmen stood grinning in place of suits of armour. Decorations littered the corridors, so much so, that it was hard to take it all in. Impkus the ghost flew past me blowing a trumpet and wishing all he passed a "*Merry Christmas!*"

In the Chamber, all the Magisteers including The Lily, were up on their table in good cheer, awaiting breakfast. Some of them still in their pyjamas! Me and Tina sat at a table and she grinned at me with her brilliant white teeth. Suddenly Breakfast exploded onto the table. There was everything you could possibly imagine, it was like a heavenly last supper. Me and Tina dined, we dined like there was no tomorrow.

When we finished, these little boxes of presents popped up in front of us. This surprised me as I wasn't expecting presents. I rarely got a present at Christmas, so this was well, utter excitement.

"Well are you going to open it?" said Tina.

"But, what is it? Who is it from?"

"From the school, I think… You have to open to find

that out," she said, ripping into her box. Inside hers was a tin of *Magic Hidden Ink*. "Oh brilliant!" She called with genuine surprise, frowning at how anyone would know to get her such a thing. "Go on, you now…"

I tore off the shiny red paper and opened the box, inside… was a key. A small, twirly key. Tina looked non plussed too. "What the?"

I took it out and twirled it round in my hands. It was a very plain, very interesting silver key. I gave it to Tina who inspected it as if it were the missing link then gave it back. "I don't know what that's for. Maybe it's a mistake?" she said.

I tucked it inside my robe pocket and carried on with breakfast. Christmas day with Tina just happened to be the best day of my entire life.

CHAPTER SEVEN

The Partington's

For the rest of the Christmas holidays me and Tina were inseparable. She would leave, saying she was going for a shower, but barely ten minutes later she would be back in the clock tower with a new idea and wet hair. We had a lot of fun. But she also shared my obsession with Malakai. He had caused us both nothing but pain and we talked non stop about what we could do next.

The day before she was due to start lessons again, everyone returned from the Christmas break. We sat and watched them from the clock tower. Tina was in Hubris form, apparently she didn't really get on with them, because they were all a bit swatty and weedy, no fun basically. She hadn't played Riptide yet, and was terrified of that day arriving because she *"saw how mullered we got."*

Having dinner in a once again packed Chamber was bitter-sweet. It was nice to see it so lively again, but some part of me really enjoyed the solitude and peace of an empty Chamber.

The night before lessons were due to start, Tina said a final farewell, properly this time for she had a weeks worth of homework to catch up on. I walked back to the clock tower, jealous that they all got to return to lessons. Just as I got halfway up the stairs to the clock tower, Partington suddenly leered out from the entrance to the stone staircase.

"Avis! At flipping last!" he cried, looking exasperated. "Do you realise how long I've been looking for you, you weren't in the specified room you were allocated..." he gestated frantically, then sighed and began rubbing his glasses. "Can we talk somewhere?" We went up the stairs a little way, into one of the corridors nearest the clock tower. I wasn't ready to give away my hiding spot yet.

"Look," he said in a fast voice. "I've managed to convince the Lily to let you back into my lessons." I wasn't expecting that. "Hunter is fine with it, some of the others a little less so, but Hunter spoke up for you."

"Did he? That was good of him."

Partington leaned a little closer as if the walls were listening. "And er, just to let you know… I erm… I don't think it was you. I mean… you're just a kid, a good kid. I know you wouldn't do that kind of thing."

I couldn't stop the smile that crept across my mouth. "Thanks Sir…"

Partington nodded to himself. "I've felt awful these past few weeks, knowing you're rattling around in here somewhere, your hard to find…"

***

I sat in class on my own, at a table near the back. But it was brilliant, so good to be allowed back at last.

Dennis and Ellen walked in first and stopped, staring at me. I smiled as best I could, until they tip toed into the room and took their seats, shooting worried looks in my direction. Then Jess, Florence and Joanna drifted in, their conversation stopping abruptly when they saw me. Simon appeared next with Graham and Robin, who was staring at the floor. Graham and Simon glared at me and took a seat as far away as possible. Robin didn't acknowledge me at all. Hunter didn't even notice me when he came in, for he nearly tripped over a pile of cauldrons by the door.

When everyone was seated and quiet, Partington swept into the room, all eyes went from me to him and back again as if to say *what is he doing here?*

"Yes," said Partington. "Avis is back in classes, I am glad

to announce."

Hunter turned and smiled at me. Robin was sat very deep in thought next to Dawn, who was doing her best sour face impression. I was pleased, when I looked around, to only see Simon and Graham's ties had turned maroon.

Just to get back to learning meaningful things was so satisfying. We started studying:

- The science of vibrations and wavelengths of a Spell.
- Magical creatures in the fourth plane.
- The four Spells of enlightenment and the history of Hexes.

Of course Straker wouldn't accept me into his lessons, so Partington took me through all the stuff I missed while I was away, which, oddly, had nothing to do with any of the work that Ernie had given me. I didn't question this however because I didn't want Partington to get cross and chuck me out, just when I'd got back.

I even enjoyed the homework each night because Tina would join me. We would sit, wrapped in blankets under the blue fire, and watch the sun set over the horizon. After we finished we would discuss Malakai and what we could do to stop him. Of course, it was all hypothetical - but I still had this burning desire to set the record straight, one day.

Gradually, I was accepted back into my form. People began talking to me, perhaps realising, in their own way, that I couldn't do something like that to Hunter. Sometimes, at dinner, I would sit back on the Condors' table, but I waited to see if Tina was around first. When I'd see her, she would start by telling me about the Spells that she'd learnt, and how they could go towards fighting or stopping Malakai.

"What we need to do is..." she said chewing the end of a carrot. "Find out where *M* goes when he comes into the school... follow him... because I *bet*, he leads us to the..."

then she'd look around, lean in, and whisper. "… *the Book Of Names*. The source of his power. If we stop that, we stop him."

I nodded along, not entirely sure if we, two children, could just *stop him*.

A few weeks after being allowed back in lessons, I was walking along the main hallway with its dangling chandeliers and blood red carpets. David Starlight spotted me a way off and scuttled away with his Eagles friends. My stomach rumbled. I imagined myself a minute into the future, tucking into a lovely pie and chips, or jam tart and custard or whatever they had on offer. Just before I got to the Chamber doors, this ghost popped up out of the ground in front of me. My first though was Ernie, but this ghost was old and wore a red uniform.

"You are required to go to the Lily's office at once…" droned the ghost, before shooting away. People around me were watching and muttering. They thought I had done something else, I just knew it. I swallowed, then turned trekking off towards the Headmaster's office as my stomach rumbled again. It was about time he told me what was going on.

The Lily's office was in the very middle of school, somewhere between the Numerology department and the Horticulture wing. The doors were massive, like great big white wings, pointed at the top and decorated with all the schools form symbols. As I tapped the big shiny ringed knocker, I had a barrage of questions and insults ready to hurl at the Lily.

"Avis *hello*…" said the Lily as soon as the doors opened, beaming at me from behind his desk. I stepped forward slowly as the door shut behind me with a click. "Come ahead, take a seat."

I had to squint. The room was big, bright and almost

everything in it was white. The chair before the Lily's huge decorative, white desk, was big and soft. I felt like a leprechaun as I jumped up into it.

"Thank you for coming. I appreciate the last few months have been… *taxing* on you. For that you have my highest sympathy and apology."

All the way up the corridor I was thinking of the best curses for the Lily and my choicest words. But now, sitting opposite him, with his hands folded, and serene eyes looking deep into me, all that was lost. His voice and body language was so calming that all negativity left me. I saw a deep meaningful apology, empathy and understanding in his eyes. Something more than words would be able to communicate.

"It's fine," I mumbled.

His desk was very organised and optimised the room. Everything in it had its own place. Light flooded in through tall, floor to ceiling windows, either side of the desk.

"Would you like to tell me, in your own words, what happened. And I want to know *everything*…" he smiled.

It felt good to tell the Lily, whose kind eyes didn't sway or judge but simply accepted. When I finished he nodded, pressing his hands together.

"The greatest men have often faced great adversity. It's what makes them great."

It was strange how he made me feel so comfortable, so able to tell him everything - I wasn't sure if I liked it.

"Now, Avis… I would quite like to know about your upbringing and family. You, I have heard, are something of an anomaly in your family."

"Yes, they are all evil, you know, the famous Blackthorns. Except… I'm not, never have been…"

"Clearly," the Lily smiled urging me to speak on.

"I don't know," I fumbled. "I suppose it was hard

growing up, they treat me like some sorry old pet, a burden to the family and the name. I can't do anything right in their eyes. I thought maybe being evil would make them pleased, but it's not who I am. I just can't do it, no matter how hard I try… I'm just not as strong as them."

"On the contrary Avis, I think there is more courage in you then there is in all of them. You stood up to them and stayed true to who you are. I would say the opposite if you were sat here with me knowing you had committed evil acts, but you didn't. In that way, you are a thousand times what they are."

I nodded unable to prevent a smile. "And do you believe that it wasn't me, who set that demon on Hunter?"

He raised his eyebrows high. "Of course I don't believe it was you. I never did."

"Then why, if you knew I was innocent, did you let people think I was the one who set the demon on him?"

"Now, I never said anything about who it was to anyone. There were higher forces at work and… I am afraid politics came into play, for which I can only apologise. For your own safety we separated you from the rest of the school while we found out what happened. If we would have told the truth, my feeling is the school would have been shut with immediate effect…" the Lily sighed and I saw lines appear on his old face. "I let Malakai in… it was a case of, keep your friends close and enemies closer… it's hard to explain," he said, looking agitated.

"But, no one told me anything, for ages," I said.

"I know," moaned the Lily. "I always try and find a solution that appeases all. Malakai is a very powerful Wizard. By letting him in, I could gain an insight into what he was doing." the Lily got up and moved around the room, long white cloak dragging behind. "I went to school with him, we were in the same class would you believe. Never would I think that he would grow to be what he is now. He threatens all that we stand for. You see, Magic is a funny old thing. For most it is an extension to life, it makes things easier, more enjoyable, more productive. But for others who let it, it can become like a drug - addictive, destructive, and can rein your thoughts entirely." He chuckled and pulled open a drawer on a huge white chest.

"You see this?" he held up a large black and white picture. "This was Malakai when he was about your age…" He held the picture up and let it float in the air, coming round to view it with me. We both stared at a plump, wide eyed, blonde boy in long, unfitting robes. But then I noticed something, something that made me quiver a little inside. On this boy's wrist, was an amulet channeller, exactly the same as mine. I glanced down at my own, the pattern was exactly the same all the way round.

"So… did you know his name back then?" I said tucking it back under my sleeve. The Lily looked away from the picture and frowned, confused by the question, so I sped ahead. "I mean, like, what was he called in school?"

"He had a few names in the first year, couldn't decide it seemed. Then in third year he settled for Malakai - god knows why, he was teased non-stop. He was an Outsider you see, didn't have the faintest clue about Magic until he got here."

I nodded, little bits of information clinging together in my brain. There was something on the cusp of being discovered. I just knew it.

"People have true names don't they sir?"

The Lily rolled the picture back up. "Yes. Everyone. But if you're thinking you will go and find out Malakai's true name, don't. I have been there and done it. He's been back and deleted all sign and notion of it," the Lily began pushing pens around the table. "Avis…" he said. "I want you to remain strong. You have a great future ahead of you, if you work hard, keep your head down, and forget the past."

I left his office buzzing. The revelation being... I was wearing Malakai's old channeller.

For the first time in ages, I skipped along the corridor back to my clock tower. I hadn't skipped in ages. I was still starving, my stomach rumbling all the way along and I couldn't decide whether to go and get some food or find Tina and tell her the revelation. Following my stomach, I grabbed a small plate of sandwiches from the Chamber and slid out before anyone saw me. Luckily, I didn't have to go to lessons because Wednesday afternoon had officially become '*homework afternoon*', which meant, of course, no one actually did any.

When I pushed open the hatch to the clock tower however, Tina was already there, standing, arms folded looking out of the clock.

"Oh Tina, there you are... *guess what*?!" I said jumping through the hatch. "I've just..." Then I stopped as another face appeared.

Robin stood looking sheepish. "Hiya mate..."

I stood dumb for a moment. Something in my head really annoyed with Tina for showing Robin *my* secret place. And another part of me confused, what was he doing here? Last time we spoke he all but cried with shock when he saw me.

"I hope you don't mind," said Tina. "He came to find me, asked me where you were..."

Robin stared at his feet for a moment and looked up, beady eyes beating fast behind their glassy frames. "I er... I'm sorry... like, *really* sorry."

"It's fine," I mumbled.

"No it's not *fine*," Robin said. "I know now. You've been

living up here, alone and… you couldn't have done that stuff… I honestly thought it was you at the time. It all kind of made sense, in the moment, you talking about demons and then one attacks Hunter after he messed the plan up," he shuffled on the spot not knowing where to look. "I've missed ya' in lessons and stuff…" He looked awkward, and swayed his long arms around, then he walked towards me and put his arms out for a hug.

I didn't do hugs, so just of stood there and patted his back. Don't get me wrong, I was glad Robin was here, really glad. But, a little part of me… preferred it to just be me and Tina. It was selfish I know, but we had a routine, and I liked my current comfortable routine.

"Anyway," said Robin, relinquishing me. "It's really hard to raise a demon and you're crap at Magic, so it couldn't have been you."

"Oi!" I said laughing.

"What did you want to tell us?" said Tina smiling wide and sitting down on my bed.

"Well…" And I explained with great gusto the recent meeting with the Lily, the picture of young Malakai and the fact that we had the same amulet channeller.

"No way!" said Tina when I finished. She stood and paced, dust rising in to the air behind her. "But… but… do you think he knows?"

"The Lily said that Malakai had been through his past and deleted stuff…" I said.

Robin hummed. "Yeah, that would make sense… didn't want people finding clues out about him…" Tina who was chewing her lip aggressively, nodded.

"We need to do *revealing* Magic on it," she announced. "Yeah, we need to find out what memories this channeller holds from when Malakai had it."

"But, it might not even be the same one…" I said. "I

mean, it looked identical but I'm not sure."

Tina shot me a dark state. "Do you want to defeat Malakai or not?"

"Well, yeah…" I said.

"Right then, we need to get to the Library at nightfall and search for a revealing Spell."

Me and Robin didn't argue, we daren't not. Tina seemed spurred on by this, most recent of clues. "It could be the only one he left," she said.

It took just over a week of searching, every night after lights out we would meet by the third floor bathrooms, opposite the Library. On the third night, we were caught by a sleepy older year who asked us what we were all doing outside the toilets.

"Just… about to go…" I said.

"We walk back together…" said Robin.

"I'm scared of the dark…" said Tina.

But after this narrow escape and tearing down countless books searching for a revealing Spell, Robin finally found it.

"Aha!" he called through the darkness. "Got it!" After a check over from Tina, we all agreed from the description that this was the right Spell. Making our way back to the clock tower we all sat around in the circle, with my channeller on the floor.

"It won't break will it?" I said.

"Noo," said Tina unconvincingly and, raising her hands at it said: "*Kerkalculevreo…*" red, popping stars fizzed in the air around the amulet with a sound like maracas. Then it hit us like a flying train. It made my head keel backwards and hit the floor, for a vision began flashing before our eyes…

A small, snotty faced kid with blonde hair and overlarge robes walked the corridor alone. He was so small and his robes so long, that he made the corridor, which was big anyway, look gigantic. He wasn't confident either, he had a permanently perplexed expression, and he walked as close to the left wall as he could get, as if he felt he may be partially invisible by doing so.

"Ello *Malakai*, arn't you cute?" said a large seventh year boy, lurching out from a nearby doorway and pinching Malakai's cheeks. "Ain't he cute lads?"

A group of boys appeared behind him in the doorway, all in green robes, nodding malevolently.

Then in a column of smoke, the scene changed.

Malakai looked slightly older, standing a foot taller and wore bright yellow, but still too large, robes. He was standing in a dimly lit underground dungeon, with an old man who was sitting at a small writing desk.

"So, I want to know Sir, if it's possible at all, to get a new channeller?" Malakai's voice had broken and he croaked the sentence nervously.

"What?! A new one?" Snapped the old man. "What do think this is? A charity?" he barked, putting his pen down. "What's wrong with *your* one?" He took Malakai's hand without asking and inspected it. "Nothing wrong with it by the looks of it!"

"Well Sir, you see it doesn't work." Malakai lied.

The old man frowned, expecting more of an explanation, but then he sighed and relented. "Pick another one then, but this won't happen again," he pointed a long, bony, dirty finger at Malakai's face. "Buy your own next time."

"Sir. Shall I destroy this one?"

"What? No! Put it back in the box."

"But sir, it doesn't work. I should put it on a shelf far into the room where no one should happen to use it."

The old man's yellow eyes squinted conspiratorially, and he spoke slowly. "Put it back in the box."

Then he made sure to watch the young boy do as he was told.

The vision faded like a dream and I sat up, blinking away the last of it. Tina rubbed her eyes and dusted her head where she now had a large dust patch. "He wanted to get rid of it?" she said. "But why?" her sparkling eyes tracked along the floor to the amulet. It was hot, and lit orange from the Spell.

Robin sat up, blinked and put his glasses on straight again. "He was a snotty thing, wasn't he? I tell you what you lot need... the Police," said Robin.

Me and Tina looked at each other, I'd never heard of it. "What's that?" said Tina.

"It's a... collection of people who work for everyone on the Outside, they arrest someone who does something wrong and lock them up."

"Sounds a bit weird to me, the Outside sounds very dangerous," I said and Tina nodded in agreement.

"Anyway, back to the point here," said Tina. "I am not sure what this vision tells us. How long was it, like a minute? The amulet must have seen more than that? I am sure it's meant to be longer... why did we only get a snapshot?"

"The book in the Library did say that it's a high level Spell?" said Robin.

"Let's try it again," said Tina holding her hands out. And again we watched the same vision. Afterwards we sat up again, nothing new had come to me.

Tina sniffed. "We're not *powerful* enough," she said pointing at our ties.

Robin grew to love the dusty clock tower in the few short hours he was up there. We did our homework together and larked around. Then, sat on my bed and watched the sun set. He said it reminded him of his home in the *Yorkshire*

Dales. He looked quite teary eyed for a minute. When darkness set in, they both left. I lay huddled in my blankets keeping warm and replaying the events of the day, as I always did before sleep. I had so many revelations to think about. The key in the box was still a strange one and my least explored. When I told Robin about it, he said we should go around and try every door in the school.

Sleep rolled over me, I had a long day of lessons tomorrow, there was talk of Straker letting me back into his class, but I wasn't counting on it. Robin had mentioned, rather squeamishly, that another Riptide match was fast approaching. Apparently, they wait and schedule most of the matches in the new year, so there would be a gluttony of exciting things happening soon. As long as *we* didn't have to play again I was fine with it.

Zzzz...

I remember rolling over in the pitch darkness and wondering what the small glowing light was. My channeller was still lying where we had left it, at the time too hot to pick up. But now, there was a feint glow coming from the inside of it. I only noticed because it was so dark. I blinked and sat up, reaching across the floor for it, rubbing my eyes of sleep and pulling it close.

I wasn't dreaming. I felt the cold sting my body as I wriggled free of the covers. The glow was perhaps the greatest revelation of all... it was the answer to the last question — *why on earth did Malakai want to get rid of his channeller?* For, written inside, in barely legible glowing ink were the words: *Property of Steve Malcolm*

That's why he wanted rid of it. It all added up in my sleepy head. He was an Outsider, he didn't know anything about Magic. But he, like me, had to get all his robes and channellers from lost property. Without knowing anything about true names, he wrote his on this amulet! Then trying to get rid of it, ended up swapping the amulet in lost property, hoping that his mistake would stay hidden, within that mass grave of old junk.

Outsiders these days are warned about their names well advance, a Wizard visits them in their home and explains everything. Now they have to pass through *The Veil*. It makes them forget their old names and anyone that knows them in their world forgets it as well, leaving them free to choose a new name. I only know this because Robin told me near the start of the year. Robin was probably called something else before, like Geoff or Peter, that's what you Outsiders are called isn't it? I laughed as I realised that Hunter must have chosen that name himself. I thought about my parents. Why did they have me, knowing that I would be a seventh son? I, of course, did not have a true name. Perhaps that's why they hated me, because I was a threat to their beloved Malakai? But as I thought about it, it all just turned a big pile of mash in my head, so I returned to sleep.

***

The poor floor in the clock tower was nearly worn out the next day. I was waiting all evening for Tina to arrive. I wish I had someway of sending her a message to make her come straight away. Eventually she did, after much looking at clocks and pacing and such. She looked annoyed, still deep in thought about the previous day, but that changed when she saw my face.

"What?" she said. I chucked the amulet to her and she looked at it.

"Inside, round the middle, can you see it?"

She looked, twisting it round in her hands. "No, what am I looking for?"

"His name, his *true name* written on the inside!"

"What?!" she said, sitting down on my bed and twisting it round and round. "I can't see anything!?"

"Last night, in the pitch darkness, it glowed only barely…"

"Glowed?" she said, putting it down. "Must have been hidden ink, after the revealing Spell… what's… what's his name?" her eyes were popping out of her skull, and I licked my lips, ready to reveal the true name of Malakai…

"S-S … Ssss!" my tongue got stuck in my mouth. "St! St! Steeeee! *Ouwwwww!*" I cried as what felt like a knife just slit my tongue!

"Oh my god Avis!" Tina cried as blood dripped out my mouth. It wasn't much, but it really hurt! "Don't try saying it again!"

We looked at each other for a moment, both realising that the name was *Jarred* - a term for a cursed name, an unsayable name.

"Ipsts jarbbbed," I said. "I'll write it…" But when I got the paper and ink, pen poised above, my hand seized up. The pen plopped out my hand and shooting pains, like needles, shot up my arm.

"Oh god!" said Tina. "Don't do anything else for god sake Avis."

We sat and stared at the channeller, thinking of a way I could say the name.

"Boes this mean, I wob'nt be able to use his name against 'im." I said as best I could.

Tina was frowning at the amulet. "What? Not sure…" she mumbled. "He was obviously really stupid, in the days where they didn't pass Outsiders through the Veil."

"Why did he use hidden ink?" I said.

"Because he was stupid, people use hidden ink to write on metal and wood and stuff because it sticks, normal ink will just run off. But why did he think using hidden ink would stop people reading it? Of course, he was an Outsider, he didn't know much about Magic then did he?" she said hardly stopping for breath. "The only way I'll be able to find out the name is if we Spell it again, and wait until it goes really dark so you can see it. Bit of homework to do anyway while we wait."

Robin came by just as the sun set and sat with us as we filled him on the latest. Then, soon enough, the time came, in the deepest darkest part of the night, Tina raised her hands and Spelled the channeller. The fizzing red stars popped again and the amulet glowed. Expecting to see the visions again we sat waiting, but nothing happened. We sat dumb looking around at each other. Tina spelled it again and again…

"Why isn't it working?!" she cried.

Robin coughed and said, rather nervously - "Ah, we learnt about this with Straker. Is there any chance that this is a *Learner*?"

Tina frowned at him. "What on earth is that?" she looked peeved that Robin knew something she didn't.

"Well, the Spell makes the channeller learn from Spells that are put on it, making it defend itself and reflect them in the future. Before he changed his amulet he must have put what protection he could on it, just in case someone did find it."

Tina huffed, "I've never heard of such a thing!"

"Nor me," I said huffing, I was the only person who knew the true name of Malakai and I had no way of saying it!

Robin swallowed. "What I don't get is… If he's been in the school, why hasn't he been back to destroy it? He knows where he left it surely?"

I had wondered that too. "Ah but…" I said. "What if he

only started coming to the school after I took this from the lost property? What if this is what he's looking for?"

Tina clicked her fingers at me. "Bingo! Only explanation. No one else in the school has ever heard of, as far as I know, Malakai coming in and doing as he pleases."

"Yeah but, surely he would have come here years ago and found it?" said Robin, causing Tina to deflate.

"Hmm, yeah that's true."

"Why don't you tell the Lily?" said Robin. "He will be able to stop your tongue bleeding when you try and say the name, and his revealing Spell will be loads more powerful."

"No," said Tina.

"Why not?" I said, I thought it was a good idea.

"If you tell the Lily then Malakai will find out, Malakai has a hold over the Lily... he must know his true name or something. If you tell the Lily, he will be forced to tell Malakai, I am sure."

We all sat silent. "Oh, I'm never gonna avenge my brother!" said Tina standing and leaning on the long arm of the clock face. "While *he* is out there... I have failed my quest!"

"What?" I said trying to be calming. "Failed? This is our first year, our robes and ties haven't even changed colour yet! You can't expect to just blow the most evil Wizard of all time out the water in our first few months at Magic school. Don't be so hard on yourself."

She turned on me. "What, you want me to wait until the last year of school do you? And then sort him out?"

"No... just, let's not rush anything."

"Avis is right," said Robin. "I mean, we know hardly anything yet, Magic wise, he'll just kill us if we try anything now."

"Not Avis," she said. "He can't kill him, he's a seventh son, and Avis knows his true name."

"But I can't *say* his name, and just because I'm a seventh son, doesn't mean he can't kill me does it?"

"*OHH!*" Tina cried into the rafters. "You're both scared!"

I shook my head. "I'm not *scared…*"

"You are! You are the only one who can stop him Avis! You are the one who can avenge my brother and all the countless others!"

I swallowed, I was scared. I was scared of Tina, who looked positively crazy, her hair wild and eyes murderous. "I think…" I said trying to slow the conversation down. "That we need to sleep on it, and search for some Spells that will enable me to say his true name."

Robin nodded with me.

"There is no *time!*" Tina cried. "Do you think if there was, I'd be waiting until my last year too?"

I frowned, what was she getting at? "I don't get it. Why isn't there any time?"

"It's the last quarter of the sign of *Handen*."

"Come again?" said Robin, who shared my perplexed expression.

She huffed, and I half expected steam to shoot out of her nostrils. "The *last quarter of Handen*, the Magical Star Sign? It's all to do with the Book of Names. At the end of the sign of Handen, the Book of Names vanishes to another place. If Malakai has the book at the end of April, he will have it for twelve years more! And I won't be able to get my brother back!"

"Get him back?" said Robin. "What do you mean?"

Tina was breathing hard. "Anyone killed by dark Magic is able to be brought back with their true name from the Book of Names…"

Me and Robin didn't look at each other, but I felt uneasy at the prospect of bringing the dead back. "Is that a good idea?" I said slowly.

"What?" Tina spat. "To get my brother back and bring an end to Malakai? Yeah, it's a pretty GOOD IDEA!" she cried. "You know what…" she said throwing her arms in the air. "I don't need you, either of you. I can do this on my own!" Her fuse had blown. I'd never seen her so fraught, and she wasn't even shouting. She was shaking with anger.

"Thanks for all the help you guys! Nice one! I don't need two sad, scaredy nerds anyway!"

"Wait," I said, my bones creaking as I stood. "Don't go…"

"Get away from me! You've proven where your loyalties lay. If you won't help me get my brother Ernest back then sod you!"

With a slam of the roof hatch she was gone.   I turned back to Robin who was staring after the roof hatch, then looked up at me with a weak smile. "She doesn't mean it mate, she's just angry. She'll come round I'm sure…"

***

"*It's clear where your loyalties lay,*" I thought. Did she mean because I'm a Blackthorn? And what was that last thing she said: "*If you won't help me get my brother Ernest back…*" Ernest? Why was that familiar?

I thought about the Book of Names disappearing every twelve years — why?

I sighed and wondered about Malakai's true name, Steve Malcolm, being Jarred. Memories of my parents kept jumping to attention. I remember them talking about removing a Jarred name, but I can't remember what it was. What on earth would they think of all this? And what would they do if I did manage to say Malakai's true name and end him? Sure, I would be in Tina's good books, very good books, but what would they do? It would show them. And… what if I managed to get the Book Of Names? I would have the power over all of them. I laughed to myself at the possibly as I drifted into a cold sleep.

***

"*AVIS!*" cried a loud, familiar voice. I woke with a start.

"What? Hello?" I looked up to see a glowing figure bobbing in front of me. "Ernie?" I said.

He looked frantic and was sobbing hard. "It's all my fault!" he cried. "All my fault!"

"What is? Calm down… tell me what's wrong!"

Ernie looked terrified. "I couldn't let her see me. This year, so hard…" he said in between sobs. "She's in the Healer's room…"

"Who is?" But I already knew the answer.

"T-t… *Tina!*"

"What happened?" I stood and threw clothes on.

"She went looking for him. Followed him. It's all *my fault!*" he wailed.

Now I knew what she meant when she said… *my brother Ernest…* "Why couldn't you let her see you?"

"I'm her… her *BROTHER!*" he wailed. "He attacked her! Malakai attacked her!"

I ran as fast as I could, ignoring the sharp pain in my sides. "It's up here!" Ernie cried zooming along the corridors ahead of me. My heart was throbbing in my chest as I skidded round corners. Finally Ernie zoomed through a set of large double doors. I crashed into them and ran inside. Then stopped still. This was the Healer's room? I stood now in awe. Dull green light was coming from, what looked like, a miniature sun which hung high in the middle of the huge room. I couldn't take my eyes away. It hung graceful and wonderful. A million shades of green swirling imperceptible strands of beauty and light. Green rays gliding downwards to people in beds. It was so beautiful. As I moved slowly into the room, transfixed, I saw the rays drift my way. As it touched me, it became bliss. All pain eliminated, all thoughts vanished, all aches and pains gone. I couldn't help but stand and stare, soaking up the green goodness.

A beautiful woman in a long, white robe walked elegantly towards me. Her blonde hair hung down to her ankles, her face radiant, with eyes the same green as the sun. And then she spoke with an angelic, soothing voice. "You are here to see Tina Partington?"

"Yes… wait, Partington?" something else smacked me in the face. Tina and Ernie's Dad was… my form tutor… Magisteer Partington?!

Ernie was bobbing up and down near a bed in the corner of the room. "This way," said the Healer.

Tina lay unconscious. Green rays coursing in and out of each breath. She looked bad. Open wounds lit her face scarlet red and her hair was matted with dried blood. The soft white clothes she had been put in were running red. The Healer dabbed at the wounds with a white cloth, soaked in a bowl of water and soft smelling potions. As the green light and the water touched her face, the wounds knitted back together. It was strange to watch. Her beautiful face returning in some part back to the one I knew. Tears welled up in my eyes now at the sight of her. Her words reverberating around my mind from the last time she spoke to me. Ernie bobbed by her bedside, sobbing into her pillow.

"All my fault," he mumbled.

"Ernest Partington? Why didn't you tell me that you were a Partington?"

"I… don't… know," he said in between sobs. "Easier… not to."

"So your the dead brother who set her the quest?"

"Yes, in my ignorance! After I *passed over*, I realised what I had done, how stupid I was to have left the quest to someone so young and innocent. The grief led me back here as this…" he indicated his see-through form.

"But you couldn't show yourself to her?"

"No. However hard I tried, she couldn't see me!" he wailed.

"And your Dad?"

"Him neither, although, maybe he once saw me. I don't know."

"She wants to bring you back to life…" I said.

Ernie stopped wailing and nodded. "Oh, I would like that so very much. To be with my family again. I don't want to be stuck like this forever!"

I turned to the Healer who was quietly dabbing. "How long will she be like that?"

"A while," she said softly.

I took a final look at Tina and Ernie Partington, then turned away. "I'm going to sort this," I said turning and walking out of the Healer's room. "I promise."

Something inside me clicked, Tina was right, I did have the power to end Malakai. All I needed was the courage. And now he'd given it to me. The Partington family had been ripped apart by this man Malakai. And the girl I… loved, yes loved… had nearly been killed by him.

As I left the Healer's room, the content feeling drained out of me as despair and anger pulsed back into my veins. I heard a man running up the opposite corridor and bursting into the Healer's room. I saw the flick of Partington's brown robes flash into the green light. As I walked further and further away the more and more determined I became to end Malakai - the evil, lower than amoeba, thing that he was.

I had the clues.

All I needed was a plan.

CHAPTER EIGHT

A Key Revelation

That first night I sat and stared out of the clock face, running it all through my mind. Robin came to see me and asked if I'd heard about what happened to Tina. I didn't feel like talking but went through my thoughts with him.

"I know his true name but I can't say it..." I said. "If I can find a way to remove the Jarred Spell, then I can say it."

Robin sniffed, his beady eyes blinking rapidly at me. "You have to be careful Avis. Don't go through with any of this as an act of revenge. This Malakai is the most evil person in the history of Magic, I'm sure he'll be more than ready for you."

"Yes. But he can't hurt *me*..." the thought had come to me before, why, when I saw him, did he not Spell me? But instead went for Hunter.

He nodded stiffly in agreement. "I get that, he Spelled Hunter and made it look like you, but why didn't he spot the channeller on your arm? If he knew it was his?"

I looked down at my channeller and then saw why. I indicated to Robin - these robes were too big for me — the sleeves overlapped my arms and hands, the channeller covered over. "And, why would Malakai even think for a moment that I would have to get a channeller from lost property? I'm a Blackthorn!"

"True that, did you know you're in that encyclopaedia of black Magic... well, your family is."

"I know." Our family was notorious, one of my great-grandparents could have given Malakai a run for his money. And then... my thoughts kept coming back to the fact that my parents had me, even though they knew I was a *seventh son*. Something didn't add up there.

"I have to do this before April."

Robin whistled. "Don't have long then."

"I just need to follow him, to find out where he is going when he comes into the school. It might lead to the book. And then I need to find out how to say his true name."

"What you gonna do if you get the book?"

I hadn't thought about that. "I don't know, it doesn't matter. I need to find out what this key does first and who it's from." I held up the key that I'd got in the present at Christmas. "Look into it for me..." Robin nodded curtly as I tucked it away. Perhaps I was pinning too much hope on things, perhaps the key was for someone else and the presents had been mixed up?

In the meantime I realised, I needed to find Ernie again.

I searched high and low for that ghost but Tina's brother Ernie couldn't be found no matter how hard I looked. It was annoying, because I had left him not two days ago, next to Tina's bed. I got so desperate I even stopped passing ghosts, asking them where he was, but, if they even bothered to answer me back, all had no idea. Each day, I would go to the Healer's room and sit by Tina's bed. She was still unconscious, but the loving Healer lady with the green eyes said that this was a good thing, more time to heal. Her wounds had sealed up nicely now and she was resembling more of the Tina that I remember. Flowers and cards littered the table and floor all around her bed. I sat for hours on end, hoping that Ernie would make an appearance. But I caught not even a sniff of him. Time was running down quickly and I desperately needed to ask him some questions. How did he die? And what did he know about the quest that would help me finish it?

Sitting in the Healer's room was good. I had to pull myself away at times for the sensation was overwhelmingly comfortable. Thoughts seemed to solidify and make sense, whereas before they were a muddled mess. The mysterious green sun seemed to suck the bad things out of you, replacing it with serenity and goodness.

A week later I was sitting, quietly watching Tina, when a thought flashed through my mind. *Use the revealing Spell on the key*!

I ran back to the clock tower, knocking for Robin on the way. He was in the Condors' dorm doing his homework with the others. Our lessons were being covered by a ghost, who kept setting more and more homework. Some of the Condors looked away when I poked my head in, but Robin saw my worried face and raced out.

"What's going on?" he said.

"Revealing Spell… on the… key!" I just about managed to say. We climbed through the roof hatch into the clock tower. I pulled the key out and put it on the dusty wood floor.

"Sit down," I said, raising my hands just above it and catching my breath. "What's the Spell?" I said, my mind had gone blank.

"Er… Kerka-something…" said Robin.

"I remember!" I raised my hands again. "*Kerkalculevreo!*" The key lit up orange, and my head flew back as a dream like vision danced across our eyes…

Ernie Partington looked very alive as he crept along the corridors. Every so often he would dart inside an alcove, or behind a suit of armour. Some way along the corridor was Malakai, drifting silently along. Then, in a flash he vanished inside a door and was gone. Ernie, with deep bags under his eyes, straightened and went over to inspect the door. Gently, he rubbed the lock, golden light fizzed around his hands, but he grew frustrated - the door wouldn't open. He stepped back and drew a wad of parchment from his back pocket and made notes. He sighed and turned back with a swish of his long, grey robes.

Then, with a whizz of white light, we zapped forwards. Ernie was on the floating island with friends, they all had silly haircuts, and some had beards. Ernie checked his watch, made an excuse to leave and walked back along the drawbridge. He was popular, people waved and cooed to him as he passed. As he approached the main hall, he scanned behind him to make sure no one was around, then screwing up his face he began rubbing his head viciously with his hands. A new face, body and clothes began to appear in place of him. Now a small man stood with a pudgy pock marked face, black robes and a Magisteer's crest. Quickly he began to walk toward the Dungeons. The small man walked through the hallways unnoticed, obviously not an important man. Yet, one boy, who was leaning over the banister rail above, saw him and set towards him calling out.

"Sir… Sir!" called the boy, running down the stairway.

"Yes?" called Ernie in a squeaky voice that he wasn't used to, then coughed. "Yes, what is it?"

"It's me Sir, Arnold? Just wondering Sir, about the homework, what is it? I thought I could do it now."

Ernie, as the little man kept walking and Arnold kept pace. "You will know the same time as everyone else."

"Oh right…" Arnold frowned. "But you said earlier I must find you and ask."

"Yes," said Ernie, stopping and scratching his head, this was an unwanted distraction. "What were we studying earlier?" he said, as if trying to remember.

"The transformation of Biglobears and Faradays into Yerpold creatures."

"Ah yes," said Ernie. "Well, do me two passages on other

Yerpold creatures and why it's important that we know."

Arnold frowned again. "Only two passages sir?" this was obviously not what he was used to and he smelt something fishy.

Sweat beads appeared on Ernie's forehead, he scanned the hallway where a dozen or so people were milling around. Slyly, Ernie raised his hand at Arnold and muttered something under his breath.

"I *see* Sir," said Arnold, who promptly ran off looking happy. Ernie smiled and carried on in the direction of the dungeons. That was close.

"But, no one has requested that key in years, I'm not sure I even have it. If I do, it will be rusted over…"

Ernie looked down at the man who was shorter even than he, whom had bags and bags of keys on chains around his waist. "I was assured you would have it by the Lily himself, but if you want me to go and tell him why you can't do your job then…"

"No! No… I can find it, all I mean is… are you sure it's *that* door he wants the key for?" the small, dirty man looked sideways at Ernie with yellowing eyes. The dungeon was dank, mouldy and echoed with the sound of scuttling creatures, Ernie didn't feel altogether comfortable. The man reached down and slid a key off a chain, and handed it to Ernie, who nodded and turned back.

The next flash and Ernie was alone at a desk. Dim orange embers glowed throughout the room. There was snoring behind him, as the other boys in the room slept. Ernie had his head in his hands, pouring over notes. He collected the sheets together, set a note down and wrote *Tina*, on the top, folded it, tapped it three times and with a poof of smoke, it vanished. Then he did the same with a thick bundle of notes.

Finally, he pulled out a key and a book. With his head

bowed over the page and right hand poised over they key, he recited the instructions. Fiery green light outlined the contours of another key next to the existing one. He placed the original inside a small green box with red ribbon. He sealed the box and began to read another passage. The box jolted and span on his desk, then shrank and popped, disappearing altogether. Ernie sat back in his chair and sighed, brushing his long hair back. He took the copied key, which was loosely transparent.

"Haven't got long..." he muttered, twisting it round in his hands. Then, putting his grey robes on, looked around the room as if for the last time. With a swish, he left. Ernie walked purposefully, grey robe flapping behind, not making much attempts at quieting his footsteps. He took the key out of his pocket and unlocked the door with a loud clunk and stood back. The door creaked. Ernie brushed his hair back, and steeled himself, before stepping into darkness.

Ernie crept down through darkness. The next second he stood, facing a large man dressed all in black, face long and skeletal with blue glowing eyes that came to rest on Ernie, who raised his hands quickly. Red, green and gold flashes scorched the air. Malakai flapped and the light burst in a shard of sparks. The two foes faced each other. With a long skeletal hand Malakai pinned Ernie to the floor. A very large book with a brown cover, older than time itself, stood on a gold mantle.

"How dare you! Coming here and interfering in *my* business!" Malakai cried.

Ernie looked charged, he whispered something and vanished, like a mirage. The next moment he was behind Malakai. "*Flutteryout!*" he cried.

Malakai flew into the opposite wall. Ernie grabbed the book, which fizzed and made horrible cracking noises. Malakai roared.

"Give that back! Don't you dare!" A whistling lit the air. Ernie stood terrified, unable to move. The next moment he was bound by thick red snaking, chains. Malakai took the book and placed it back on the mantle carefully. Ernie struggled against the expanding chains.

"You will never get away with what you're doing. I will make sure of it! I know your plans. I won't stop until your gone!" said Ernie before a red chain bound his mouth.

Malachi chuckled. "Oh please... I've heard it all before."

Another flash of white light and Ernie stood motionless, bound in red chains, at the top of the tallest tower in the school. High pitched wind whistled around the open top. Malakai came to stand and look down at the drop into abyss. "Any last words?"

The chain around Ernie's mouth disappeared. Ernie's eyes were large, but he didn't look like a man about to die.

"You know nothing! There are thousands of other people ready to take my place. The plans I have this year are already making their way to the right people. I followed you the whole year and you haven't spotted me. You think you're powerful, you think your special, you think your power gives you a right to rule! It doesn't. You're weak, your lust for power comes from a loss of love. And I pity you."

Malakai's blue eyes dimmed, and his head tilted to the side. With a lazy flick of his finger, the red chains fell off. "Maybe, but you're the one whose about to die..."

"I'm not afraid..." Ernie smiled as wind whipped his hair and clothes.

Malakai huffed and swiped the air. Ernie slid across the floor. He didn't struggle. He just kept his gaze with Malakai and in silence, slid off the tower.

The vision stopped in a flash of white light, my head jolting. I blinked and sat up straight, my head spinning. Robin blinked at me. Neither of us said anything. As I sat there, I wondered about the pointlessness of Ernie's attempts at taking the Book Of Names. He seemed to submit too easily, as if it was all just a game. The way he fell, smiling, keeping his gaze with Malakai. Whatever his plans were, I didn't understand them. Even Malakai seemed deterred by Ernie's unusual behaviour.

The key, in the box I'd got for Christmas, was from Ernie. Did it flow through time and only arrive here in time for Christmas? Or did he plan for it to arrive just at that moment?

"I don't understand how he sent me the box with a key in it," I said. "I mean, when was he at school?"

Robin looked very disturbed by everything he'd seen. "It's a very powerful Spell. I'm sure I've read about it somewhere in one of the old Library books... or was it Straker who was talking about it? It's something about committing an item to fate, or destiny or something. And leaving it up to Magic to decide who the next owner should be."

"Right..." I said. "I suppose the next thing to do then is find Tina's notes."

Robin left soon after. I continued to sit cross-legged on my bed starring at the darkening sky. I'd been Tina's friend for ages and I didn't even know where her dorm was. Some investigation was needed.

The next day after lessons, we walked around the school choosing some of the more unoccupied corridors. "You do realise what would happen if we get caught in a girls dorm?" said Robin beady eyes flickering.

"I think that is the least of our problems," I said. "What form is she in?"

"I don't know... Oh, yes I do, or at least I know a way we can find out... the Riptide wall," he was right, the Riptide wall was where all the forms in the school were listed, so you can see when your games are scheduled.

Me and Robin marched to the hall where the Riptide wall was. There were a few people around, but most were taking a stroll outside. It was a lovely sunny day and the light streamed in long rays through small windows onto a high wall, filled from top to bottom with sheets and information. Each form had their form name, flag and colours with the people in their form listed below. Robin began scanning the large tapestry for the names in teams. It took flipping ages. Some of the names were so high up I couldn't see them. But after a while Robin said:

"Aha! Found it! She's in the *Hubris* form. Ergh, they wear pink."

"Don't matter about that. Where's their dorm room?"

"Erm... let me see..." said Robin, who was on tip toes, running his finger down the sheet. "Girls... dorm room number... is... 314c!"

"At last!" I said. Then, I stopped before the stairs. "Where is room 314c?" Robin shrugged.

We must have searched for hours, we even missed dinner. Starting on the first floor, there were lots of 300s, but no 314's. The room numbers were not obviously placed, something I've noticed before, but it made it tremendously tricky to try and find a room using *logic*. Eventually, down a light and bright corridor lined with pictures of famous witches, we found it. Doors on one side read 698, 635 and 612e and the doors on the other side were 313, 377a and 314c!

"At flipping last!" I said.

"Hey," said Robin. "They are all at dinner arn't they? If not, we should come back another time."

"No, we go now. If there is anyone in there we make excuses." I didn't know what excuses these will be - "*sorry I was just looking for Tina's dead brother's notes on how to end Malakai*" - but I was sure we could come up with something. What mattered now was being as quick as possible. Like Robin had said, April was barely a week away.

I took the handle slowly and went inside. The room was just like ours, same layout, same fireplace, but different curtains, different bedspreads and different carpet.

"Now which one is Tina's?" We scanned around, and hunted for clues. There was no guessing what we would find here.

"This girl has more books out than you're allowed," said Robin standing over a nearby bed. I walked around the room, which was a lot tidier than the Condor girls room.

"And the bed is really messy! She's got all her homework sticking out of her sheets."

I smiled. "Let me have a look at that," this bed was closest to the window, the sheets were the same as all the other girl's, if not a little less cared for. And, looked like they hadn't been slept in for a while. Robin was right, there were sheets of parchment sticking from beneath bedsheets. More stuck out from the edges of a locked desk.

"This *must* be hers..." I scanned the books that lay in piles next to her bed. There were too many to list, but read things like: '*Characteristics of Black Magic*' and '*Things You Didn't Know About Magic*', amongst others. I pulled the parchment out of her bed and collected them into a pile. Robin whispered a Spell, unlocking the desk and pulled the other sheets out collecting them into a large pile. They were most definitely Tina's, I recognised her handwriting. Some of the notes listed Counter Spells and possible hidden places in the school. As I quickly flicked through the papers, I noticed some of them were older than the others, and the handwriting different.

"These must be Ernie's notes," I muttered. I also spotted a list of people written by Tina, with the pros and cons to each person and whether they can be trusted or not.

There was a big question mark next to my name. A little stone dropped in my stomach.

"I think someone's coming," said Robin.

That night, after me and Robin had our fill of some kind of meat hotpot, we sat under an improved fire created by Robin that supplied enough light to sort through the papers and put them in order. I put all Ernie's notes into a relatively organised pile. Then we did the same with Tina's. Afterwards we sat and read them through together.

Ernie's notes went into detail about Malakai and his past. It said that he was bullied at school and that initially, after school, he set out to avenge those bullies. The power he felt from quashing those people led him to finding a taste for it. He wasn't particularly clever or special in school, he kept to himself and got by as best an average Outsider would. When he left school he became a loner, hiring a shack from an old woman in a remote part of snowy Slackerdown, the fifth and most forgetful Magical Kingdom. It was here, where he descended into some kind of Magical madness, working all hours of the night and day, developing new Magic and plotting his revenge against those who had crossed him in the past. Ten years later he was very well-known to the Magical community. He built strong networks with evil people, with a string of rich old women leaving him money in their wills.

There was a page of Ernie's notes dedicated to acquiring a key. He noted down several shape-shifting Spells, and what to tell the caretaker, noted as "*Parker*" that would make him hand over the key. Ernie also talked in long passages about possible ways to conquer Malakai - "*read all the books*

Malakai read, so as to learn counters to his Spells" But when he came to list those books, there was a big angry question mark.

"Ah!" said Robin. "This is what Tina was talking about the other night!" He showed me the piece of parchment, which had a complicated drawing on it of the AstroMagical Star Chart.

"Look," I said. "She's mapped out when the Book of Names must have arrived, and when it leaves."

Robin gulped. "She was right. End of April…"

Me and Robin read until the chickens began clucking and dew settled on the school grounds. During lessons the next day I tried to do all the ghost Magisteer asked but couldn't help falling asleep on my desk by midday. Some of the others did too; Hunter, Dennis and Dawn were all sound asleep, less due to tiredness and more down boredom. Robin was a machine when it came to work and took the time during these boring lessons to pour over notes which he kept hidden under the table. I was too tired to think and dozed in and out of consciousness until dinner.

That night, we took the notes tucked inside Robin's bag to the Healer's room and read over every note by Tina's bed. Robin was amazed at the wonderful feeling of clarity he got from the room and wondered why the sun was not in the middle of the school for everyone to benefit. Tina looked a lot better now, still pale, but I could see improvement. I was hoping Ernie would pass by, he was the one we needed to see. Even looking over the notes now, with the helpful green light, none of the connections were making much sense. For instance, a lot of what Ernie wrote only he would understand. This included random Spells, strange cryptic phrases and question marks over everything.

A few weeks later, nothing had changed, Tina was still in the Healer's room unconscious. But I grew accustomed to having Robin around. He was bloody clever and made connections I never would have on my own. Although we had all these notes, I had a plan that had been festering in my head for some time now, and I couldn't seem to get rid of it, no matter how hard I tried - something that increased every time Robin would remind me how long we had left.

"Only three weeks left until the end of April mate…"

"I *know*."

The thing was, I knew that in stopping Malakai, I could save Tina. So, to fail in stopping Malakai was to fail saving Tina. My mind jumped around all over the place for days at a time. The revelation that Tina was a Partington was still hard to digest. Why hadn't she told me that her Dad was my form tutor?

Each night, me and Robin would sneak off to the Library and see if we could find a new book. Robin would suggest revisions to Spells, changing them into Spells that were harder to counter. Obviously it would be more dangerous, but it was worth the risk. For an Outsider, Robin sure was clever.

But I still didn't tell him what my plan was, or anyone in fact, because I knew what he would say. All I knew was I had to do something. I could plan and plan and plan, but it would never feel like the right moment to challenge Malakai. I was twelve years old, knew barely enough Magic to pass the first year and the majority of the school hated me, so I wouldn't exactly be held up as a hero. But sometimes, I thought, you have to do things for others that might not benefit yourself.

Half term came out of nowhere and Robin, rather apologetically, went home for a week. Just before everyone went home, the ghost that was taking our lessons told us that Partington would be back to teach us again when we all got back, everyone cheered, much to the annoyance of the ghost. It would be good to get back to learning interesting things again.

I missed Robin the first couple of days, we'd spent so much time together - deciphering all those notes - that now, I felt very alone again.

In the mean time, I was collecting my own very nice stash of notes. I had worked on changing three Spells, which we were told from day one, to never ever do. If you change the content of a Spell, without knowing what you're doing, you could blow yourself up. I had to take a risk though and find something that Malakai would not be expecting. To counter a Spell, you need to know the name of the Counter Spell, which is pretty easy. But if you've invented your own Spell, then its a whole lot harder to counter, or block. Now, I'm not so arrogant as to assume Malakai would not know how to block my Spells, but it could buy me some time.

In the proceeding days of half term, I kept to myself. I took my notes with me to the Chamber and ate while reading. I still received scorning glances from around the room, but I'd learnt to ignore it quite well now. Anyway, I had bigger things to think about.

Hunter decided against going home this half term as he had too much work to do. Strangely, he seemed a lot happier now, after his accident. He liked Straker's lessons, as he was now trusting them to perform practical Magic. I sighed and wondered when Straker would let me back in his class, he knew I was innocent.

"Yeah, he's a stubborn, strange man..." said Hunter leaning in. "And a bit weird," he laughed biting into a large belgian bun. "So what you doing Avis? I see you walking around and going to places but I have no idea what you're doing. It's not anything... *evil* is it?" He raised his eyebrow as icing dripped down his chin.

"No, ha, very funny." I was only really used to speaking to Robin and Tina, so now my social skills were pretty terrible. I found it awkward and clumsy holding even a normal conversation.

I saw Ross walking around looking stressed as he revised hard for his exams. Sometimes I would catch his eye and he would look away smiling. Perhaps he left me alone now because he thought I was evil? I had a sneaking suspicion that David Starlight and the rest of the Eagles form were avoiding me too. I'd seen David, on his own looking glum, walking towards me in the corridor the day before, when he saw me he turned down an opposite corridor and hurried away. Maybe my evil plan had the desired effect after all.

After a long boring week of sitting on my own in the Chamber, deciphering old notes and brainstorming my plan — Robin finally returned. I heard his voice in the main hall and ran out to greet him. He had his suitcase floating behind him and I noticed that he looked a little more fattened up, rosy cheeked and cheerful. I needed to have whatever he'd eaten. My belt hardly fitted and I kept having to make new holes.

"God I'd missed that place," he said. "I love Yorkshire."

The next day we were back in lessons with Partington. He was cheery, but I could tell it was forced. Deep worry lines covered his face and his clothes looked unwashed. To start, he was quite dreamy and asked vaguely what we'd learnt with the ghost.

"Not a lot!" called Dennis and the class laughed.

"Why were you away Sir?" said Dawn, the big blabber mouth.

Partington swallowed. "Oh just… family stuff. Never mind that." I wondered if they knew that his daughter was Tina?

After a few minutes Partington returned, in some part, to his old self. He cracked a few jokes about the ghost and launched into an interesting lessons about Hexes. I think it was doing him good, teaching us, it took his mind off Tina. Now I looked at him, I saw the resemblance.

Wednesday morning I woke up early, wrapped tight in a hundred blankets. The wooden floor hard and cold beneath me. The sun had just poked over the horizon and through the rays that trickled in through the clock face I saw a small rat scurrying through a crack in the wall. I sighed and sat up.

Today was my Birthday. I was thirteen. This year, I wouldn't be chased around the castle by my siblings and forced to open booby-trapped presents. This year I wouldn't have to cut an exploding cake. This year, I wouldn't have to hide in the dungeon all day because Rory thought it would be a good idea to give me a baby Wolf-Raptor.

Invariably, I ended up at some point on my birthday, crying. This year, would be different. I wondered if my parents were going to send me some presents? Or a present? Or maybe even a card? Anything would be nice.

If Tina was here, she would have got me a card.

I had noticed around the school that on someones Birthday their friends got them a big badge to parade around with, letting everyone know it was their friends Birthday. Then in the Chamber, a big cake would come out and everyone would sing *Happy Birthday*. But only for the popular ones, or people with friends, or people who weren't suspected of attempted murder. So my hopes weren't high.

In fact the day was pleasant. Partington taught us all about enchanted furniture, which I found fascinating. I contributed to the class in fact, because my Great Uncle Farrybold, who lived with us until a year ago when he passed over, was an eccentric antique dealer and was always bringing home huge bits of furniture, like sofa's that sprouted unlimited seats, wardrobes that chose your outfit for the day and even a hairbrush that grew back hair on bald men (it didn't work on him).

He was killed by an antique billiards table in the end, which collapsed on him when he said a trigger word. It was a shame, he was always nice to me, when he remembered who I was.

Partington stopped me just as I went to leave that lesson and asked if he could have word. He sat down on his desk and shut the door by flicking his hand. He looked at me and suddenly the thing we both shared came to the front of our minds. Tina.

"I know that you are up to something," said Partington pointedly. "I don't know what, but I know that you need to be careful. I've seen you walking around the school with that look on your face. And I know that you're good friends with Tina." I shifted uncomfortably, unable to look at him directly. "You know something, and I don't expect you to tell me. I had warned her many times that actions have consequences. It was no one's fault except hers. Also, I've been reading some of your notes…" Partington held up my Main Book, which allowed him to see my writing. I shuddered. I think I had accidentally wrote on the parchment that Partington could check. I swallowed, not wanting to know what he had read.

"Don't worry, wasn't anything bad. Just some Spells that I don't think you should be doing."

"Yes, Sir."

"You do know," said Partington. "That you can come to me with anything, don't you?"

I nodded politely. "I do, Sir." I wanted to tell him about Malakai, the Book Of Name's and my plan. But, I just couldn't. I couldn't bring myself to tell him the truth, that I knew his dead son Ernest and planned to follow through and complete his quest.

"She's under a curse..." said Partington looking up at the ceiling. "*He* put her under. To make sure she won't wake."

I was sure that he was talking about Malakai, but I frowned, unsure. "A *curse*, Sir?"

"Yes. He's a nasty individual is *Malakai*," he looked at me now. His red, blotchy face gazing at mine, trying to spot any giveaways. I matched his red and bloodshot eyes with my blankest expression. "And your not to get involved with him either. Not as revenge or anything, you hear me?"

I had to look at my feet, I didn't want to lie to him. I shrugged. "What do you mean - a *curse*? Like, she won't wake up?"

He looked away from me, sighing. "No, not unless it's broken."

"How? What I mean is, *why* did he curse her?"

Partington stood and began shuffling papers. "Don't know."

Before I knew what I was doing, words began tumbling out of my mouth. "She was doing what Ernie told her to..."

His eyes moved slowly down to me. "Impossible..."

I felt a trickle of sweat down my back. "No Sir. Ernest sent her the plans, she told me."

He didn't move still. "Plans?"

"Yes, plans of... *ending* Malakai."

Suddenly, I saw the whole mess dawn across his face. "*Of course...*" I think I had just put one of the last puzzle piece together for him. He sat down again slowly. "That explains a great deal," he said gravely.

I stood there for ages, feeling awkward. I didn't know

what else to say. I had already given away far more than I should have, what would Tina say if she were here?

Partington began muttering. "Can't believe the Lily stood for this. No choice, I suppose. Silly, silly T… and Erns, that's what he was up to, all that time…" Partington stopped muttering to himself and looked up. "I never knew how he died. But now, it's obvious. He didn't *jump* off the top tower. He was *killed*. I knew it. I always knew it. Just never realised in all that time what he was doing. I knew something was up with him, caught him sneaking around at night in the school, but he would never tell me why… he went after Malakai… and got himself KILLED!" Partington slammed a fist on his desk.

Something was working it's way into a conclusion in my mind, a question I had been wondering this whole time: *why was Ernie going after Malakai? What possible reason did he have?* But then I saw - Partington was rubbing his ring finger. And a memory of Ernie going straight for the Book of Names.

Partington talked through his hands. "Must have been eating him up inside, the whole time."

"What was, Sir?"

He pursed his lips. "The death of their Mother. My wife… she was killed by Malakai."

I couldn't say anything, my mouth dried up. I suddenly felt so sorry for him. This lovely man who had nearly lost everyone he cared about to one person. Malakai had killed his wife, that's why Ernie went after Malakai… but also, more importantly… he went after the Book of Names. Tina had said she wanted the Book of Names to bring her Brother back, maybe Ernie wanted the book to do the same for his Mother.

"When he was fourteen and Tina would have been three… Malakai decided that Marcela was far too powerful, she was in the opposition Government, and in opposition to his cause. So he got rid of her. The Government marked the death as an '*accident*'. It was a travesty! And now my daughter is under a curse for which I, nor anyone, has any idea how to break!" His face dropped and his shoulders sank. I wanted to shake him, make him see that he had powers greater than me... he could stop it, he could break the curse. But he looked so small and shrivelled up, that I feared he might never stand up again.

"Can't the Lily help, Sir?"

"Pah!" cried Partington, his back rising. "Chance would be a fine thing, he's has no power against Malakai, not anymore!"

"Why not?"

Partington shrugged. "Malakai has got some hold over him, I don't know." I was beginning to think I did know. More, in fact, than the adults in this school.

I left feeling awful. Even though it was my Birthday, I didn't care. I had to find a way of breaking the curse over Tina. I was annoyed, if I had the courage and initially agreed with her, then she would never have stormed off and got herself in trouble. I also thought that Malakai must have cursed her for a reason - maybe she knew something and this stopped her from telling anyone. And why didn't he just kill her?

I had just under two weeks to find a plan and a solution before the Book of Names went back into Malakai's possession for another twelve years. And Tina... if I didn't find a way of removing the curse then she would remain under it indefinitely.

When I got back to the clock tower, a glowing figure awaited me. Ernie's face was glowering at me.

"Why did you tell him about ME! YOU HAD NO RIGHT!" he zoomed around the clock tower at lightning pace.

"I didn't tell him about you, I told him you left Tina the quest…"

"YOU SHOULDN'T HAVE!" he said zapping into the bell. *DONG! DONG!*

"STOP!" I said, fearful my secret place would be found out. "He wanted to know why…" I called.

"I know! I heard you!" he stopped zooming around and bobbed up and down in the corner. "I heard, I was there… he's right, there is nothing we can do about the curse. The only person who can remove the curse is Malakai… no one and nothing can remove it. She will be like that for twelve more years!" He zoomed across to the clock face, sobbing.

"What? Why twelve years?" I said, following him.

"He knows what he is doing - nasty, clever man - the Book of Names will vanish at twelve minutes past twelve. If he is near it, he has Magic to know where it goes and can follow it to it's next residence, which could be anywhere! Therefore, he will be virtually unobtainable after this point…"

"I don't get it…" I said truthfully.

Ernie huffed. "Oh LOOK! The Book of Names is in the school *now*! That's one of the *places* it goes. So Malakai, for the last few years, has been forced to come here to do his work with it. You can't move it, or take it somewhere else. The opportunity to end him is here and now while he is in the school! God knows where he will be next! It could be anywhere… No one will be able to find him… and then we can't make him take the curse off Tina! And she will be like that until her death…" he sobbed hard into his fluorescent hands.

I feared that the only reason Ernie was so animated was because he felt guilty. Guilty because he knew that this was all his fault. He shouldn't have sent Tina his papers. I checked the notes on my bed while Ernie sobbed. One page of Ernie's notes detailed twelve possible locations where the Book of Names might go. Hailing Hall was on there along with places it had been previously, along with seven locations with a question mark by them. Before, when I read this, I had no idea what it meant.

My mind flittered about between facts and plans. There was a definite plan in my head, I just couldn't extract all of it. If I could find a way to remove the Jarred Spell and say Malakai's true name, then I would be able to... make him remove the curse and surrender the Book of Names.

"Ernie," I said.

"WHAT?"

"Do the same rules that apply to us, er, living... apply to ghosts?"

"Like what?"

"I don't know... like can you do Spells?"

"No, not really. Most Spells tend to pass straight through me."

"Hmm..." things were kicking off in my mind, so many ideas. "If I want to get hold of you, how can I?"

"I don't know, I don't work in appointments, or summonses."

"But if I really need you?"

He cocked his head and narrowed his eyes at me. "Just do a Summons... *Vocataste*-Ernest," he said bitterly, jumping into a dive.

"One more thing... How did you become a ghost?"

He sniffed. "Because I felt *guilty* for leaving Tina the QUEST OF COURSE!" He dived through the floor and was gone, leaving his voice to echo around the clock tower.

CHAPTER NINE

The Final Plan

Ross was concentrating very hard on his upcoming end of year exams, where he will most likely, qualify as a P.W.W - *Professional Working Wizard*. He was taking them quite seriously, getting himself ready to join Malakai's team, no doubt. I noticed a lot of people around the school concentrating very hard. The last years were doing everything they could to get some peace. Whereas it suddenly became a game for the years below to do everything in their power to make noise and mayhem wherever the seventh years were studying. It got to the point where Magisteers were patrolling the seventh years' dorms to make sure people didn't pass. And they made them these Magical protective spheres wherever they went, so they could work without being disturbed by anything. They looked like big glassy bubbles. Francis Buttery, from two years above, said that it blocked out all noise and people, and played soothing classical music. The P.W.W exam is notoriously hard, and if you don't pass you're buggered.

But all this special treatment just caused more people to do everything they could to penetrate the thin, glassy, protective bubbles. One fourth year boy, Ramid Khan, actually managed to slip inside Evan Roberts glassy sphere, but then started to panic when he couldn't get out! Evan, with three other seventh years in his vicinity, stood together and sent whizzing sparks at his bottom. He wouldn't be that bravado again for a long time and needless to say, sitting down would be a slight problem for a week or two.

I didn't see the Lily out at all any more. Usually, at meal times, he would be at the Magisteers table, talking to anyone who approached, but recently he was keeping to his office. I wondered why. I toyed with the idea that I should tell the Lily everything, perhaps he could help? But then Tina's voice echoed *"No…"* inside my head.

I had seen very little of Robin since he returned. He had been roped into helping Caretaker Ingralo, a big and gruff man who didn't expel much more than grunts and orders. People are chosen randomly to help Caretaker Ingralo, like a kind of jury duty, five people are chosen a week. And this week, of all weeks, Robin pulled the short straw. Obviously, last years are exempt, and everyone moans like hell when it's their turn to help. Apparently, by all accounts, Ingralo is a bit of a slave driver.

Robin came to the Clock tower the second night, after cleaning and mopping the hallways for ten hours straight. Poor guy looked exhausted and was swaying on the spot.

"I got… blisters on me hands, and feet… and he don't let ya' have a break!" he said, clutching onto a wooden beam.

"Sounds awful," I said leafing through notes.

"Listen, I tried to get out of it, best I could, so I could come help you, but there's no way out… not with this guy."

"It's fine…" I said. It was a blow, I needed Robin. "But you'll be finished by the end of the week? I'll need your help then, you might just be crucial to this plan working."

There were so many social occasions popping up that I was struggling for excuses. Hunter was celebrating his Birthday and having a party in the Condor's form room. "It's amazing I made it to thirteen!" he said winking at me.

We also received a Riptide schedule and were expected to go to every game! Unless we had a good reason, like cleaning the school or doing end of year exams - which I didn't. Thankfully there were no games that we had to play in, I speak for all of us when I say there was a collective sigh of relief.

After a whole weekend in the Library, I came across a couple of things that I found immensely intriguing. The first was a simple but quite brilliant Spell. I nearly yelped with surprise when I found it hidden in a book all about water creatures…

"… to approach these creatures who sense humans by their thought frequencies given off by the brain, a Spell is required which hides this: Avertere, forces whatever looks at you to not register your form. But more, it hides your thought frequencies, which the brain rather haphazardly gives off at all times. The Spell is not full proof, one can be spotted out of the creature's peripheral, this may alert them, but when looked at directly you will not be spotted, thus they think they are seeing things. Immensely useful in approaching marine wildlife, some Wizards have experienced it working well on other Wizards…"

This was a revelation. It meant that now I could walk around, especially to the Library, without being disturbed. But also, I had read that Wizards, mostly the highly trained ones, could sense what you were thinking, and your next move, by reading the thought frequencies that your brain leaks out. What I never knew was, thoughts are emitted as vibrational waves, just like a Spell, or a radio wave, which can be interpreted just like a radio antenna interprets a radio wave and turns it into sound! I had no doubt that Malakai could read thoughts, even people like Partington had a good grasp of it, and the Lily was a master, I was sure. This Spell, would be very useful - especially if I combined it with something else.

I found another really interesting book, down one of the darker corners of the Library, about the *'Evolution of the Wizard'* - something I had already learnt at First School, plus a little with Partington, but this went into extra detail, for example I never knew that as a Wizard I was a *"Homo Noeticus"* — not a *"Homo Sapiens"* like most of you. Wizards are the next step in Human evolution! Or so this book reckoned so.

It reminded me of an assembly we had a few weeks ago, led by Magisteer Dodaline talking about Outsiders. She said that more schools like Hailing needed to be built to keep up with the demand of Outsiders waking up as Wizards. She didn't say why though.

Later, I came across a chapter in this book about *True Names*. It must have been a rare book because I'd never seen another book about them. It said how all Outsiders now had to pass through this Veil a few weeks before they started school, which made them and their family and indeed anyone who knows them, forget their old name completely. Also, I thought that if you knew someone's name, you had power over them… but what did that mean? Malakai is all powerful anyway, he could kill anyone he wanted to. Why did he need to know all True Names?

This book had several illuminating passages: *True names, discovered in 1243, are commonly misunderstood today. Initially, it was thought, if one found out the true name of a Wizard then you had an all encompassing power over them. In actual fact, this is largely mythical. Knowing one's true name does not give one infinite power. In fact, if you know and say a true name of an enemy, and they know not yours, then whatever Spell you direct at them will trump theirs. You have a huge level of control over them, some say you take over as the master of their destiny, but this is an exaggeration. Merely, where the power lies, is in the sharing of the true name - for if one shared a Wizards name out, the power of the Wizard will wane both physically and actually - great power had lay in knowing a Wizards true name and threatening to share it, this in itself can guarantee their compliance in all you require.*

The high Wizard Tyreko, who came to high power in 1655 was sent mad by a past misdeed and killed many Witches. Santi Venart, a training Witch who once knew Tyreko seduced him using love Magic and found out his true name. She shared the name "Egbert

Richardsward" far and wide. Overnight, Tyreko reduced in size, shrinking to four feet. He aged fifty years and resembled a swamp creature. He died shortly after, being set upon by roaming vagabonds.

Over the years, many myths and legends have not aided the truth when it comes to true names – some still believe that one who knows ones true name, has the power to send another to a place worse than Hell – a kind of purgatory, or collection centre, that one can store all those whom one knows the true names of. While this might be possible to someone of prestigious talent, it's not likely, or a given whatsoever. True names were brought forth by Magical Nature, to ensure that no one got too powerful… if they did, like Tyreko, there was a means to control them back to safety. This may seem contradictory explanation, True Names are a complicated Magic, and are not to be messed with. Thus the phrase "He needs to be Tyreko-ed" comes.

My head was spinning after reading. I scanned the rest of the book but nothing was as concise as that, but it did go into information about how true names are found…

How Santi Vernart found Tyreko's true name is not known, some say she made him confess to his new love, which would be plausible owing to her extensive practice in love Magic, others think she had help from the infamous Council of Indigo – who have helped end many sent wayward by the effects of black Magic – but some think there is a book, hidden by ancient Magic, that records all true names. It's been referred to under several different names; Gillet's Book of Truth, Hallert and Jivaldo's Newly Born Names, Wizard Namero and simply; The Book of Names, plus many others. Although only myth, many profess that this book is real, many more have seen it – a book by Selibrius Xanderious details that the book travels between twelve unknown locations, every twelve years at the end of a quarter. Many agree with Selibrius, others state that such an item as a Book of True names is dangerous, especially in the wrong hands and should be destroyed.

My eyes were drooping. I had done so much reading, I felt exhausted. It wasn't just the reading but the fact that my brain was working overtime thinking of a plan, or a way to use all this information. On the way back from the Library at some silly time in the morning, I spotted Robin and a few others crawling along the corridor floors with toothbrushes. The large caretaker, with his belly hanging out, was smoking and reading the newspaper and occasionally barking orders. Robin didn't spot me, so I slipped away down an opposite corridor fearing I may be roped into help.

Sunday night I slept like a baby, moonlight streamed in through the clock face. It was getting warmer now that Spring was arriving and I didn't have to sleep with so many blankets. I dreamt long, winding dreams - Tina's mum was in them, facing Malakai, next to Ernie and Tina, Partington watching on as they were all pushed off the tower. Then, the passages of the book began reading back to me... *where the power lies, is in the sharing of the true name... the power of the Wizard will wane... send another to a place worse than Hell - a kind of purgatory...* I saw Tina banging against cage bars, stuck in a tiny prison cell, screaming, but no sound came out. ... *Great power had lay in knowing a Wizard's true name and threatening to share it, this in itself can guarantee their compliance in all you require... whatever Spell you direct at them will trump theirs...*

I woke in a cold sweat, a straight line of sunshine hit my face. I think, finally I knew exactly what I had to do...

In class that morning I sat in silence with a fully formed plan in my head. There was no going back from this one. From dawn, to the start of lessons, I wrote the whole plan down in one go, skipping breakfast and putting the final touches to it as I turned the corner to class. I put one particular page of my notes in a envelope and wrote Robin's name on the front. On another, I addressed it to *Partington* and put in all the remaining notes from Ernie and

Tina.

If I told anyone what my plan was, I knew instantly what they would say. That's why I didn't tell a soul. I remained calm, knowing that, if I did this correctly, I would free Tina from her curse. But I was tired, my head felt heavier than a Hubris's backside and my eyes felt like they were being bathed in stinging nettles. What I wanted most of all was to curl up in my dorm bed - that luxuriously soft, cloud-like mattress. Not the blanketed wooden floor I was currently on, which was about as soft as a brick pillow and comforting as a curse laden teddy bear. Robin also looked tired, he was fast asleep and dribbling on the desk.

Three days remained and I started panicking. I was pacing the clock tower, kicking up dust and pouring over the plan. The more I went over it, the more I saw the gaping holes in it. For instance, the key - I needed to know what door it unlocked. There must be thousands of doors in Hailing Hall and it would take me all year to try it in each lock. I tried to recall what the door looked like in the vision we'd seen of Ernie, but it could have been any number of hundreds. They all looked the same.

I knew who would know where the door was… Ernie of course. I knew this already, but I had been trying to find the right words to make him help me, but they wouldn't come. For some reason, I had a feeling that he would be unwilling, especially after what he said last time.

"*Vocataste*-Ernest!" there was a loud whooshing noise then a small pop as Ernie appeared in front of me in a misty white flash.

"Brrr…" he said, shaking himself. "I still hate that."

"Ernie," I said. "I have three days left to save her, you have to help me."

His watery eyes didn't move. "Depends what you are

planning."

"I need you, on the last day of April at midnight, to deliver these letters to Robin Wilson and… Magisteer Partington."

He looked at me sharply. "Are you joking with me?" he said in a small dangerous voice.

"No, I promise. I need you to swear not to look at them, but deliver them, make sure they get them at that time."

He sniffed. "This Robin I can do, but not my father. He can't *see* me."

"He will…" I said, smiling. "Deliver his second." He nodded stiffly, but he looked mighty suspicious. "Also, I just need to know one thing. I need to know what door it was that this key leads to."

As his eyes dropped to my key, he let out a screeching "*OHHH!*"

"What? *What!?*" I cried.

"I should never! EVER!" he wailed. "Have sent you the key! It was foolish, selfish!" He began wailing and soaring around the clock tower.

"What do you mean? Ernie, all I need to know is what door it leads to. Then I can end all this!"

"No, you can't! You think you can, but you can't! I have got others into much trouble, I cannot do it again. I will not tell you what door that key leads to," he cried. "Never, EVER! I have done enough damage for a lifetime!"

"Wouldn't you like to see your Mother again?" I said. The self loathing wails, suddenly stopped. Head in hands, his face looked up through pale white fingers. I jolt of fear trickled down my spine.

"YOU *DAAARRRREEEEE!*" he flew across the room at me. His face changed. Now a monstrous, demonic version of Ernie's. Eyes bulged, mouth opened black and huge. Terrified, I screamed and jumped to the floor. He flew round and round above my head hitting everything he could as chunks of wood and debris reined down around me.

Until, finally... there was silence.

Dust and wood continued to fall, but Ernie had gone. His screams reverberated around the broken roof rafters, leaving the clock tower, my plan and Tina's freedom, in shatters.

Sleep did not grace me that night, or indeed the next day. I spent all night in the Library looking for a blueprint of the school. In some vein attempt of finding this door. I wondered about summoning Ernie again to see if he had calmed down and would tell me yet. But I was still terrified after the last meeting. I continued to contemplate it as more and more books returned nothing.

I was so tired and so stressed, that when I saw dawn rise through the Library windows I wondered if it was a joke? How did the night disappear so quickly? There simply were not enough hours in the day or night! Why did we need sleep anyway? What was the point of it! I was panicking. I ran back to the clock tower and spoke the summoning Spell again. I would forfeit my safety just to find out where this door was. But as soon as he popped into the room, he vanished instantly. Leaving a trail of white smoke, and a foul smell.

I swallowed and again said the summoning Spell... again, he vanished.

The third time, he appeared, before I felt a cold fist connect with my mouth.

BANG!

I hit the floor hard.

The bang on the head seemed to wake me up, more thoughts entered my throbbing head. What if I could find out where Tina was attacked by Malakai? That would surely be the area of the school where the door was? Who was the Magisteer who found her?

Hmm... I hummed to myself... Tina would know. Tina would *know*? What if, and this was a long shot, what if I could tap into her memories and find out the last place she was? Maybe, and oh this was clever — I could do a revealing Spell on her clothes, or something she had on her at the time?

I set off for the Healer's room. I climbed down from the Clock tower, full of drive, taking the wooden stairs down five at a time. I took the dusty under passages and squeezed through the gap in the wall and back into the main school. A few people were up, coming back from their morning showers and some on their way to breakfast. I think I needed a shower, but I had no time for that. I would just have to put up with being whiffy.

I pushed open the doors of the Healer's room. Thankfully, no one was around. I slipped inside and closed the doors. The Healer looked up with her huge pristine smile. I drifted along to where Tina lay, green light flooding through me. Some of the green strands were latching onto me and I felt the energy tingle my skin.

The Healer saw this and frowned. "Are you looking after yourself?" she said.

"Yes," I said. In truth, I hadn't eaten a proper meal for weeks. I'd had to make another hole in my belt to stop my trousers from falling down and I'd had so little sleep that I mistook my toothbrush for a pencil.

She continued to frown, her eyes watching the green strands. "You have to take care of yourself, to be able to take care of others," she glanced at Tina. "Jade doesn't lie."

"Who?" I said.

"Jade," the Healer flicked her eyes to the pulsing green sun.

I knew what she meant, but how could I just stop and have a lovely sleep and a hot meal, knowing that Tina might never wake up? I stayed for an hour, the Healer sat patting Tina's head for a while and talking in some funny language. Whatever she was doing, it had some effect, as Tina's body seemed to emit this kind of white fuzzy light.

When she left, I looked around Tina's bed for something she might have had with her when she was attacked. All her possessions were not here though. Not even her clothes. Partington must taken them.

But wait… she was wearing a ring, I think it was her channeller. I'd never noticed it much before, but I am sure Partington had one that looked the same. It was silver and slim, with black indentations all the way around. I couldn't make out what but it looked like names.

When the Healer left the room I took Tina's hand. I felt guilty and my heart began racing. I slid the ring off her finger and lay it on the bed next to her. Glancing around, I knew I didn't have long, for the Healer would be back any minute. I raised my shaking hand over the ring and said the Spell.

My head flew back in the chair. But this wasn't right. The vision was surrounded by choking, black smoke. A laughing voice echoed in my head and I saw Tina fall to the floor, Malakai's skeletal frame standing over her. Then his blue glowing eyes looked at me. Awful choking black smoke filled my lungs and I woke. I lifted my head and choked my guts up! Oozing black gunge came out of my mouth and nose. It was like nothing I had ever tasted. I felt sick and ill. Thick green light began to encircle me as I coughed and coughed.

After an hour, I was better. The Healer returned to the commotion and called me an idiot as she put the ring on the side table. She gave me a bowl of stuff to breath in, covering my head with a towel.

"Idiot, idiot..." she kept muttering. "What were you thinking? She's been cursed, all her possessions are cursed. What did you think would happen? Do you think people wiser than you hadn't thought about performing a revealing Spell on her possessions?"

I looked up from under the towel, feeling small... Black goo, not as much as before, was slowly making it's way out of my lungs.

"I'm sorry," I said for the thousandth time.

As I left, the Healer comfortably content with all the curse goo having gone, I pushed open the door to leave. At the same time, Partington was coming in.

"Ahh!" I said, scared.

"Oh Avis," he said smiling. I felt awkward as we stood in the doorway together. "What's that black mark on your face?" he said.

"Oh, just... erm, not sure." I said, rubbing at it as the Healer cleared her throat loudly behind me.

"Well, I thought I'd come here for a while before we meet in class, seems you beat me to it."

I nodded. "Yes, Sir."

"You do know we don't have lessons... it's a Riptide game. We will be making our way down as a form. Now, go and get some breakfast."

"Yes Sir," I said nodding.

The door closed.

No class?

A Riptide game?

I sighed, this was not part of the plan.

Bummer.

I made sure I had some breakfast, even though it felt like the croissant I was eating went down like dry cardboard. I couldn't eat. I was slightly hysterical. In just under seventeen hours it was the end of the sign of Handen and the Book of Names would disappear. My attempts at finding out where the door was had failed and in my desperation I did a revealing Spell on a cursed channeller. That had to be one of the more grim experiences of my time here. Malakai knew what he was doing. If he killed Tina, evidence would remain and talented Magisteers would piece the clues together. Yet, by cursing her, no one could find out anything. I scoffed down some boiled eggs and soldiers as best I could. There wasn't many people in here and those that were, worked away inside their bubble or were asleep on the tables. Poor things. Robin came in just as I was about to leave and stared at me with a glazed look.

"You ok mate?" I said dreamily.

He didn't say anything for a second, but then blinked, shaking what was the best impression I've see of a zombie away. "Yeah," he said. "Er, food… class."

Poor thing looked like baby troll, and I should know, Dad keeps one in the dungeons at home. I helped Robin pick out some breakfast and put it in a napkin for him to take up to class. On the way he nibbled his iced bun with spider legs - he didn't seem to notice and muttered incoherent things about sleep.

"Pick your feet up," I said. He was dragging his feet, which I hate. "I know you're tired but there's no excuse."

The bun seemed to perk him up a little, so too did the hot cup of sugary tea. When we got to class, everyone was sitting there ready with their Condor scarves and Riptide banners and there was a general buzz of excitement about the first Riptide League game of the season. I was jealous of how well slept they looked. My plan was to get this over with as quickly as possible and get back on with my plan.

"Who's gonna win then?" announced Graham. "Let's do a gold bet."

"Yeah I'm in on that," said Simon. "I'll bet ya' fifteen gold pieces that the Centaurs will beat the Manticores."

"You got yourself a deal!" said Graham.

"I hate Riptide," said Ellen. "It's so violent."

"Oh, you're just basing your hatred on what we endured at the start of the year," said Jake, who's English had improved so much it was a shock to hear him speaking. "At least *we* are not playing."

"Not until next year," said Gret smiling viciously.

"Yes well," said Partington, sweeping into the room. "We will get more practice before we play again. I will not have another capitulation like we saw before. Right come on."

We traipsed out of the school and into the grounds with the other forms. I now began recognising faces and people from around the school. At the start of the year they kind of mixed into one unrecognisable mass. But now, I could put a name to the face, like Brian Gullet who was known as the brainiest kid in our year. His tie colour seemed to change every week. I didn't know what level he was, but I didn't see anyone else in our year wearing a pastel purple tie.

Hunter was kind of known as the funny one, along with Jamie Brown and Kenny McCarthy - those three were hilarious together.

There was a bunch of kids who never spoke too, and always looked depressed. I was glad I wasn't their friend. The main one, the miserablest, called himself John-Paul Hampton and he just shrugged at everything.

There was the Riptide lot, including Joanna, Gret and Jake, who along with Hannah Klide, Bernie Boppet and Jack Zapper, had joined in with the upper years and played matches at lunch and free time. To be honest, there were a lot of different Riptide cliques - it was flipping popular, and they were all mega excited about this game. Some of them were wearing horse's hooves and waving a gold Centaur flag for their friends in the Centaur's form. Others were supporting their friends in Manticore, with red flags and this weird looking lion, man, scorpion thing emblazoned on it.

I recognised a lot more Magisteers now as well. Straker had a reputation, some loved him, most hated him. Whereas Partington was known as a bit of a loveable leftie. There was Magisteer Underwood, who arranged all the Riptide games, she was the Magisteer of Magical Creatures. We had her in third year apparently and she looked nice enough, with her long patchwork brown robes and bright blue hair. Magisteer Commonside taught Numerology and Magisteer Yearlove taught Spell-craft, which is the forging of Spells. He was a charismatic man, tall and muscular and very good looking — with dark eyes like a wolf-raptor, black hair and a thick black beard. He always seemed to have a small gaggle of girls following him.

I was so tired I felt like I was in some strange dream. I thought about running back to the castle to save Tina. But, there was simply no way out of this. The Magisteers and sixth years, walked alongside the crowd, down the hill to the stadium. They would spot someone instantly if they tried to bunk off. I couldn't believe I was being dragged off to watch a Riptide game when I could have been searching the school for the door. It was incredibly frustrating.

The stadium was… rickety. I hadn't noticed that before and it made me nervous because we were quite high up. No doubt a lot of Magic had been used to keep it in place. Wizard builders always did a bit of bodge job, just patching anything up with Magic. Never trust one. My parents always get Outsiders, and just wipe their memories afterwards. We stood about ten rows up, coming out of the long wooden stairway and finding a spare row near these moody third years. The Magisteers were all standing together across the stadium from us, on this kind of extended wooden plinth. Simon and Graham were going over stats next to me, Dawn ordered three ice creams from some poor ghost who was dressed up as an ice cream girl and Jake and Gret debated tactics. Now the stadium was full. The atmosphere, noise, and buzz of excitement was exhilarating and soon enough I found myself pulled into the spectacle.

The Manticores came out first as this little leaflet popped up in front of us detailing the team and information. They were in the fifth year, wore red shirts and black robes and were an awkward bunch, some looked mean and up for the fight, whereas a few others looked rather nerdy and scared. They made their way onto the pitch to face Magisteer Underwood.

Then the Centaurs walked out, dressed all in shimmering gold, the crowd roared, as the stadium lit up with golden flags.

"They're the Champions from last year!" called this excited boy behind me. "I want them to win…"

"Pah," said his friend. "You're just a plastic fan. You choose whatever team wins so you can share in the glory."

"Not so, I said a couple of years ago my allegiance was with them."

"What before they won anything? Whatever," said the snooty one.

Straker stood out of his chair as the Centaurs took their place and they all saluted him. What was that about?

"He was their tutor last year," said Robin. "Straker never stops banging on about it."

Underwood suddenly cried aloud. "Take your positions.

As we let the habitat change!" Their was a fizzing sound as the green grass faded away and blinding white light lit up the pitch. Replaced with rising mud mounds, thick green bushes, and a couple of very large oak trees. The crowd *Ooooed*. I felt really nervous for some reason, perhaps I was remembering what I felt when I stood there, awaiting the flounders to be released, not having a clue what I was doing. There was just time while they prepared to look at the leaflet.

The Centaurs are last year's Champions. They won the league by 7 points, and the 'R Cup' comprehensively. Their top scorer was Marshall Compton-Campbell - A graphic of a mean looking boy whom I was sure I'd seen before, swivelled on the page. *Flanked by the leading assist scorers of the season Gemma Icke, and Jenson Zhu.* Another two graphics of a pretty girl, slim and slender, and a small Chinese boy swivelled round. I pointed them out to Robin on the pitch. They were really warming up hard, led by their team captain, this huge girl about five times the size of me and as many wide - who then proceeded to take her place next to the fountain. *The Manticores have never won a league title in the whole history of Hailing Hall, but their form Tutor Magisteer Commonside is confident that this is the year that fortunes can change: "The numbers are in our favour for certain." He said when quizzed. Their top scorer is Hayden Carmichael with four, and in last season's campaign they managed one Libero-Manus...*

"Whats a Libero-Manus?" I said confused.

The boy behind me spluttered. "You don't know what a Libero-Manus is?" He had a cocky look to him and looked to be in the fourth year with his yellow robes. His friend frowned at him, obviously used to his annoying nature.

"It's when one team gets all of the other team in the air," he said as if it was obvious.

"Ah I see," I said curtly. "Thank you."

I read on.

Whereas the Centaurs managed a total of seventeen Libero-Manuses throughout the season. The odds are firmly stacked against the Manticore's in today's game.

Graham looked as sick as a dog after reading the leaflet and Simon was grinning broadly and relaying what he could buy with fifteen gold pieces.

The Centaurs new Magisteer and coach is Oliver Trunwood, Magisteer of Magical Illusion, but a keen coach who has led six forms to glory in his thirty three years at Hailing Hall.

"Your balls will appear in your bold hole in five... four... three..."

The whistle blew and off they went as a great roar erupted from the crowd. Suddenly they were off in a great rush of light and noise. Spells instantly whizzed up all around as three of the Manticores shot up into the air and flew back to their bench. The Centaurs' blue flounder soared across the pitch where a flying Marshall Compton-Campbell caught it and slammed it into an unguarded bolt hole.

"ONE-NIL!" cried Underwood, whose voice was magically increased and carried across the stadium. One Manticore hid behind one of the Oak trees with the red ball, but was immediately surrounded by five gold shirts. He managed to Spell one into the air, but immediately found himself in the same predicament, dropping the red founder, which was now sailing across the pitch to Jenson Zhu, who kicking off a mud hill, Spelled the ball to his teammate Gemma. She caught the ball jumping over two Manticore players, Spelling them in mid air with her left hand while freezing the ground with her right. The oncoming Manticores slipped and sprawled across the ice. Gemma, with incredible agility, chucked the ball through her legs in mid air to Marshall, who Spelled a Manticore into the air and tossed the ball into the bolt hole.

So this was how Riptide was meant to be played!

The Manticores didn't stand a chance. The Centaurs were just too good. Their captain was barking orders continuously and soon enough a loud "LIBERO-MANUS!" rang true across the stadium. The crowd stood and applauded, but the Centaurs didn't hug or smile, they looked resolute and focused, their captain calling out to them, "Four more games!"

The Second match, ten minutes later, was played on this habitat like the Outsider's *City of London*, with all these garages, concrete roads and lampposts. It was very interesting. I'd only ever seen London on TV. Robin said he didn't like London, he'd been there before with his family and managed to get totally lost and no one could find him, so refused to ever go back.

The Centaurs repeated their winning ways, trampling the Manticores 5-1. The epic partnership of Compton-Campbell, Zhu and Icke obliterated any reserves of confidence the Manticores had. They did score however with "Herbert Hanningshire!" being called out to a mute applause as he darted round the back of the large Centaur captain and put the flounder in the bolt hole. She immediately Spelled him, raising a wall of fire all the way around him so he couldn't move for the rest of the game.

The third match and the Manticores put up a much better fight. They became more physical. When Gemma Icke was in mid air, one Manticore turned her boots to lead and she plummeted to the floor, slamming her face into a wooden bridge, and they still lost 3-2. The large Centaur captain was sent off by Underwood for:

"An illegal Spell!" She had set a swarm of Wasperats on three of the Manticore forwards and the game had to be stopped temporally while they were removed.

Half way through the fourth match, me and Robin were sharing a box of *Sweet Newt Eye Popcorn*. I decided I really liked the Centaurs. Some people around the stadium were moving seats, so I didn't take much notice when someone new stood next to me.

When I turned and glanced to see who it was, I nearly dropped the popcorn. David Starlight was looking grim, wrapped in a purple scarf and watching the game. He sidled closer to me.

"Hey Avis," he said. I didn't know what to do, what did he want? Was he going to put a Spell on me and embarrass me in front of the whole school again? "I just need to tell you something."

"Okay," I said, still wary. Robin was too, he kept shifting around and sniffing - he always did that when there was someone around he wasn't keen on.

Robin sniffed. "What do *you* want?"

"I wanted to speak to Avis, and you I suppose. You were there *that* night," he looked grave.

I frowned, curious. "Go on…"

"Well, look, I told Straker that it wasn't you who did that to Hunter… *eventually*. But, it's just."

"Spit it out," said Robin.

"Just wait…" said David whispering and looking around as the crowd roared at another goal. "I saw *him*, that night, *Malakai*," he mouthed. "So I knew it wasn't you. I told Straker it wasn't… anyway… this is about, something I saw the other night," he played with the end of his scarf. "I was coming out of the boys' bathroom on a midnight toilet dash. I had to go to the old ones, because they closed the toilets near us, and as I came out I saw… *him*."

"Who, *Malakai*?" I whispered.

David nodded, his face hangdog and limp. "Yeah."

"Why are you telling us this?" said Robin suspiciously.

"I just thought, well, I think he saw me… and I don't want what happened to Hunter to happen to me. And if we all go to Straker and the Lily, everyone who's seen him can tell them and let them read our memory, they will see we aren't lying! And they can stop him coming here and attacking me! And others of course," he added.

"Pah," said Robin, turning to me. "He's only telling us so he can get his ass off the line."

"What was *he* doing?" I said, inspecting David's patchy face for clues.

He blinked. "Just going through this door, when he turned I think he *saw* me…"

Something dropped in my stomach. "Did you say going through a door?" David nodded. I turned to Robin, the eyebrows on my face must have been raised very high because he blinked rapidly trying to work it out before I told him. I turned back to David, speaking quickly. "What door? Where was it?"

"It's the door near the old bathrooms…" said David in a small voice.

"No, no, more specifically than that!" I said, my voice rising.

"I don't know the exact door!"

"If you don't tell Avis," said Robin. "Then you will be *got* by Malakai, that I can state for certain, but if you do tell him where that door is, I'm pretty sure you'll be *spared*."

David looked from Robin to me before getting some parchment and a pen out of his pocket.

Me and Robin looked at each other with incredulity, we knew what door this was. Neither of us could believe we'd forgotten! It was the door that Tina had first attempted to get through at the start of the year, the one we saw her outside, near the boys bathroom!

"We have to get out of here and get to that door!" I said

to Robin who began to look around for a way out of the stadium. I had already noticed that it was particularly strict. There was a sixth year guarding every entrance and two ghosts! But then, Robin tapped me, his face white as a snow.

"What?" I whispered. His eyes were fixed on a place just over the rim of the stadium, in the distance. "What Robin?"

He pointed. "It's him."

I followed his gaze. My heart beating fast, as chatter and noise around me faded. Adrenaline began pumping through my body. It was Malakai. Gliding along the surface of the grounds, hidden only by a long hedge. He was making his way into the school to stake his claim on the Book of Names. And I was the only one who could stop him.

I jumped across the gang way. "Oi! Watch it!" called a couple of third years.

"Sorry, sorry!" I said, pulling Robin by the sleeve along behind me. We had to get out of here and get to that door. I tried to sneak past the sixth year guarding the stairs down.

"Stop," he said. "Where you going?" He was tall and bullish, with eyebrows that could rival Magisteer Simone.

"Toilet," I said.

"Sorry, don't believe you. Go back to your stand please."

Me and Robin lumped back to the stand. There was a great roar of light and fireworks as the Centaurs gained another Libero-Manus! The sixth year guarding the exit began jumping around.

I began to panic, this churning ball in the pit of my stomach, time was fast vanishing and we had to get out of the stadium. "I didn't realise we would be here all day and night!" I said.

"I know," said Robin. "I expected to at least be able to leave for the toilet!"

I cursed the fact that I had even come to this match, I should have just stayed in the clock tower and fulfilled the plan and saved Tina. The sun was setting and a cold chill moved in. I looked all around for potential exits but all were guarded. I watched as one boy, a first year like us hopping around on the spot pleading with them to let him to go to the toilet.

"Please!"

"No… orders are clear, no one is allowed go to the toilet during matches," said the sixth year. I realised the only way I was going to get away was to create a distraction. The ball of panic in my stomach grew as Robin showed me the time. It was time to act, even though everything in my body was screaming *NO*!

"Robin," I passed him the letter. "This explains everything you need to do. Don't open it yet. And give this one to Partington when you see him. Open it at 11pm…"

He blinked at me as there was another loud roar of applause for the Centaurs. I turned away, and held my hands directly above my head. "*Avertere…*"

I knew it worked because Robin began looking all around, his eyes darting here and there for me, but averting away from where I actually was.

My heart was thumping so loud in my chest I almost thought it might eclipse the noise around the stadium. For a moment, I just stood and watched. Everyone's faces so entranced in the game, even the Magisteers. Flags and scarves waved in the air across the rickety hexagonal stadium. I hoped I would see this again. But, this was it, taking a deep breath I raised my arm high into the air.

"*Beratater-Lut…*" my channeller lit up white hot with the effort of the Spell as directly above the pitch, a bright orange circle appeared. Then, a spectacular thunderstorm erupted above the habitat.

CRASH! BANG!

Long streaks of blue light lit up the sky, scorching across the stadium. There were muffled screams from all around the stadium as people ducked. Magisteers stood as one and raised their arms. The Centaurs and Manticores ran for cover as Magisteer Underwood began scouring the pitch for the culprit - thinking that it must have been one of the players. I took my chance, as the bullish sixth year guarding the nearest exit left his post to help. I jumped up onto the rail and, balancing nimbly, ran all the way along to the stairs. I jumped the rickey stairs three at a time as the crowd in the stadium began to boo whomever had just ruined the game.

It felt incredibly lonely going back to the school. Tiny gas lamps popped on up the hill as darkness set in. Large black clouds overhead thundered once more then stopped. I jumped the last of the steps and climbed the hill back to school. I could hear all the people in the stadium still shouting, annoyed and confused as to what just happened. The large black cloud overhead began to rain. I made it inside the main hall just in time. The school was eerily silent. No noise, no movement, nothing. I had just one pit stop to make…

"Hello again," said the Healer. "Has the curse cleared up?"

"Yes, thank you," I said. "Just came to see her one last… I mean, to see her again."

I took a seat next to Tina's bed. Green light folded around me once more. Tina's wounds had completely healed now, all that remained was tiny, barely noticeable, white scars. She looked so peaceful.

"I know I am a weakling, that it takes you to be cursed for me to be able to tell you how I feel. But, I… really care

189

about you. More than anyone else I've ever met or had the privilege of knowing. I had a dream a few weeks ago, at least I think it was a dream. You and me, we, grew old together. And we, told our Grandchildren all about the time we saved each other, in the first year of school," I sighed. "Please don't wake up and be mad with me. Just know that I had to return the favour. You saved me, so I must save you."

I stopped talking. She lay peaceful and quiet, her chest rising and falling, eyelids fluttering.

A few ghosts gave me confused, apathetic looks as they whizzed past me in the corridors, carrying their dirty laundry and huge boxes of dirty dinner plates. My heart was hammering. Something in the back of my mind was telling me that there were holes in my plan, there had to be, there had to be Magic that he knew that could counteract mine. Perhaps he would just laugh in my face. But, I had to take this chance, there would never be another opportunity like this one again. The clock in the bell tower began to chime, calling ten o'clock.

CHAPTER TEN

The Golden Escalator

This was the door I had been searching for. I just knew it. The one I had forgotten about the first time me and Robin caught Tina behind that suit of armour. I wondered what would have happened if I hadn't have spotted her there. How would things have turned out?

How could something so wooden and plain lead to something so unknown and mysterious. Yellow light flickered from gas lamps on the wall behind me. The key felt cold and dead in my hand. I pulled the string off round my neck and checking the corridor one last time, put it in the lock. A loud clunk echoed along the corridor. I twisted the golden handle slowly, readying myself for him. Inside was darkness, it was impenetrable. All I could hear as the door shut behind me was the beating of my own heart. The stairs leading down were uneven and I had to hold onto the wall to remain steady. I was going down to the same place as Ernie had in the vision, I just knew it. After a long way down I finally saw light. Flickering yellow firelight, just a dot at first but growing. At last, they stopped. I tip toed along a long dark passage towards the light. Then, I faced three entrances. The light was coming from straight ahead. But in the alcoves to the left and right were small rooms filled with stuff, hidden by greying cloths. Up ahead, the passage got tighter, the walls closing in, the ceiling just an inch from the top of my head.

And then I saw him... The huge, hunched figure of Malakai.

I put my hand over my mouth. Gas lamps around the side of the room hung wonky, casting a dim light over the man who stood seven feet tall. He was stood bent over a tall lectern, on it I could see the edges of a humungous old book. Silver instruments lay half covered in dirty cloths around the filthy, cobwebbed room.

He hadn't spotted me - I could Spell him now, the one I'd agonised for months over. I raised my hand.

"Don't even think about it…" his voice rumbled.

My heart jolted as his long white face turned slowly, independent of his body. "Avis Blackthorn…" I was paralysed by fear, frozen to the spot as if a shard of ice had run down my spine and freezing me to the floor. His glowing blue eyes bored into me. "And how did *you* get in here?"

"I… I… a key…" I managed. The Book Of Names behind him was shimmering with golden light.

"So it's the runt of the Blackthorn family!" he said. "Come to get revenge for his poor, little, meddling girlfriend."

The blood began boiling in my veins as he mentioned her. "How dare you talk about her," I said, my voice rising high.

He didn't move. "Is that why you're here? To *stop* me?" he mocked.

"Yes!" I called.

He let out a raucous laugh. "You?" he continued laughing, his skulled face rocking. "All I needed was you to do something like this and it would give me the perfect excuse. I promised your parents that I wouldn't harm you, even though you're a *seventh son*. They are very *useful* to me." His words whirled through my head. "Yes, your brilliant parents do have one weakness. Their remaining ounce of compassion. But *now*…" he said, chucking his huge skeletal arms in the air. "Now you have forfeited that promise. Under my terms and conditions your are now *in my way!*"

I had to act. "Go ahead, do it! See if I care!"

"You were already this close after that stunt - pretending to be *me*. I could have set that demon on you…"

My legs shook and I did everything in my power to try and steady them. "Instead, I realised how much more fun it would be for everyone to think it was *you*. I mean, who on earth is going to think it was *Malakai*?" he laughed to himself.

"*Flutteryout!*" I cried. A white light burst from the amulet as Malakai toppled. I lunged forwards as quickly as possible, hands outstretched for the Book of Names. A single sharp swipe sent me sprawling backwards against the wall. "DON'T!" I called as Malakai who rose instantaneously, raise his arms. "I know your TRUE NAME!"

Malakai stopped dead. A long hand an inch from my throat.

"What?!" he said deathly slow. His boiling hot breath scorching my face.

"Yes," I said panting. "I know your true name. St-Steeeee… *Owww!*" My tongue cut again. But Malakai stepped back, dropping his hand. For the first time I saw fear in his eyes. "I will stop you from getting the Book of Names!" I said as blood dribbled down my chin.

His blue eyes dimmed. "*How?*"

"By telling everyone your true name."

"You can't even say it!"

"Curse me the same as Tina, go on, then we'll see who can say it!"

"Curse you, pah… No, no, no, I am not that stupid. I'll kill *you instead*…"

I felt a horrible sinking feeling. "You can't. I'm a *Blackthorn!*"

"You've forfeited your name by attempting, pathetically, to thwart ME!… Goodbye Avis Blackthorn."

Then, it happened. His hands shot into the air. I saw as

if it was all slow motion, happening to someone else. Crackles of blue light, like tiny stars, danced in his hands as a high pitched whistle filled the air.

"No! Please!" I cried. In an explosive burst of twinkling light the stars shot towards me. I screamed as light erupted through the room. The pain was unbearable. Every pore in my body on fire. I felt myself writhing on the ground, the room spinning violently, all I could think of was the pain!

And then quiet.

Deadly, heavenly quiet.

I felt my last breath leave me.

***

I sat up.

Malakai was looking over the book, hunched back rising up and down.

A crack split the wall to the right. White fluorescent light, smattered with transparent mini rainbows, began to fill the room. Malakai hadn't noticed and now I knew why. I was *dead*.

I looked around. I was hovering just above the floor. Below me was my body, lying in a sorry sprawling heap in the dirt. The strange thing was, I wasn't shocked. All my pain was gone, in fact every pain I had ever had was gone. It was as if I didn't even realise some of the aches and pains I was carrying around with me. All I felt now was a gentle, relaxed, peaceful bliss. My thoughts felt the same.

The crack in the wall widened with a splitting sound, spilling more starry light into the room. A strange noise suddenly came across me as this time, golden light reflected off the walls. A huge golden escalator appeared through the crack. Without thinking I drifted towards it and stepped on. It moved upwards slowly, through the crack and up into the clouds. The hole in the wall sealed and that sorry room disappeared. All around me was the most wonderful, lustrous twilight with a humungous starry sky with soft clouds moving daintily. The midnight blue spread into violet and indigo the higher we climbed, the texture like that of running paint on parchment.

I turned to look back but the crack in the wall was but a dot. In the clouds above, a girls sleeping face suddenly appeared. It was Tina. Then I remembered... I was meant to save her... the thought felt foreign. Attached to human emotions I no longer had. Overriding guilt started somewhere where my stomach had been, then spread to my heart area. I felt guilty for leaving her, for she would never know the beauty of death.

The escalator began to jolt and stutter then slow. My thoughts began returning, my form changing. The silky translucent entity I currently was, began curdling. Turning gloopy and wet... I was becoming a ghost! Now I remembered why. The closer the escalator moved back to earth, the quicker my old thoughts returned, hardening in my mind in the same speed that my form took to turn into a ghost.

The book I had read about ghosts said that you become a ghost if you have a strong emotional anchor on Earth. Tina was my emotional anchor and... I had planned that, yes I did, I remembered now. The plan returned in full form into my ghostly mind. I felt kind of flimsy, half in this world, half in another.

The crack in the wall reopened wide beneath me. I stepped off and back into that room as the crack sealed with a snap. Malakai, who was pouring salt in a circle around the Book of Names, now looked round. My ghostly form emitted a blue glow in this dim cave. Then, he laughed a loud piercing cackle. It struck something inside me, hurting me as the blue glow dimmed a little. I concentrated, fighting the urge to float away though the walls and hide.

"You should have *cursed* me," I said and Malakai stopped laughing. "I don't know if it struck you but I *wanted* you to kill me."

"And why would that be?" he put the salt down and faced me.

"Because, you forgot one thing. You put a Jarring Spell on your true name, but that doesn't apply to... *ghosts*." I smiled watching his face drop, then I pulled the channeller from my bodies' limp wrist.

"NO! *NO!*" he cried. "How? *WHERE DID YOU GET THAT!?*" I just smiled. "No impossible, impossible..." he repeated.

"See for yourself," I said, chucking it to him. He caught it and began waving his hands over it. The soft glow of his true name glowed on the surface of the metal and he gasped a long, rattling breath. "Now..." I said, floating forwards. "If you dare do anything other than what *I* say, I will use your *true name*." I said gravely. "More so, I will broadcast it to all other ghosts."

I remembered what I had read in one of the books: ghosts have a telepathic link to each other and somehow, I could tell all the other ghosts in the school Malakai's true name. They would share it with the living and Malakai would be reduced to nothing. Suddenly, a bell rang high and true around the school.

Bong, bong, bong, bong, bong, bong, bong, bong, bong, bong, bong, bong... Twelve bongs. It was midnight! The Book of Names would be disappearing in twelve minutes! Golden light began accelerating around it.

"I want you to remove the curse from Tina!" I said urgently.

Malakai chuckled. "I *see*, valiant and loyal to the very, very end," he said. "Well tough. I could kill her in a second."

"Kill her and I will end you," my voice rose. "Remove the curse you set on her and I won't use your true name." I bobbed up and down slowly, sensing his scrambled thoughts. I began to speak softly. "Believe me Malakai, I've seen what happens to a Wizard when their true name is used against them. I doubt you haven't seen the same?" I nodded towards the Book of Names. "Not very nice is it? I could sacrifice a girl, if it meant saving the Seven Kingdom's. I wonder what would happen to all those that despise you when they realise you were defeated by a *boy*?" His glowing blue eyes never strayed from me. "I would love to watch you shrivel up, leave you to wander the Magical Kingdoms, a small shadow of a man you used to be. Wouldn't last very long, would you? This way you at least have the choice to do the right thing."

"So many chances to kill you," he muttered. "And against my better judgement. I knew you were different from them. Dangerous to me, you think differently. You cannot be controlled like them. I failed myself. I should have killed you."

"You did," I smirked.

"Your parents convinced me to leave you be," he sighed deeply and carried on. "Perhaps they are traitors, very clever traitors..." He kept talking slowly, breathlessly. "Seventh sons are rare, very rare. I can control everyone, using this book, except seventh sons. Your *true names* are unknown..." Then his whole tone changed, suddenly he let out a cry: "*PERCEIVUS!*" He cried. Streaks of red and black smoke shot across the room at me.

"STEVE MALCOLM!" I called. The red and black smoke Spell squirmed to the floor like a writhing snake.

Malakai stood arms aloft, frozen to the spot.

"I warned you," I said as he backed away against the wall.

"I'LL KILL Tina. And your parents! Your entire family!"

"Go ahead, like I care… Death is not to be feared."

He was panicking as the book began shining brighter and brighter. Golden strands leaping into the air. There was so little time left. I had to act fast.

"*Steve Malcolm*," I said again and Malakai screamed. Out of nowhere invisible fists began barraging every square inch of him. His tall form bent double with the shock. "Steve Malcolm… *Steve Malcolm!*" I repeated over and over, burning fury exploding out of me. All the injustice, all the loneliness, all the unhappiness… all because of this man.

"STOP! NO! *AHHHHHHHHHHH!*" his cries echoed monstrously. Malakai's tall black form began to shrink. His skull mask fading translucent. His black robes ripping and falling away as the invisible hands stopped. He was bent forwards, breathing heavily.

"Had enough? Have I… *convinced* you yet? Or do you want *MORE*?!"

"Please…" he managed. "Fine… you win… please… I will remove… the curse, if you let me… go…"

I folded my arms and smiled as his glowing blue eyes looked up. "I think you are mistaken," I said. "I hold the power here."

His head dropped deeper as he sobbed. His Magic and disguise that he used to cloak himself as '*Malakai*' were fading. I could see a partly-bald head and a mousy, frightened face. He was just a man, his eyes small and black, blinking tears. His skeletal hands reverting to small, chubby, flesh ones. His tall torso shrinking to that almost less than mine. The golden strands from the book started leaping into the air. "Remove the curse NOW!" I called.

Malakai raised his hands into the air and recited something breathlessly. Gloopy black stuff began shooting into the room through the walls and into his outstretched hands. Malakai swayed on the spot as the curse left Tina completely. I knew because, well, I saw her. Through the walls of the school, which turned as see through and ghostly as me, my vision zoomed in on her in the Healer's room, waking with a cough and splutter.

Malakai looked up at my smiling face and coughed up a lump of black mucus. "Who is the real winner?" he said. "You will still be dead and I will remain."

Then... voices.

"Avis!? AVIS!? WHERE ARE YOU!?" Running footsteps echoed up the passage way. Malakai whimpered, looked back at the Book of Names, and prepared himself to flee.

"Goodbye *Steve Malcolm*..." I said.

Malakai began swirling. But not before invisible fists started battered him through the black column of smoke before, with a *whoosh*, he disappeared. The last thing I saw was a small, bald, crying face realising he'd lost.

My job was done. All of a sudden, my ghostly form began shedding it's gloopy, ghostly wetness. I had done what I had come to do - Tina was ok.

The crack in the wall opened large and wide flooding in glorious white light. I moved weightlessly towards the golden escalator which welcomed me back like an old friend.

"AVIS! There you are!" cried Robin, who came skidding into the room followed by Partington and Ernie. Their eyes darting from me, to my body on the floor.

"Quickly Robin!" cried Partington. Robin checked his watch, yelped, then ran over to the Book of Names pulling out my letter containing the instructions.

Ernie darted across to me. "Avis wait! Resist the lull of death... please!" But then Ernie gasped. His form began changing too.

"She's alright now," I said. "She was our emotional anchor. And now she's better."

Ernie was panicking. "She might not be, we don't know... I haven't seen her," he lied.

Partington ran across to help Robin. The letters I had left them gave precise instructions on how to use the Book of Names to bring back the dead. I felt myself going weaker and weaker as my ghostly form shed, yet the golden escalator shined bright golden and inviting.

"AVIS! WAIT! YOU MUST!" called Ernie, but his voice sounded far away.

Robin began saying Spell after Spell, throwing this arms around. Partington lit candles and poured salt and drew chalk symbols on the floor, all at the same time. "Thirty seconds!" called Robin, who began to read furiously.

I hoped they failed. I wanted to go. I put one foot on the escalator.

"TEN SECONDS!" The Book of Names began to float in mid air. Robin and Partington stepping back as the pages began flapping violently.

"Avis..." said a new voice, one I hadn't heard in a long time. I turned and saw...

"Tina?" She was looking at me, eyes swimming with tears. "Stay..."

It was too late.

Golden fire erupted across the room as wind and light blew my head back. Then, everything went dark.

***

I woke with a face full of dirt, coughing and spluttering. I didn't move for ages. Slowly, I felt all the aches and pains return like annoying old friends. I sat up really slowly and looked around. For a minute my vision was foggy. The lectern was rocking, the Book of Names gone. Plumes of dust was falling slowly back to ground.

I didn't understand… I was supposed to be dead. It should have been impossible for Robin to bring me back, because my name isn't in the Book of Names. That Spell to bring back the dead using the Book was meant for someone else. So how was I sitting here, back in my body?

Partington was slumped against the wall watching me. "There's cutting it fine, and then there's that…" then he stopped. He saw something else out of the corner of his eyes, his head turned slowly and looked at something, or *someone*, in the passageway entrance.

If I hadn't seen him with my own two eyes, I wouldn't have believed it. Ernie was sat blinking and inspecting his hands. His own flesh hands.

Partington looked like he was going to have a panic attack. Tina looked from Ernie to me, unsure of what she was seeing as Robin sat rubbing the dirt out of his eyes. The crack in the wall was gone and a huge part of me wished I'd stepped onto that escalator earlier.

Ernie looked up. "Avis," he said. "You did it! I can't believe you did it!"

Partington's eyes were huge, trying to take in every morsel of Ernie's body. "Ernest?" he said. "You're… here… *alive*?"

They both stood gingerly and for a long moment Partington just stared at his son. Maybe trying to work out of Ernie was real, or part of some dream caused by a bump to the head. Eventually he decided on the former and pulled him into a rib cracking hug.

"I can't believe it," Partington cried as Tina joined them. I wasn't sure if they were laughing or crying - both, I think. Robin caught my eye and grinned.

"But how? Why? Who?" said Partington. "Thought we'd... lost you *forever*..."

Ernie looked over Partington's shoulder at me and Robin. "It was Avis," he said. "Avis could see me, while you two couldn't. They both worked it all out."

Partington and Tina turned to face me and Robin, their eyes swimming with tears. "Oh boys, you clever, clever, brave boys!" cried Partington hysterically, coming to hug us both, long tears forming streaks in the dirt on his face. "How did you *ever*?! *Malakai*? And Ernie... the Book of Names!" he didn't know what to say first.

"Avis?" said Tina looking confused. "But... your a seventh son? How did you... get back?" she looked at Robin.

"Well actually," said Robin. "He *is* in the Book of Names."

"What?" I said. "But, I can't be... I'm the *seventh son* in my family. Even Malakai said so."

Robin rubbed his glasses. "If that's true, how do you think I brought you back to life? I saw it... it appeared just as the book was disappearing. But I've forgotten it now." Robin blinked looking around, as if the answer may be on the walls. "How strange..."

"Well you will forget it," said Tina matter of factly. "The Book of Names won't let you remember them! And this is interesting, the Book wanted you to bring Avis back." Her eyes were swimming with adoration.

"Perhaps..." said Ernie. "Or, it could have something to do with Avis knowing and saying Malakai's true name?"

Partington cleared his throat. "Could be. Let's keep this conversation for a later time. Let's get out of here."

As I stood, I heard my joints and bones click. My body felt a hundred years old. "Take it slow Avis..." said Tina. "Your going to ache for a while, that body has died, it needs time to recuperate."

"Whereas mine," said Ernie. "Is brand new. I feel great!" he gave a twirl.

Tina hugged Robin, then me. "I can't believe you did it," she mouthed as we began moving slowly back through the passageway.

I felt strange. I was so glad Tina was ok, Ernie too, and well, my genius plan had worked. But my heart yearned to be on that escalator. As we left the room I saw Ernie look longingly over his shoulder at the place where the crack in the wall was. He felt it too, I just knew it.

"Where do you think the Book went next?" I said stumbling behind, my voice croaky.

"Wherever it's gone," said Robin. "Let us hope it won't be found for a long time, not by Malakai, not by anyone."

"You have freed countless Wizards from curses and spells, you do realise that."

"You're gonna be famous," said Tina.

"Hmm..." I said. "I'm not sure about that." I felt awful, don't get me wrong, my chest ached, my legs hurt, my head thumped, but, I was so glad it was finished. Malakai, the man who had been a shadow over my family since I could always remember, had been reduced to nothing more than a mere mortal. He'd got away, but I'd completed what I set out to do - and now, she was walking right beside me, a little weak, but we were all fine, just fine.

You see, I knew that I could not challenge Malakai in Magical skill, but I did know his true name, largely by accident. Yet I couldn't say it. After reading about ghosts, I learnt something that most Wizards don't pay attention to — spells don't apply to ghosts in the same way. The only way I could say his true name and weaken him, was if I was a ghost. I didn't want to completely end him, because then Tina would remain cursed. I gave Robin the instructions, telling him to open them just before midnight so he wouldn't tell everyone and spoil my plan. I'd found a book that gave direct instructions on how to bring back the dead using a true name. What I wasn't expecting was to be brought back myself.

CHAPTER ELEVEN

Ernie's Story

I kept waking up in a sweat but seeing Tina's green lit face staring at me in the bed opposite. "Shhh…" she'd say, soothingly. "It's ok."

When dawn stretched in through the tall windows, the Healer came around the beds with hot drinks and food on a floating sheet of green light. I sat up slowly and ate, under stern orders from the Healer, a bowl of gloopy green stuff. As I swallowed, I felt it going all the way down, pulsing pure energy to the ends of my fingers and toes. The Healer smiled. I felt much better already.

Partington, sat opposite, propped himself up in bed then said he wanted to know everything. Ernie in the bed next to his dad, was inspecting his legs and prodding his knee caps. I sighed, not sure where to start. Robin, in the bed to my left, finished the green stuff, handing the Healer his bowl and then put his glasses on smiling round cheerily.

So I told them everything. With the green light pulsing through me it felt cathartic to relive recent events and telling my captive audience all that I had done. After I finished, and after much gasps and intake of breaths we all sat back for a brief moment of silence. Partington, the oldest out of us all, was simply bursting with questions.

"Well…" I said, answering his third in a row. "People only come back as ghosts if they have an emotional anchor to earth."

"I *see*…" said Partington enthralled, sitting before me like some disciple in prayer before his master.

"But, I couldn't have done any of what I did without Tina, or Ernie, or Robin, or you Partington. Don't you see, I just *finished* the job. It was Ernie's quest first, then Tina's, then mine… I basically followed their notes."

"And the key?" said Partington. "To the door, was from Ernest?"

"Yes, from the past," I said.

Ernie cleared his throat. "Just before I went, I made a copy, in case I failed. I put a *Destiny Charm* on it."

"My god," said Partington clapping a hand to his mouth.

"What's a *Destiny Charm*?" said Tina.

"It's errr…" said Robin, cleaning his glasses with his shirt again. "Well, a flipping hard charm that leaves Magic the guardian of an item. Then, it follows the *Seven Flows of Magical Destiny*, through coincidence and serendipity, and then it appears to the right person in the right place at the right time."

I blinked impressed, how did Robin know that?

Partington turned to Ernie with a pained expression. "Oh Ernie… you went after Malakai because of… *Mother*?" Ernie nodded, looking down at his feet.

I admitted my concerns that Malakai was still at large, mostly to fill the uncomfortable silence that had befallen. His threat of coming back to finish the job now preying on my mind.

"Pah! He won't be coming back anytime soon. Anyway, if he does, we'll be ready for him," said Partington raising a fist in the air.

"And he'll be scared of you Avis," said Robin.

Yes, I thought, *but, I can't say his true name anymore.* I kicked myself, I should have telepathically sent his name to all the ghosts. Not that I knew how to.

"You know, when this gets out, and it will…" said Tina grinning at me. "You'll be famous Avis. What are your family going to think?"

I grimaced. "I dare to think."

"But Avis you will be the face of the uprising against Malakai! We can begin to dismantle his empire. Once this gets out it will be just what people need, they will have the confidence to confront him. His main power is gone! He doesn't have the Book of Names anymore, he's weak."

"He'll be looking for it though, I bet ya," said Robin.

"He will," said Partington. "Ernest is right though, Avis. If you become the face of the uprising, having already conquered him, you will give so many Wizards the hope to stand up to injustice again. And that's very important."

"I am not the right person to be the face of any uprising, believe me! As I said, I just followed on from your quests. I'd prefer anonymity."

Ernie looked fit to burst. "But!"

"He said he wants anonymity," said Tina defiantly. Her stare enough to make Ernie and Partington back down. "But, there might be an alternative..." she said. "I mean, we'd have to figure out the right story, but, I don't see why it wouldn't work..."

It was agreed and a Magical pact had been formed. If anyone even so much as breathed what we'd agreed to anyone but each other, then something very nasty would happen.

"And you are sure that is ok with you Avis?" said Ernie.

"I am one hundred percent sure." It was a great plan, I had to agree.

"Right," said Partington as the Healer nodded that we could all leave. "Time to tell the world..."

***

A special assembly had been called in the Chamber. I was sitting next to Tina and Robin, sipping kiwi juice, my heart thumping. The Chamber was packed to the brim and buzzing with excitement that an impromptu assembly had been called. They were all whispering, trying to guess what it could be about.

The Lily prowled the front of the Chamber and once silence fell and addressed the packed room, beaming wide.

"It has long been known…" he called. "That the man known as *Malakai* held a deep Magical power over a vast portion of our Society. He was schooled here, at Hailing Hall and all of you have heard of him, his evil ways and mysterious plans that we would all be entering into, with little choice," he paused. "I am pleased to say then, that after an altercation in the school last night, Malakai's powers have been *severely weakened*…" talking broke out. I saw Ross's livid, confused face as he looked round at his friends. But then cheering. The whole school began cheering and screaming with joy.

"*NO WAY!*"

"*HOW?!*"

"*Impossible*!" People cried, hugging each other.

"Hush… hush!" cried the Lily over the impenetrable noise and excitement. "Let me introduce then… our hero. The person who did it, the one who has saved countless lives, not just from death, but from a life of martyrdom. Now, let us listen to his fascinating story… Ernest Partington!"

The crowd roared and screamed as Ernie stood from the Magisteers table and walked confidently to the front. The whole school stood and cheered for ages. I smiled as he looked over at me. Tina was clapping and screaming all at the same time, she glanced at me once or twice to see if I was jealous. I wasn't… not much, this was for the best. Huge drapes and posters fells from the rafters with Ernie's face emblazoned across them. Ernie was a crowd pleaser.

His good looks endeared him instantly to the girls and his confidence and bravado gave the boys a new hero.

"So that's what happened…" finished Ernie. "And now, I can finally retake my last year of school." The crowd stood again and applauded. Some were crying, astounded at the brilliant story. And it was a brilliant story, mostly made up by me.

Ernie had recounted to an enthralled audience how as a ghost he couldn't be seen, how he lived in the clock tower and one day stumbled upon an old amulet with a name written inside. It was the true name of Malakai, the one who had killed him.

"And I soon worked out, with some help, that I was the only one who could stop him… Ghosts are the only one's who can say a Jarred Name."

We left the Chamber. Everyone in the school so excited that they began running around the castle sending firework Spells whizzing into the ceilings and off into the grounds. I realised that there were more people who's lives had been touched by Malakai than I'd realised. Even the Magisteers joined in the celebrations, until the castle was a mass of colour, noise and excitement. The Lily was standing on the staircase above the hall, he caught my eye and winked.

***

The last three months at Hailing Hall were what I thought coming to this school was supposed to be like. In other words, it was bliss.

Ernie had managed to get himself on the front page of the Herrald for a whole week. We hardly saw him, as he was continually in meetings with journalists who wanted their five minutes with the now infamous Ernie Partington. Suddenly any doubt I had about not revealing it was actually me dissipated. The newspaper was very flattering about such a young, clever, handsome boy, yet still ran with the headline *Ghost-Boy defeats Malakai!*

Of course, Ernie wasn't impressed with it, the papers referring to him as *Ghost-boy* hit a nerve I think. Still, the school was walking on air, housing an A list celebrity. Someone who had won back the liberty of thousands of Wizards across all the Seven Magical Kingdoms. You know, I almost kept forgetting that it was me that did those things. He was the man of the moment and Partington was so proud. He knew it was a sham, but I think he was just pleased to have his only son back.

I was glad now that I didn't die. Just for those last few months at school. It took me a week or so to fully recover from dying, but after, I felt normal again. I slept in the Healer's room a few more nights, under her orders, I didn't complain. The sleep you could get in that room was unbelievable. When me and Tina left the Healers room after a week, Tina now fully recovered and back to her normal self, we danced and skipped along to the Chamber where we indulged ourself in a huge meal with three puddings! It felt so good to eat!

"I want to get Robin something special," I told her. "You know, for his heroics…"

"Aw, your such a cutie…" she said pulling closer a copy of the Herald. We flicked through the paper and she showed me lots of stuff at the back with tiny order forms. "These catalogues are my favourite, I was obsessed as a kid!"

I had to admit, my attention was caught by the many Magical things that the back of the newspaper housed. A few things that caught my attention like:

Tait's Walking Bookcase, have your books nearest you at all times! This Bookcase folds up into a piece of wood big enough to fit in a breast pocket. When tapped will open out into full-size, thus allowing all your books to follow you wherever you go.

"I'd like that!" said Tina, her eyes wide.

I couldn't help a smile. "I was just about to say that…"

"Or what about this…" she said pointing.

We sat and had a think. I couldn't order anything from the Herrald as I had lost all my gold on the train here. But then I kept getting this thought, tickling my brain - when I walked through the passage way towards the Book of Names, there were rooms to the left and right stacked with goodies and treasures, Tina didn't need convincing.

"Got the key still?" she said.

"Of course," I said. "But what if Mal… what if *he's* down there?"

"Pfft… do really think he will be?" she said laughing.

As we left the Chamber, I saw David Starlight, sitting quietly on his form table doing homework, he caught my eye and grimaced, looking away quickly.

Tina unlocked the door and slipped inside as the cold, damp draft hit us. She held tightly to me as we went down through the blackness. Soon enough, we stood in the small, cramped room to the left. It took Tina over five minutes to find a Spell that would illuminate the room. Finally, one worked. Small clear stones dotted in the walls all the way around lit with dim, pulsing white light. "Hmm interesting…" she said.

"Why?" I couldn't see what was so interesting, the light wasn't even very bright.

"Well, Wizards stopped using Quartz to light a room about two hundred years ago… this room must be blooming old!"

Tina began pulling the dusty rags off with gusto. This caused plumes of century-old dust to erupt everywhere.

"Ahh!" I cried coughing.

"Oh give over, you baby!" she laughed.

But once we had a look, we realised this really was a treasure trove of stuff that Malakai, or whoever else, had collected.

"Don't touch anything," said Tina. "On pain of death."

"Ok... what the heck's that?" I said, looking at a tall thing that looked a food blender.

"That looks like a *Dehouser*," said Tina with awe. "It makes a house collapse in on itself and collects it into a tiny ball. Look! There's some inside." There sure was, it looked like some sort of gum ball machine.

"Oh wow!" I said picking up what looked like a pair of dirty old shoes.

"What?" said Tina.

"These..." I said, unable to believe what I was seeing. "These are a pair of Seven League Shoes!"

"No way!" she said, grabbing them to take a look.

She turned them over, the soles were covered in the number seven, and inside had a label: *Seven League Shoes, use me carefully.*

"They don't make these anymore! There's only seven made, in the whole world! My Dad's always wanted a pair..."

"Avis..." said Tina looking at something. "I think I've found the perfect present for Robin."

Soon enough, all our lessons had resumed. Things had got back to as normal as normal could be.

I was back in my dorm room with the other Condor boys. Back in that comfy bed, homework by the fireside, communal trips to dinner and ridiculous chats about boy things.

"You and this Tina are a item yes?" said Jake, smiling at me across the fireside. All the boys looked up over their parchment, smirking.

"Pfft," I said. "Naa, we're just friends." But my face burned red.

"Well, if you are just friends you won't mind if I ask her out then?" he said.

I hope he was joking because I felt a jealous monster rise in my stomach at the thought. All the boys were silent for a moment. Then, the git laughed. "Your face!"

"You sod…" was all I could manage in a small voice, but relief flooded back through me.

"Well, Hunter's doing pretty well for himself," said Graham. "In fact, it's caused a bit of tension in classes. He's been seeing Jess and Florence at the same time."

I gasped. "No way! Where is he now?"

"Probably trying to apologise to them both!" said Graham as the boys laughed.

There was a moment of pens scratching across parchment, before Jake looked up at me again. "So… if your friends with Tina Partington, you must have some *insider knowledge* about Ernest Partington?" All eyes looked up, except Robin who smiled wryly over his homework.

Dennis crooned. "Ah, I wish I was Ernie's friend… do you think you can introduce me Avis?"

I laughed. "I'll see what I can do Dennis." Simon didn't look up, he was jealous, I just knew it.

"How well do you know him?" Graham placed his parchment down and was leaning forwards. I pretended to scratch away at my homework, being all mysterious, but the truth was I hadn't thought up what to say. How much did I tell them?

"Bah…" I said eventually. "Not that well, just, you know,

when he was a ghost… and er that's it really."

Jake placed his homework down now. "So, you knew him when he defeated Malakai?"

"Erm… sort of…" I muttered, looking at Robin for help.

"Because," Graham said. "I remember when you said you could see Malakai out the window that time."

Jake narrowed his big eyes at me. "Yeah, and we was all talking and wondering about you when you disappeared after that *accident* with Hunter."

Graham nodded fervently. "And Hunter said himself, in so many words, that it wasn't you that attacked him, but someone else… someone he wasn't allowed to say?"

"What are you suggesting?" Simon said, turning on Graham. "That Avis was framed by Malakai, so teamed up with a ghost to defeat the most evil Wizard of all kind?" he scoffed.

"All I'm saying is, if it was Malakai who attacked Hunter, that means Avis was blamed for attacking Hunter, even though it was easy for the Magisteers to work out that he didn't do it! And we were all led to believe it was him… I mean it made sense at the time, he was talking about all these evil plans."

"And, he vanished somewhere during the Riptide match, even though the exits was sealed off… the night that Ernest came back to life…" said Jake.

"I am here you know…"

Jake turned back to me. "I know you are. I am just saying that we are not stupid, we have all spotted these… what you call them?" he clicked his fingers trying to find the word.

"Anomalies?" Simon offered.

"Yes, these anomalies… we've all noticed. We just want to know the truth."

"Come on guys," said Robin. "Let's just chill, I'm sure

Avis will tell you what happened in time…"

"Yeah I know," said Graham, sitting back. "Sorry mate didn't mean to get carried away like that. It's just, you know, you can tell us - we are your form. We're not gonna say nothing…"

I nodded and soon enough the scratching of homework restarted, a little tenser than before. My mind was working overtime not to compromise the story. I'd worked so hard making up Ernie's story, that I had had completely forgotten about my own.

Partington was in an immensely good mood and taught us lots of brilliant stuff, preparing us for our second year at Hailing Hall. Over the remaining weeks our lessons began winding down with more free time. Which was nice, because me, Robin, Tina and Ernie would meet up out of our respective classes and go for walks round the grounds, have dinner together and go to the weekly Riptide match. I liked the routine.

Partington told us that, in our second year, he would only be our form tutor. We would be going off to have lessons with lots of new Magisteers and learn loads of new, exciting things. Everyone was sad, but he reassured us that we would see him every morning for form.

Just before dinner that night, in the Condor dorm, I told Robin to wait behind.

"What? What is it?" Robin said, looking worried.

I laughed. "Nothing to worry about mate."

"Oh right," he said. "Good, no more drama please."

"I erm, just wanted to give you this," I pulled out the little wrapped parcel from under my bed and gave it to him.

"For me? Why?"

"Why? *Why?* For saving my life? For bringing back two dead people in record time!" I said as he smiled. He took the parcel and unwrapped it, pulling out a pair of old, wire framed spectacles.

"Now, they don't look like much," I said. "But these are a pair of…"

"I know what they are," he gasped. "Wow, thank you mate, but… where did you get them?"

"Secret. I just never got to properly thank you, cos' you know you were the *real saviour* that night. If it hadn't been for you… well."

He swapped his glasses for the spectacles. "Woah!" he called, jumping backwards. "Weird! I couldn't wear these all the time!"

"I know right, weird aren't they!" I'd tried them on in the passageway. When you put them on, they revealed every bit of Magic that had been done in the vicinity. The most recent Magic shows up bright and colourful, whereas historical Magic shows up faded and grey. It makes your eyes hurt seeing all the bright colours of recent Magic, but immensely useful and cool if you know what your looking at.

A week later, I was down at Breakfast early. Me and Tina had agreed to go out in the grounds together all day. Just me and her. I met Tina in the empty hall. She was looking very casual in a pink hoodie and her hair perched up on the top of her head.

"Your late…" she said.

It was a hot and sunny all day. We found a spot by the lake and lay in the sun, chatting and watching the ducks.

"What a year," said Tina. "That curse he put me in, did I tell you, I could hear what people said to me, sometimes."

"Really?" I said, feeling my face grow red. "What was it like? Being cursed I mean?"

"It was *weird*," she said gravely. "I was in this horrible, nightmarish place, completely on my own. It was all grey, and dusty with rivers made of black gunge. And then these bars would just fall down and I'd be trapped in this tiny prison cell. But sometimes I'd wake up and hear people. But I couldn't open my eyes, or move, or talk... I never want to be cursed again." She looked up at the bright blue sky wincing. "Never thought I'd see that again... thought I was gonna stay like that. No offence, but I didn't think you'd work out a plan like that, and... die for me."

"Yeah well, like I said, I owed you."

She smiled her brilliant shining smile. "Come on, lets go for a dip!"

"Erm..." I said, looking at the big, cold river.

"Where's your adventure?" she clicked her fingers and a rope appeared, attached to the tall tree above. Then, she jumped on the rope and swung in a high arch through the sky. She let go at the height of the arch and soared through the air, hitting the water with a gigantic SPLASH!

"Get in Avis!" she called bobbing above the surface.

I had to really didn't I? I tried to look cool as I soared through the air. And failing as all the water went up my nose. Tina laughed.

We bobbed in the cold water and I tried my best to stop my teeth chattering. "It feels amazing to have Ernie back you know," she said. "Some people say you shouldn't mess with the dead, but... this felt like the right thing to do."

"I know what you mean," I shivered. "Erm... there aren't any dangerous things in this water are there?" I swear I felt something touch my leg.

"I don't know how I can ever thank you enough..." she came closer.

"You don't need to," I said. "This is enough." My heart was hammering so hard.

"I don't know how you thought of it all and... had the courage to face him like that. I just froze."

For the rest of the day we lay, drying off on the grass together. As we lay, the noise of people playing outside the school drifted through the air. Tina's hand slowly found mine.

The next afternoon, me, Robin and Tina met up for Dinner in the Chamber. Ernie had loved his new found fame at first, but now I was sure he was using Magic to evade being seen by anyone. "If I have to sign another autograph I will spontaneously combust!" he said. "I am sure I signed Arthur Cook's book twenty times already!"

Then, a shadow fell over our table, as Ross followed by Hamish and Gascoigne, stood over us with a strange glare in his eyes.

"You happy with yourself?" he said a little loudly. "Hanging around with the *enemy*."

"Enemy?" said Robin.

"Cork it lamppost!" said Ross, as people in the Chamber started looking round. "Yeah, the *Partington's...*" he pointed at Tina.

I whacked his arm away. "Don't point at her."

"And that *Ernie*. He's the one who... to Malakai... what do you think our parents will think? Think they'll be happy with you hanging around with *him*?"

I stood up slowly, my head barely up to his shoulders. "I don't care what they think... strikes me, he did us a favour."

"Yeah, and how do you work that out, runt boy?" Ross looked really angry, his eye was twitching.

"Don't talk to him like that," said Tina.

Ross exploded. "SHUT *UP*!"

I swallowed, he was dangerous when he was angry. "I said... don't talk to *her* like that..."

"And what are you gonna do about it?" said Ross, prodding me in the chest.

A voice behind Ross rang true. "Avis has enough manners to never harm a brother. So I am thankful that you and me, are not related." Ernie, now standing, was inspecting Ross.

"Oh look who it is," said Ross. "And what are *you* gonna do *ghost boy*?"

All eyes in the Chamber were now on Ross and Ernie. "Go on Ross, show him who's boss!" said Hamish in his deep nasal voice. Ross, gee'd on by his friends, raised his arms and threw a Spell at Ernie. A whizzing green bolt of fire shot across the Chamber.

Ernie didn't even blink. With one nonchalant click of his fingers, a black circle of water appeared before his face. The spinning green fire Spell hit it and instantly dissipated into smoke.

Ernie winced as if he was sorry for the lack of challenge Ross showed him. Ernie clicked his fingers again. A fizz and a crackle lit the air. Sticky brown tape flew out of nowhere and bound Ross's hands, feet and mouth.

Everyone in the Chamber launched into applause. "Pick your fights," said Ernie, leaving Ross writing around on the floor with Hamish and Gascoigne attempting pathetically to Spell the tape from the writhing Ross.

"Brilliant…" I said high-fiving Ernie, then watched as Ross's friends carried him out of the Chamber like he was an old carpet.

***

In no time at all, it was the last week of school. You could sense the emotion in the air. The last years had finished all their exams and proceeded to fly about the school, sending Spells whizzing all over the place. They went crazy! Hunter, Jake and Ellen were all picked up and thrown in the air (playfully of course) as they ran through the Chamber and were told off by Magisteer Dodaline.

With three days left I was sitting by the fire in my dorm alone, finishing my last homework assignment and wondering why I missed the clock tower so much. There was a knock and Tina came in, sitting down on my bed.

"Comfy…" she said. "Listen Avis, what are you doing for summer?"

I sighed. "I don't know." I put my pen down and sat next to her. "Thought I'd just go home."

"Are you sure that's a good idea what with, everything that happened?" I knew she was worried about what Ross had said.

"They don't know it was me."

"Yeah, but Avis, Ross knows you've been hanging around with us… the *enemy*."

"True…" I reasoned.

She bit her lip. "So come and stay at mine."

My heart gave a little flutter. "Wow, thank you, I am sure I will, but…"

"But what?" She looked offended.

"But, I *need* to go home, I need to face them… it's hard to explain, but after this year and all that's happened. It wouldn't feel right ignoring them. I need to… face them."

Tina nodded. "I get it. I do. But, just so know you can come to mine whenever you want."

"Thank you…"

Funnily enough Robin had said the same, in as many words. "Come and stay at mine this summer, you'll love it in Yorkshire!" I politely declined, saying the same as I said to Tina, but promised if things got tough, or I just wanted to come for a week or so then I would. Obviously I didn't invite them to mine, as it might scar them for life. Literally.

On the very last day, emotions ran at fever pitch. Hailing

Hall was all of our homes now. We all piled into the Chamber for the end of year assembly. I sat next to Robin and the rest of the Condors at a table spilling over with food. Jess and Florence sat opposite each other, staring in opposite directions with Hunter further away from them still.

Ernie had joined a sixth year form, the Phoenix's, with their charismatic form tutor Magisteer Nottingham. They were receiving jealous glances from the other sixth year forms. Obviously they wanted the celebrity in their form.

The air was buzzing. We ate and drank for what would be our last meal together for months. I had a bit of everything because there was so much to choose from! I gorged myself until I felt particularly fattened up, much to the delight of Tina, who worried about how thin I was.

Soon enough the entertainment began. The third years took to the stage to perform a play, as was customary at the end of the year. I'm not sure if it was supposed to be a comedy, but that's what it turned out to be. The stage looked incredible and was littered with Magical illusions: holographic backgrounds like clouds, floating furniture and even a dragon. Vivian Kirkwood, a small, uptight, serious boy and the narrator of the play, walked out onto the middle of the stage. Just as he opened his mouth he fell straight through the trap door, there was a second of silence, then a thud. It was absolutely hilarious.

The play continued in this calamitous vein for the entirety. They kept getting lost on the stage, due to an overpowering cloud illusion Spell which also caused several coughing fits. Vivian narrated the rest of the play in a neck brace, one boy accidentally came on without any trousers on and Curtis Blackwell managed to swing his sword so hard, it flew off, hit a fire bracket and set the curtains on fire. Magisteer Mallard, the director, stood by with his head in his hands.

Eventually, we gathered that the play was about the famous Wizards Jermain and Shaun-John, who invented most of the modern Spells we have today. But I don't think I've ever laughed so much in all my life. The great warrior Wizard Jermain was played by Gerry Sanders, a boy smaller than me with the most high pitched, squeakiest voice in the world! At the end, the curtains fell over poor Colin Clapper before he could get off stage, so he just stood awkwardly until he was forcefully escorted off my Magisteer Mallard.

"And NOW!" bellowed the Lily taking to the lectern. "We crown the champions of this years Riptide League! Please put your hands together for…" everyone in the Chamber began drumming on their tables. "…The CENTAURS!" The room erupted in cheers as golden confetti exploded in the air above us and rained down. The Centaurs stood proudly from their table and walked to the front amid a standing ovation. Clasping each other in celebration and beaming wide, the Lily put solid, dazzlingly golden medal around each of their necks. Jenson Zhu, Gemma Icke and Marshall Compton-Campbell received the biggest cheers. Then the huge golden cup in the shape of an *R* was handed across to the big team captain - Ingrid Bloater (I did find that quite amusing, and nearly choked on my cake when that was announced.) She took the cup and raised it high in the air as golden fireworks erupted from the ground, nearly scared me half to death. Robin was annoyed because a firework case went in his drink. Magisteer Straker was on his feet applauding, he looked more animated than I'd ever seen him and even wiped a small tear from his eye.

"That's two years in a row!" announced the Lily. "So lessons to be taken from the Centaurs, for all of you."

"Doesn't matter how many lessons in Riptide we have,"

said Robin. "We'll still never win!" Jake and Gret shot Robin a fierce glance as Simon clapped Graham on the back.

"You owe me another ten gold pieces." Graham grimaced and reached for his gold bag.

After pudding, we moved on to the school awards. The Lily took to the lectern again.

"And now for the Hailing Hall School Awards! Given out to pupils who we, the Magisteers, think deserve it… Firstly, the award for best kept dormitory. The winners are… the Hesserbout form!" A girly scream shot into the air as the fourth year Hesserbout form jumped up collecting their certificates and Magical boxed prizes.

"What's in them do you think?" I whispered to Robin.

"Ernie said they usually give a pot of Everlasting Ink, or something…"

"Really? Is that all? I'd be well annoyed if thats all I got for keeping my room clean all year."

The Hesserbouts retook their seats as the Lily bellowed again. "And the award for the form who excelled in their studies above all others this year are… Jaloofias!" A table of snooty looking fifth years stood and gave bows and courtesies. "Well done Jaloofias," finished the Lily as they sat back down with their small boxes.

"Now, we have a couple of special awards to give out… It's important in this school to be, not just academically astute and clean, but to have something else. Sometimes life requires you to be more than just clever, more than just determined, more than just skilled. Sometimes it requires a multitude of skills, skills that come from being a good person and deciding what the right thing to do is, even if it means sacrificing something that you hold dear." The Lily's eyes subtly swayed towards our table and my heart began hammering. "The next winner then…" he called. "Goes to some*body*, who under extreme pressure, triumphed. This special award goes to… *Robin Wilson!*"

Robin froze in his seat as the crowd erupted all around us. He turned to look at me with absolute terror plastered across his pale, be-speckled face.

"Go on!" I said pushing him up. Robin limped to the front of the Chamber. The crowd clapping and cheering even though they didn't know what he'd done. Tina was standing on her chair, clapping and whistling as loud as she could, until Magisteer Dodaline pulled her down.

"What did he do?" said Hunter.

"Well done Robin," said the Lily, clapping him on the back and turning him to face the Chamber. He looked like a frightened deer, being held up before a room of hungry wolves. The Lily ordered silence again. "Robin Wilson, you have displayed qualities which the average person should be severely jealous. Not only did you come here an Outsider, oblivious to the knowledge of our race, and adapted yourself quickly and knowledgeably, so much so, that most of the Magisteers thought you were a born Wizard, but also you forgave, at a time when all others didn't and wouldn't. Not only that further, but you saved two lives, with little time, no prior knowledge and performed what is one of the hardest Spells known to Wizardkind. That deserves a special prize, and a special round of applause." The Lily threw his arms into the air and the Chamber erupted.

Robin took his seat back next to me, a small leather box under his arm. Eyes all around watching him curiously as he sat down, wondering what on earth he did to deserve such a special award.

"Next is a three way award. For three people who, playing David, took on Goliath, with selfless determination. These people have shown amazing attributes in morality, guts, and perseverance at a time when all seemed lost…"

the Lily smiled. "Something that takes immense courage and belief. So, can we have Ernie Partington, Tina Partington and Avis Blackthorn up here please!" I swallowed hard and closed my eyes. Everyone on my table began clapping me on the back.

Why was this happening? Had Partington told the Lily?

"Your turn now mate…" said Robin pushing me up. Tina looked shell shocked too and copied my jelly leg walk to the front, joining Ernie.

The Lily was much taller when you stood next to him and he smelt like lavender. He shook Tina's hand, then mine. Handing us both a small, black hexagonal leather box with our names written in scrawling golden ink. Now he turned us to face the room. A sea of eyes watched us, across a huge room that flickered orange firelight and muti-coloured robes shimmering rainbows across the walls. I locked my shaking legs into place and tried to muster some saliva in my dry as a bone mouth.

"It takes tremendous courage to…" *Please don't say what we did*, I kept thinking. "…to stand up and do the right thing even when others would tell you otherwise," nodded the Lily. "We know why Ernest is up here. For what he did, we must be eternally grateful. And Tina, who single handedly took over her brothers quest so amicably, helping to restore him to mortality. Without you're helping hand, Malakai would still be at large…" then, after a long applause, the Lily's tone changed to a crippling sincerity as his eyes rested on me.

"*But*… a *special* thank you must be said for Avis Blackthorn. Someone with a name that we all judged." Many faces dipped apologetically as the Lily looked around. "With some… bad luck, this year, Avis was wrongly accused of the attack of his form mate, and friend, Hunter. What I was saddened to see, was the quick judgement of those who know better. As you are all well aware, Malakai paid several visits to our School this year, which fortunately, was ended by Ernest. However, in one of these visits he stumbled upon Hunter, Robin Wilson and Avis. It was Malakai who attacked Hunter…" There was a huge, long gasp, and then whispering. Hunter looked proud, for he had survived a Malakai attack. Jess and Florence were looking adoringly at him. As I stood there, legs shaking, I saw Partington grinning at us like the cheshire cat. David Starlight didn't know where to look and Ross, livid, stared at the ground.

"Poor Avis received the blame, as was Malakai's intention. Yet he dealt with the painful accusation with valour. He dealt with the months of solitude with staggering spirit, and he dealt with his enemies with tremendous daring. I can categorically state that Avis Blackthorn is a *good Wizard*!"

There was utter silence for what seemed an age. Head's turned and whispered, blinked… then smiled. All of a sudden a giant wave of cheering and applause exploded like a canon. Surges of emotion ran through me to see the whole Chamber applauding. The Lily had let on a lot, but I didn't mind. And now, the greatest gift he could give me — the treasure of being known as a good Wizard was granted. I was a Blackthorn yes, but I was a good Blackthorn and my family would have to deal with that.

After a long mauling of claps on the back, hair ruffling and teary apologies, I retook my seat. Tina and Ernie joined me and Robin on our table and we had a long, blissful afternoon drinking Mango Perry, nibbling scrumptious food and talking. Towards the end of the afternoon, the Magisteers all stood up as one. The next moment, a bonanza of trumpets blared out across the room from nowhere. The tables and chairs expelling us from their seats and slid to the sides of the room with a scraping noise.

"Seventh years!" called the Lily. "You've completed your time with us. I, the Magisteers, and your fellow pupils who have shared in your time here, will forever remember you." Sniffs and welling of eyes soon began as the Lily walked solemnly through the middle of the Chamber.

"When things get tough, or difficult out there, always remember you belong to the growing Hailing Hall family. Now go and be great Wizards!"

Ghosts floated into the Chamber in one mass of white and blue glowing light as suits of armour around the side of the Chamber began blowing on wind instruments that appeared out of nowhere. We all applauded as loud as we could, as the seventh years, through lots of tears and hugging, slowly began to make their way out of Hailing Hall, as, surprisingly, the ghosts began singing!

We thank you for you time with us,
We hope you've learned your fill,
It's your time now to enter the world,
And make it a better place, still.
Take all that you've learned here and turn it into good,
Make people's lives and all their strives properly understood.
Go forth now all equal,
We give you our thanks,
Now you are a part of the schools sequel,
Go join your new ranks.
For all that you taught this place,
We thank you,
Forever learn and live with grace,
We hope you've learned your fill,
It's your time now to enter your the world
And make it a better place still...

It was an emotional experience. The seventh years looked so sad to be leaving what was their home for the last seven years. And yet there was an excitement at entering the Seven Kingdoms as fully trained, Professional Working Wizards. I shook and wished warmly as many people as I could. Some smiled when I shook their hands, ruffling my hair and wishing me well. Robin too was grilled by one or two about what he did. He remained as vague as possible, before someone else would shake his hand and ask him the same.

I spotted Ross who wasn't shaking anyones hand. He was looking down at the ground and made his way out of the double doors alone. We all followed the seventh years and the Magisteers out of the Chamber and into the courtyard. Carriages were lined up in neat rows, ready for the seventh years to go home, or indeed, wherever they were off to next. I knew of several, Kellie Kirkyard, Timothy Howard, Ahmed Omran and Helen Ulysses who were going travelling around the Seven Magical Kingdoms and the Outside, I overheard them in the Chamber talking about where they would meet. How exciting, what an adventure!

The Magisteers stood as one, with their arms in the air. A pool of white light lit the sky and, at its full height burst. A gigantic rainbow split the sky, arching across the school. It was so bright it cast a technicolor glow across the grass courtyard. Then, carriages began launching into the air, as seventh years waved their scarves out of windows and soaring off into the rainbow and away to start their new lives.

Me, Tina and Robin collected our luggage from the hall and stood together as Ernie joined us (he didn't have any luggage). No one said anything, we just stood in silence. This was the end. We all hugged and I heard Tina start sobbing.

"I'm staying here with Dad," said Ernie. "Gonna help

him pack." He sighed deeply and looked around at the sunny, green fields. "It will be nice to see home again, I'm sick of this place," he laughed.

"I'll wait with you," said Tina.

Me and Robin said our goodbyes to the Condor form who stood nearby. "Hunter…" I said shaking his hand. "Take care, see you next year…" he pulled me into a hug.

"You will Avis…"

I repeated the same to Jess, Simon, Graham, Ellen, Jake, and all the others. I shook their hands, hopefully next year I would get to know them a lot more. Fireworks erupted into the air all around us as the Magisteers stood at the foot of the hall and waved their goodbyes and hugging some teary eyed first years.

Partington was standing and waving at us as hard as he could. "SEE YOU NEXT YEAR!" he bellowed as the Lily tapped him to quieten down. We all laughed.

A big black carriage suddenly soared through the air, dropped and pulled up next to me. The door opened.

"Blimey," I said, recognising my parents best black carriage. "It's my parents best carriage!?" I looked around for Ross, perhaps it had mistaken me for him. But, he had already gone.

Tina wiped her eyes then hugged me so tightly I thought my ribs might crack.

I swallowed, trying to suppress the thought that I wouldn't see her face for the next couple of months. "I'll hopefully see you before the start of next year… all of you."

"Please do!" said Tina. "Or we'll come looking for you!" she said, tears streaming down her golden face. Robin kept blinking and cleaning his glasses. "Oh!" called Tina. "If we meet up, we can go shopping, get you some better clothes!"

"Erm… ok?" I said.

I shook Robin and Ernie by the hand once more and got into the carriage. Partington whistled from the hallway entrance and waved again. I looked around at the place that had become my home, before taking my seat in the most luxurious carriage my parents owned. It didn't even require moody horses, it drove itself. I lay my suitcases down and wound the window down. All across the courtyard were tearful goodbyes, hugs and carriages shooting into the air. I saw the boys of the Eagles form all saying their goodbyes to Straker, who mellowly bowed to each of them.

Hunter seemed to be deep in conversation with both Jess and Florence, while Gret and Jake got into the most gothic carriage I've ever seen, adorned with Golandrian drapes, gas lamps and mean, black horses.

Then, my carriage shot into the air so fast I thought I might have left my stomach on the school grounds. I leant out the window and waved to my friends. My best friends. Tall, clever, be-speckled Robin. The taller, handsome, charismatic Ernie. And of course, the teary, mad, beautiful Tina. Maybe someone up there does like me, before I started school, I wished more than anything to make a friend. And, well, I'd made three of the best friends I could have ever wished for.

In a few seconds they turned into mere specs. We hit the rainbow and multi coloured glitter filled the carriage. The sky was full of carriages like a flock of black birds dancing above a fountain of exploding Magical fireworks.

Hailing Hall looked even more amazing from above. The clock tower, my home for those long, cold, solitary months, started to ring out. I smiled and waved goodbye to it. In a way, I would really miss that clock tower.

The trees, all having uprooted themselves were now waving their gigantic branches at us. In a carriage opposite me, David Starlight glanced across and caught my eye. For a moment, I thought he might smile. But then, he just ignored me and closed the blinds. Charming.

The box the Lily had given me sat on top of my bag. I took it and sat back. A little confused, I opened the curious box. I pulled out... the pair of Seven League Shoes!

How on earth could he have possibly known?

I sat back and relaxed. I had no idea what I was going home to. My parents sending me their best carriage was a good sign, but who knows with the Blackthorns? I put the Seven League Shoes on, just in case, and closed my eyes.

To be continued...

Did you enjoy reading *"Avis Blackthorn Is Not an Evil Wizard!"*?

If you enjoyed it then I would be honoured if you shared your thoughts on Amazon.

If you would like to contact me about anything, then please email:
jackwilliamsimmonds@gmail.com

I look forward to hearing from you.

All the best,

Jack Simmonds

CPSIA information can be obtained
at www.ICGtesting.com
Printed in the USA
LVOW03s0141010817
543282LV00005B/371/P